*Totally Bound Publishing books by Ellen Mint*

**Happily Ever Austen**
Pride and Pancakes
Rash and Rationality
Madeline's Park

**Coven of Desire**
Retail Hell
Claw
Snow Print
Fang
Whisper
Badge

**Collections**
Some Like it Haunted: Ink
My Bloody Valentine: Love's Curse

# Coven of Desire

# BADGE

ELLEN MINT

Badge
ISBN # 978-1-80250-958-8

Interior text design by Claire Siemaszkiewicz
Totally Bound Publishing



Published in 2022 by Totally Bound Publishing, United Kingdom.



Totally Bound Publishing is an imprint of Totally Entwined Group Limited.

# BADGE

# Dedication

Ink lovers, this book is for you. He's got his claws on the mike and isn't giving up without a fight.

Thank you to my almighty alpha reader Kristi, my word-whipping editor Anna, and my ARC team. They helped to whip and spank this book into shape.

# Prologue

Hell is not other people.

Despite what any French playwrights have believed, hell is far less creative and far more destructive in its torture. For the realm of hell was, is and shall forever be nothing.

It was into an endless void—stolen of all color save a swipe of morose blue, putrid green and clotted-blood red—that I'd woken. The act of waking was the only new experience for me. Being a creature of sin, I'd never found much need for respite, be it in a bed or entangled in a pile of limbs upon the marquis' settee. Hell did not alter its rules to accommodate my kind.

Change died in the land of the damned.

Each day—and I use the term loosely—my eyes would open upon the endless expanse of my personal torture. Or perhaps it was the same for everyone. Raising my head, I marched through the labyrinth of nothing. I let my claws scrape against stone walls only a man's length apart. Sparks struck in my wake, but any splash of interesting color or light was dampened by the ever-present fog. It seeped from above and below, twisting my mind so if I did not focus, the floor and ceiling inverted.

Still I walked.

For the past four centuries of my purgatory, I had yet to see a fellow damned or hear a voice crying from the darkness. For all the talk of demons down in hell conspiring to take humans' souls, they seemed to be of no mind to do any active torturing in their domain. Perhaps, after a few millennia, they had grown tired of the game and retired to a tropical island, leaving the restless dead to punish themselves.

"Good morning," I called to the death tree. Stripped of all leaves and bark, it was the same sickly gray of the world, its serpentine branches splitting the wall apart as it strained across to the other side.

I'd done every manner of damage to the tree. Broken each branch, hacked through the trunk with my nails until it lay sundered on the ground, lit its dead husk on fire and watched it turn to ash. Each day it was fully restored to its sickly glory. Now, we'd let bygones be bygones and I'd like to think become something of friends. As much as a sin of lust and an insentient plant could be.

Taking a right at the tree, I came upon the only reason I was able to move. A stone statue fashioned in the form of a shapely woman stood beside the wall. Her hands were outstretched beside her breasts and a single drink rested inside.

It was not water clutched safely in her fingers, but desires answered. Small ones—a smile from a child or a belated birthday card—but it was enough to keep me ambulatory for another day. I sipped slowly, savoring the one difference in my day even though it too was monotony. As I sucked upon the stone woman's fingers, I stared up at where her head should be. The entire face had been cleaved off, leaving me to wonder who my lone beneficiary was. While the tree and I had our issues, I'd only felt fondness for her—even if it was her gift that kept me from fading to dust.

"Thank you, my dear," I said, strength trembling through my body.

To think, I'd once controlled the arms of kings and queens from the comfort of their beds. Now I was reduced to lapping sustenance from the crooked fingers of a stone woman. If humans only knew the true cruelty of hell, perhaps their world would be a kinder place.

Little more remained in my prison of nothing. The walls twisted around, guiding me back to where I began, which would only restart the cycle. It was unending, unchanging, unbreakable. Gray stone, gray skies, gray ground, gray…

A light no bigger than a pinprick pierced through the blandness. I stared at it hovering above my head, the tiny star a speck, but a speck of orange. Even so microscopic, it glowed among the gray. At first, all I could do was watch. The world I'd known for four hundred years had finally changed. For better or worse didn't matter—the mere fact that something was different sent me running.

The speck hovered above the tree, the light flickering among its dead branches. I clasped the trunk, using my incubus claws as pitons, and climbed. As I went, the tree's trunk sizzled to black ash.

"Forgive me, my friend, but it's either me or you." I climbed faster, the tree below me dissolving away. There wouldn't be much time for me to reach the speck of light. Branches tore at my body, ripping away flesh and feathers, leaving me tattered and heaving when I reached the top of the tree.

Clinging to the tallest branch, I stared at the speck, now the size of a pea. The trunk below me swayed, ready to fall to pieces and send me careening to the stones below. It didn't matter. Straining, I reached a claw out to the light, and as the tip of it touched…

"—spirits, we ask that you join us tonight."

A voice that wasn't my own rent the air. I hadn't heard another's tongue in so long, my jaw dropped at the sound.

"I don't like this."

"Shut up, Gabe."

Had I finally punctured through to another part of hell?

"On this All Hallows Eve…" the first voice, a woman at a guess, intoned.

"That's tomorrow," a pedantic male chimed in.

"It's close enough," the woman snarled back. "We call upon the spirits to give us your name."

No, this wasn't hell. Only a mortal would be foolish enough to simply ask a spirit for their name. I'd found Earth!

A great crack broke from below and the tree's fall began. With the last of my strength, I leaped off the branch. My good friend the tree shattered the bricks, toppling the wall. But I reached for the small hole hanging in the sky…and wedged a finger inside.

Lights flared and darkness—blessed, eternally missed darkness—swept away the gray. I breathed and scent returned to my long-withered nose. It stank of barley, confections, dirt…and hormones. *Yes!*

I twisted my finger, the dusty memory of what she had taught me returning. Fire sought out wicks and twenty candles cast the room in light. A bevy of young adults stared at me, their human faces twisted in various rictuses of horror and shock.

Their garb was strange. One wore a toga improperly tied, another a flimsy dress for a lady-in-waiting. I could make neither heads nor tails of the man in all silver with a box for a face. Though I quite approved of the other man's naked body slathered only in red paint save a single pair of micro-pantaloons. These humans, always evolving, never staying static for long. *Oh, how I missed you all.*

"Who…who are you?" the leader of the amateur seance asked, her once-staid voice squeaky as a mouse. She pointed a finger at me, her body trembling with such ferocity it caused a pointed black hat to tumble off her head.

"I am the spirit you summoned," I declared and widened my stance. In doing so, I caught a piece of wood below my feet covered in letters and the words 'yes', 'no' and 'goodbye'. Curious.

"Holy shit, it worked!" one man shouted.

Then another cried, "Why is it naked?"

I cocked my hip and smiled. "Do you wish to rectify that problem or press your advantage?"

Three of the four blushed. Not bad odds after being out of the game so long.

"Who are you?" the leader asked, not answering my question, but not rushing to cover my nudity either.

"Why, I am an inc—"

The chain on my long-abandoned memories shattered, dragging me back to the moment I had been pulled straight to hell. They'd never been so numerous before, stinking of pitch and smoke, unstoppable. How many more yet lived in this future? I wasn't safe.

What if they were lying in wait? What if they too would find the tear in the realms and banish me once more?

I tossed my shoulders back, spreading my wings of shadow. The humans gasped, and I turned to flee, when a pillar of light punctured the skies. It came from a tall building in the distance. Once again, the universe provided a solution to my problem.

"Thank you for freeing me," I said, "but tell none of what occurred, and I will spare you all."

The humans gaped in terror, a most respectful answer, and I flexed my wings. Wait, it wouldn't do well to face the enemy so immodestly. I turned to the man in red and ordered, "Give me your trousers."

# Chapter One

*Ink*

A hand pierced the grave, shattering the witch's pentagram as it strained for the sky. Lightning crackled through the dark clouds above, the fully emerged arm somehow perfectly lit despite the night around it. While the sorceress cackled in glee, the dirt fell away, revealing a face of ashen pallor with minor skin inflammation and a withered nose.

"Ah, he suffers from the great pox," I said aloud, and a shushing broke from the blubbery lips beside me. There was no doubt a person was attached to said flopping skin bags, but I could not discern them in the darkness. The air bulged with barely coherent desires, the shadow in the chair beside me wishing only for my death.

A shame, for after two thousand years I had yet to ascertain any way to cause such an end. I began to lean over the divider keeping us separate, when a palm graced my knee.

The chasteness of the touch nearly caused me to chuckle, when my bond whispered, "Watch the movie."

I folded my arms. Having already dispatched the box of chocolate balls, I had grown bored of this display of flickering images ten minutes in. I tipped my head to her, spotting the blond locks of the wolf to her other side. He seemed to be enraptured with the tinny trite, a full fist of popcorn raised to his mouth. I intended to tell her I'd had my fill, when her eyes darted to me.

*Please let me enjoy this.*

Her desires did not require my talent of reading through the colored fogs surrounding the gray mass of humanity. I felt her request singing through every nerve and a smile replaced my smirk. Taking her hand, I raised it to my lips and whispered against her knuckles, "As you wish."

She rubbed my knee once more and left her palm upon my thigh. The greens and purples of the giant screen reflected off her fingers, each digit delicate and also hard as stone. She'd chipped a nail recently, no doubt the damn specter's doing. I clasped my hand over the back of hers and held tight when a finger jabbed into my shoulder.

The wolf had raised his hand from Layla's shoulders in order to prod me. "This is the best part," he said in a harried but exuberant voice.

I jerked my gaze to the grumbling guardian of silence beside me, but it remained resolutely still. *I see, so Calvin can speak whenever he wishes, but I must be held to a higher standard.* Humans never could wrap their minds around the concept of justice.

Rather than pick a fight, I turned my gaze to the screen. The syphilitic man was moaning, no doubt from the pain he now found in urinating. Around him circled the sorceress, her silver cloak flapping in a wind that did not move the trees in the background. She spoke gibberish Latin and lightning lit up the white sky. In an instant, all of the graves cracked open like elevator doors and people climbed out.

"Is she attempting to build an army of undead?" I scoffed. "No villain worth their salt would waste time with such a foolish plan. You have, at most, three days before rot causes your army to bloat, then explode. Even less in the summer."

"Will you shut the hell up?" My neighbor greatly disapproved of my logic, even if it was sound. Humans were basically walking candles—one light and the whole of the army would go up in smoke, leaving the sorceress alone and awkward on the battlefield.

"Ink..." Layla leaned closer to me when the man with the pox leaped forward and bit off the sorceress' nose. As I said, a very foolish endeavor. My smug righteousness only lasted a moment when Layla gasped and clung tight to my leg.

My heartbeat increased with hers, a flush of those endorphins she devoted her study to rushing from her to me. While the undead man crunched on the offscreen sorceress' body, my bond turned to look at me. Pink tinged the soft tan of her cheeks, the dark depths of her eyes wide in shock.

She glanced to where her nails tried to dig through my flesh and blanched. "Sorry," Layla said, but before she could retract her hand, I pressed it tighter.

"You need never apologize for that," I said, catching her chin. I pulled her closer and whispered against her lips, "I am built for your punishment."

The kiss sent a wave of spicy pink desire through me. It radiated down my tongue, encouraging said nimble organ to toy with Layla's lip. As I plunged deeper and tasted of her mouth, the desire pulsing from her transformed to a sultry fuchsia. I let my touch land on her shoulder, all manner of horrific undead attacks forgotten. Each traipse of my fingers winding down the ribbons on her blouse toward her breast sent a touch of satiety through me. It was little more than a bite, a nibble really, but the fuel fed my fire.

Layla's wily hand had found itself trailing up my thigh then retreating. She fought the internal war far too many of my prey carried the mantle for. *What I desire versus what society deems proper. Ever at odds, never satisfactory.* The whole concept of morality had been invented to keep people anxious, unsatisfied and in search of a cold bath. But within my bond, the electric desire was winning out.

I took her breast in my hand and Layla bit down to silence her moan. That seemed to shatter the mood and she froze, causing my elaborate dance to pause as well. "Ink, we should…"

"Take advantage of the flickering ambience of mutilated corpses in this foreboding dungeon?" I whispered, tucking back her hair and tracing around her ear. She closed her eyes, lost in the simple pleasure of my touch.

Alas, it was my neighbor who once again could not cease to thrust himself into my affairs. "Will you shut your fucking mouth already?"

I scoffed and shook my head. "No. I do not believe I shall, and you are the better for it."

The man, for his visage grew more evident in the rising light of the screen, folded his hand into a fist. He popped it up as if he intended to knock my teeth out, which only caused me to smile. Whatever nerve he thought to have had fled, and the man rose and abandoned his seat in the back of this darkened theater.

As he stomped his feet and cursed under his breath, his shadow cast over the screen, hiding away the funeral march.

"Down in front," I called to his retreating form.

"Now you've done it." The cursed specter slipped into the vacated seat, proving I was never afforded a moment of peace in this world. He managed to look smug despite being without a body and forced to stand in the aisle.

"What? You think he will challenge me to a duel? Even with two of his sturdiest gentlemen at his side, it will be nothing more than a jumping behind the pub."

The ghost only stared ahead, not saying a word to me, but his eyes flickered to Layla who was quickly losing the thread of desire. That would not do. I had seen little of her in the past week, though I'd had more than my share of the vagrant ghost we'd acquired. Whenever I would reach for her, either the wolf or the dead man would be there first. Typically, I could work with such a scenario, but the ghost was without form and the wolf…

I sighed, staring askance at the man doing his best to ignore his own animalistic urges and the tenting in his trousers. What everyone needed was to break this tension with a day-long celebration of the joy only three bodies could bring. The ghost could sit and watch for all I cared.

"My bond." I pulled aside her spirals and breathed heavily in her ear. That sent the heat rolling once more and she clenched her fingers tighter to my thigh. "Why hesitate?"

Her deep eyes opened wide and she stared as if in shock that I could yet read her mind. "I know…" Gently, I dropped my finger to the top of her cleavage.

"What you truly..." I swept it down between her breasts and over her belly.

Where her thighs split, I clutched onto her skirt, and began to raise it. "Desire."

Layla squirmed in her seat, her eyelids heavy as she succumbed to my logical charisma. I abandoned any prelude of remaining in my seat and turned to press my cock against her thigh. She struggled to fight a gasp and I drew my touch up the hot spread of her underthings. I never needed to test if she was wet, but I quite liked the glide of the proof of my pull and how she flexed to let me in.

As I tugged aside the edge of her panties, I leaned into her ear. "Go on," I whispered, toying with the succulent lady lip at my finger. "Tug on him."

The wolf turned, his eyes blazing with a hunger I knew he too was fighting and failing to ignore. For him, it ran either burning red or muted yellow. Tonight, it burned hotter than the flames of Hades. Cal took Layla's cheek and pulled her in for a kiss just as she reached for the waistband of his jeans...and slipped under. His groan trembled through my hunger, smelling of a feast but failing to satisfy. I paid it barely any heed, Layla's response to him far more delectable.

Her body burned with a rising tide of desire, and my innocent little flick of the bean wouldn't do. I abandoned the seats entirely and took a knee to the floor. The wolf was trying to not thrust his hips in his seat even as he rolled a hand over Layla's breast and panted. Their deep kiss broke and she looked at me in shock.

"What are you doing?"

"I'd think it'd be rather obvious," I answered. Her heart thundered like a rain of timpani. I wrapped my hands under her thighs, clenched her hips and pulled her to my mouth. The underthings meant nothing to the slip of my tongue or the press of my lips. I licked and sucked around, under and over them, soaking her already drenched panties to total saturation. Layla raised her leg and placed it on my shoulder. As she did, Cal reached over to run his hand over her thigh and lift it higher.

Her hand worked fast under his jeans, bringing the unresolved tension to a proper crescendo. I too felt the swell inside, the only way I knew sex to feel. The slumbering hunger sharpened its fangs, my metaphorical mouth drooling while my literal one supped upon the beautiful woman's clit. She arched her back, pressing more of herself to me and pulling her head down the chair.

I glanced up a moment, delighted by the response, when I spotted the ghost standing behind watching. No, he was whispering words to her, no doubt ones stolen from better men. But they seemed to be working to bring Layla to a frenzy. I dipped deeper, every pulse of my tongue filling my body with the strength of a dozen men.

When she began to clench, nearing her climax, my first instinct was to stop. Not in pleasuring her—that I could do for days without end. No, I nearly paused in pulling her energy lest I take too much. But that was the joy of taking a witch to bed—there was never an end. Her magic fed me, letting me feast without risking her loss.

"Ink..." Layla whimpered. With one hand, she clung to the wolf's impressive John Thomas. With the other, she wrenched on my hair, ordering me to finish her off. Gladly.

I dipped back for the last taste that'd fill me to bursting when a bright light blinded me. Blinking against the harsh rays that highlighted the nearly empty theater seats ahead of us, I turned to find a man not yet old enough for a hair on his chin dressed in a crimson uniform with his arms crossed and a glower on.

"Hello, my good man," I said, rising to my feet. He flinched as I held my hand out to him. "Would you care to join us?"

# Chapter Two

*Ink*

"Thanks, Ink."

I'd never seen my bond in such a furrowed state of apoplectic embarrassment. She cast a hand across her eyes to aid in the disguise as all three of us, plus the specter flotsam, marched from the theater at the behest of the movie guard. He hadn't offered up much by way of challenge, but Layla did not seem of a mind to unleash her spells upon him. Perhaps she was in a generous mood.

I held open the door, allowing Layla to exit. She placed a hand on the cool glass and I slipped on a proud smile. "You are welcome."

Her eyes narrowed and she wrinkled her nose, but before I could offer a repeat performance, she slipped out into the dark night. I was about to follow when two hundred pounds of wolf muscle slammed into my shoulder. It was a mere trifle, no doubt damaging Calvin more than me.

But as I stood my ground and met his snarling blue glare, he said, "Yeah, thanks."

I tipped my head, my heart brimming with their gratitude, when the ghost walked up next. Smiling directly at Daniel, I raised my head and walked out, letting the door swing closed in his face. For a moment, the foolish dead skidded on his toes and raised his hands up as if a full plate of glass trapped him. Then he too scowled, his fine features twisting in a knot as if he believed the ferocious scowl would shift him into the childish tiger on his death jacket.

*Why is everyone in such a foul mood?*

"My bond." I reached to take her hand, but she wrenched it back faster than an asp.

"Don't. Not after that."

"What? Lavishing you with my expert tonguing?" I laughed at the level of my skills, but my bond merely glowered.

"You're not supposed to. That was a… Gah!" Layla clawed at the air as if she were puncturing a balloon, then spun around to walk ahead of all of us.

The wolf ratcheted his eyes to the heavens and he raised his chest with arms crossed. "Anywhere else you want to get us banned from? Maybe whip it out at an ice cream parlor?"

"You place the blame upon my shoulders?" I gasped in shock.

Layla pivoted fast to stare me down. "No one else tried to finger me at the movies!" Her words carried crisply across the dark air, drawing the attention of a cluster of people huddled around their large, all-metal carriage. Layla cursed under her breath at the eyes on her, and she raised her scarf to disguise her face.

"And you were the one who desired it." I fought back, refusing to let my reputation be besmirched. A rampaging sex fiend I might be, but I only fingered, licked and thrust where I was wanted.

"Great, so you can't turn it off for even two hours now?" the wolf argued not to me, but to his paramour.

"Like you didn't pull my hand down your pants." The ever-simmering fight once again found flame, Layla turning her ire on the wolf.

"It was the man the demon antagonized who went after the usher. If he'd kept quiet, none of it would have happened," the cursed ghost chimed in. He'd slipped behind Layla, needlessly pawing at her hair without moving a strand, but staring over her shoulder in my direction.

"Ah yes, I forget that while my comments are unwanted, you blathering on in Layla's ear the entire time in the dark is perfectly acceptable."

He too crossed his arms. Each of the fools looked like stone guards outside a crypt. "No one else can hear me," Daniel said.

The wolf clucked his tongue. "Just those of us who don't count, apparently."

"Cal." Layla groaned.

"He wouldn't shut up. Every ten seconds it was 'oh, that's a plot hole,' 'that effect is so cheesy.' All I wanted was to watch a fucking movie with my girlfriend."

Daniel scoffed. "That wasn't a movie. It was regurgitated gore for the mindless masses."

The wolf roared at him as if he would leap onto the ghost and reveal his innards to the world. While I would happily sit back and enjoy such a scene, alas it was not possible as Daniel's entrails had long since been eaten away by worms. Layla slapped a hand to Cal's chest and let her other hand float limply inside of the ghost's.

"Can we not have a full-on supernatural brawl in the middle of the street?" She pushed back on her boyfriend's chest but he wouldn't shake off his fangs. "Cal, your ears are pointy."

Layla gestured toward the sprouted wolf ears, gray and white hair already peeking through. The wolf had enough sense to slip back and cover his head, shrinking away the proof that he wasn't as he appeared. "And, Daniel…" She turned to him. To the people passing by she appeared to be talking to thin air. Layla stared at a couple rubbernecking at the tableau, while I gave a small wave.

Shifting her stance and dropping her hand, she whispered to her nails, "If you don't like cheesy horror movies, then don't come."

"That is what she indicated," I said, causing everyone to look at me in confusion, then glare when the joke hit.

"This was supposed to be one night out after…" Layla whipped her hand in a circle to summarize the adoption of the ghost, the attack of a water djinn and the realization her mother yet lived. The djinn was all that concerned me. For a creature of such power to be in this realm, and worse, be doing the bidding of another, did not bode well for this world. More importantly, creature politics could suck me up into a mess I'd quite like to avoid.

"So can we all just let it go? For now. I'm so…fucking tired." The sensual glide of my bond's voice cracked to broken glass and her head hung low. Both the wolf and ghost comforted her, the latter running his hand across her shoulders while the former hovered. She put on a smile and our merry band resumed its way to the car.

As Layla walked beside the wolf, nearly all her weight placed upon his wide stature, I drifted behind alone. "My bond," I called, uncertain of what I wanted until she turned to look. I smirked when the ice-eyes of the wolf stared back at me. "Perhaps you would do well to put down the burden you needlessly carry."

She stared at her handbag, then me in confusion. Tapping my forehead, I explained, "You've been fretting with desire to tell the mutt something."

That caught his attention. "Oh?"

Layla lunged back and clasped her hands to her heart, covering the locket that carried a piece of the ghost inside. "It's nothing," she said.

"So much nothing you told the demon?" The growl returned to his words, practically grinding them to dust. He cast his eternal glare upon me and rippled his lips as if I would be unnerved by a fang or two.

"Cal…it's not… This isn't the place to talk about—"

"The red wolf."

One could hear the drop of a pearl necklace three alleys over from my declaration. Shock rose in my bond's eyes, as if I hadn't been tuned in to her mental flogging about the subject for nigh on a week. It was the werewolf I couldn't be certain of. His chest ceased inflating, the whole of his body frozen. Perhaps he hadn't heard, or he'd misunderstood.

"What do you mean 'red wolf'?" Claws punctured the night air and caught around my throat. It tickled, but I managed to keep the laughter down. "How do you know about that?" he snarled in my face.

I braced for a howl from the rapidly forming fangs, but it was Layla in a soft voice who pleaded with him. "How do you?"

Cal tossed me aside. I stumbled but a moment and used the time to adjust my cuffs as he focused his needless ire upon Layla. She peered up from below her shrouded brow, unable to face the beast, and asked, "Who is it?"

The human shook off the fur, his head darting back and forth to note the other mortals stumbling from the theater into the street. "This isn't the place," he snarled and took off.

"Then where is? What are you hiding?" Layla gave pursuit down the alley connecting the theater to an abandoned furniture store.

Finally, blissful silence. I took in a breath, savoring the night without the unending undercurrent of acrimony.

"Why did you do that?"

Well, it had been nice for a moment. I did not deign to glance to the ghost, looking away from the bickering couple to a most curious van. Were there many animals prowling a city that required capture in the middle of the night?

I owed no explanation to anyone, much less a remnant of a life poorly lived. But the bastard hovered in my line of sight and refused to move. I could wait until Layla had walked far enough away, but it sounded as if she and the wolf had stopped to scream it out.

Staring into his dark eyes that reminded me of a debonair man of the seas, I said, "Because I was tired of them pretending that their world wasn't cracking apart."

Daniel rotated his head to be obstinate. "No. You did it to break them up."

It was no skin off my perfect nose if she should choose to sever her bond with the wolf. I would at least be afforded peace without this disquieting press of guilt singing through my head. In my unending experience, human couples were little more than two people bound together by law who'd happily kill the other if they didn't also have to bury a body. It was only a matter of time before the scales fell from their eyes.

"You did it to hurt her."

Indignation burned through me, the human flesh crackling to the demon skin below. I raised myself higher, talons sprouting from my elbows and wings of shadow bursting through the air. "You know—" Before I could speak another word, the ghost vanished. No doubt he had been pulled to Layla's side like the obedient lapdog he was. "Coward," I muttered, tossing off the demon façade with a flick of my wrist.

I had no intention of involving myself in their hysterical drama. But alas, any fun I'd have alone could only be of the looking variety. Slipping to the market to observe a delicious cake could be entertaining for a moment, but being denied a slice for time unending was beginning to chafe at my most delicate bits. I tipped my head to the side, listening for my bond's ever-beating heart. It was steady, but quickened with anger and a flush of shame.

"What I wouldn't give to find a human lacking the latter," I whispered to the night when the door on the mysterious vermin-catching van opened.

That man looked strikingly familiar. Even with a cap tucked tight to his face, I recognized the sharp stoop of his nose and the roundness to his cheeks. Where had I seen him? My memory did not return while he inspected the interior of his van and removed a net and…a gun? An old danger trembled through me, the sensation clanging every warning bell, telling me what was before me could only be a—

"So it is true…" A woman's voice, rich with charm, punctured through my revenge haze and straight to my core. I pivoted on my foot and found her hiding in the shadows, a wide-brimmed hat obscuring her features.

She took one step into the light, revealing a scarlet red heel. I stared upward, fearing more trickery from either the locals, the other realms or the hunters. But as she raised her head, my jaw dropped.

A smirk lifted the lips red as spilt blood. "You escaped hell."

"Lust?"

# Chapter Three

*Ink*

There were few beings in this world that unnerved me to my marrow. The djinn, whose own wish-granting scheme interfered with my work, celestials, for obvious reasons, and her. "I see you've traded in the ebony for gold," I said, pointing to the cascade of blonde hair.

Her smile cracked apart the ruby lips, revealing the fangs of a creature who'd toy with its prey for five days before killing it. She was in many ways my mentor, my oldest friend and the greatest threat to my freedom. Lust patted her hair as if it were an ermine mink curled around her neck. "Look at you, my Eros. How long has it been?"

"The fire at the theater in sixteen-something."

"Ah yes, dear Henry did not see that one coming." She chuckled and tented her fingernails together as if she'd been the one to send the Bard out Viking style. "I must say, you were at your most exquisite with a ruff and silken doublet. But this layabout businessman outfit plays to an easier-to-digest crowd."

I smiled with Lust at the shared memory, but neither of us let it reach our eyes. "How did you know I was in hell?" I put to her, earning a slight bob of the head for catching her on a half-truth.

Lust plucked a small mirror free from her bag and stared at her reflection like Narcissus. She knew how to time it so anyone questioning her would be thrown off kilter, but I was used to her tricks and girded myself. "It was Pride. I forget which one."

"Ah, yes, Pride never seemed to travel far from the empire's ships."

"It left me in such endless despair to hear my beloved Eros had fallen." Lust clasped a hand to her bosom, her voice breathy in a skilled trap that'd ensnare most feeble-minded mortals.

I snickered at the idea and leaned closer to whisper, "And you took an entire kingdom to bed to distract you from the pain."

She lifted her shoulder as if I had caught her in a secret. We were cut from the same cloth, though Lust was far older than even I. She liked to claim she was the first sin of our kind, though it was possible she'd had the others banished for the title. I'd never cared to test her claim.

After retouching her lipstick, she snapped the compact shut with the same force of a whip cracking buttocks. "Imagine my joy upon discovering you had somehow slipped the inescapable bonds of hell to return to me." Lust curled her hand around my biceps and pulled herself closer until her cheek grazed mine.

I craned back to stare at her, finding familiar darkness in her eyes. She blinked them rapidly, testing the limits of her lashes. "How in the knotted realms did you manage to escape?"

Ah. That was her quest, of course. "With my usual cunning"—I wound my arm out of her grasp to raise both with a flourish—"and charm."

Lust chuckled mirthlessly. "Dear Eros, your cunning was always without grace and your charm…well, that is at least above mediocre, thanks to me."

I quirked my head at her cagey answer and drove to the heart of the matter. "Have you come to pump me of my secrets?"

The light glinted off her pearly teeth. "Way I've heard it told…" She placed a finger to my sternum and slowly danced each tip down my body. "You've been busy doing some"—Lust's touch stopped right above my loins as she leaned close enough to finish—"pumping of your own."

Lust retreated her hand to my hip but refused to slip away, and I lingered just as close. Her dreamy smile snapped to a groan. "Really, Eros? Yet another witch binding? Have you learned nothing?"

An uneasy feeling tried to swipe away my core being. I had no word for acting with the opposite of the charm, elegance and wit of an incubus. It was as if everything that made me a sin had been drained away, and it only occurred in her presence. "You don't understand," I whispered, shrinking at her disappointed glare. "When I emerged from the realm, I was lost, uncertain of this world…"

"Weak." Lust groaned as if she had come from the very idea.

I glared at her for such a reaction but kept my tongue still.

"My poor, dear Eros. Adrift in this world, without a tether to keep you safe, you fell into the first trap of those awful gatekeepers. I understand." She ran her fingers back through my hair, tousling the strands like an empress inspecting her newest silks. "You must be suffering from fits of terror."

"I'm quite content, truth be told."

The delicate touch cinched tight, Lust tugging my head back as she advanced. "Bound to a witch's teat with no escape save her good word or death. And we all know what happens if she dies."

*I am dragged broken-nailed and shattered-winged back to hell.* A tremble shivered up my spine at the memory of nothing, of long stretches when I could neither die nor slip into madness. In the nothing, I became nothing.

"You poor dear." Lust caressed my cheek the way a mother would her babe during a storm. "Ensnared by yet another cruel witch and forced to live on her bread and water alone. It is too much for a sin to endure."

"Oh, I can assure you, she is a fragrant wine and honeyed cake." Between the sheets, at least. Outside of it, Layla bounced between sour vinegar and bracing whiskey. I couldn't say which was better.

That wasn't the response Lust wanted. She tugged my head about like a puppet on her strings, but I gave no reaction and she let me loose. "Are you saying you're pleased with this arrangement?" She spoke as if scandalized by such an idea. "One of dreadful, unending *monogamy*?"

I laughed, fixed the hair she'd attacked and adjusted my cuffs. "It is anything but dreadful in a witch's bed." On occasion, the wolf would join in too. "If you're quite finished, it has been a pleasant opportunity to reminisce with you, Lust, but I think given the current circumstances it would be best to—"

A scream ran out through the streets. *Layla!* She was in a fight with the wolf. He'd be there at her side should interlopers dare to join. I felt the constricting of her heart not from loss, but fear and…something more.

Hands clasped around my shoulder. I reached back to break them both, when Lust's blonde hair swept against my cheek. "They're rather fragile, aren't they? A little cut here, a fall there and you're right back to hell, Eros."

My bond had been toying with powers beyond even my skill. Werewolves and pernicious hunters were one thing, but the Marid was another creature entirely. Never mind whatever this Mr. White she could not cease prodding was. If I cut ties now, before she leaped without looking one too many times…

Another guttural scream broke free and I took off running.

"If you change your mind, Eros," Lust called from behind, "you know how to find me."

# Chapter Four

*Layla*

I was going to murder that damn demon once I figured out how to murder technically not-demons. There had to be a spell to get him to stop acting like a drama-stirring pain in everyone's ass.

I put aside all thoughts of how I'd torture Ink now that the cat was out of the bag and about to explode around us. Cal didn't so much march as slam his feet down the alley behind the theater.

"Who is he?" I prompted. I'd been waiting for him to tell me, but he'd kept me in the dark about his time alone at the cabin in the forest. Or what I'd thought was alone until I had accidentally peeked in on his memory of stalking a red wolf.

Cal tossed his shoulders back, the two blades merging as if he were about to tip his head back and roar. I braced myself for that, or for him to shift and run. Instead, he crinkled his hands and collapsed his chin to his chest. "Damn that demon."

"Ink is…on everyone's last nerve. I don't know what's gotten into him lately. He can't stop…" There I went again. Every time I tried to get Cal to open up, he'd swing the conversation around to anything else. The tension had been inescapable and ready to blow from the moment I banished that cursed Marid. I wanted to convince myself it was the addition of Daniel to our group, but I couldn't lie any longer.

I hated that he was keeping a secret from me.

I hated that I was keeping a secret from him.

"Just…talk to me. I'm your…" My throat constricted at the word I'd happily tossed around without a thought. That was before. Before I had stolen into his memories and kept it from him. Before I had learned my mother wasn't dead but had abandoned me. Before I had realized I wasn't good enough to be loved.

His angry stance didn't fade, his eyes blazing and muscles that could crush a boulder locked in fight mode. "It's my brother."

Eli, the gentle and unstable brother, was dead. As for the other… "I've seen Mark with fur. He's a black wolf, not red. And not as big as this one, either."

Cal's wary aloofness snapped. "You saw the red wolf?"

*Ah shit.* Heat burned on my cheeks at the festering lie I'd been carrying for far too long. My fingers found their way inside my bag, running back and forth over the spine of my spell book while I glared at anything but my boyfriend.

He reached a hand out and, for a brief moment, I almost flinched. But it was to cup my cheek and brush back my hair. "What happened? Did he try to hurt you? Were there others?" Cal demanded fast. All I could do was hem and haw.

"I didn't *see* see him." My throat turned raw. Dana had warned me to not fuck this up, and I'd done it in record time.

"What?" he prompted, his voice dead save for an edge of concern.

"I saw you...seeing him?" In my mind, turning it into a question would lessen the blow. It took a moment for Cal to piece together what I had confessed, and when it hit, his anger exploded.

He leaped back, landing on the balls of his feet, while he tugged hard on his hair. "You...you used your fucking magic on me?"

"Not on purpose!"

"You're spying on me?"

"No!" I wanted to reach for him, to find some way to dampen the rising tide of anger, but when my hand fumbled for his, Cal yanked it away. "I have never spied on you."

"Except for when you thought my brother was a murderer."

"Like I'm the first," I muttered to myself, only enraging the beast. At his glare, I pointed to my arm. The bruises were long gone, but it was hard to forget the iron grip of a werewolf that despised me. Now there was another one out there. Another brother he'd never mentioned before?

For a beat, the anger in Cal's eyes lessened as he stared at where Mark could have done far worse if it hadn't been for Ink. I had good reason to be wary of werewolves, most of all for him. Every time he was around his own kind, they wanted to kill him. How could I protect him if I were left in the dark?

I opened my mouth to try to explain when Daniel popped in behind me. "That foul-mouthed buffoon decided to walk home," he said with a toss of his head. Only the blue hair highlight shifted before falling back to the same place it usually hung near his left eye. He took in me and Cal facing off, and in a cautious voice asked, "Have we determined a means of eliminating the red wolf?"

"No," I said to him.

Cal screamed over top of us, "You are not dealing with this! Either of you or the damn demon. This is my—it's not your concern."

"How is it not?" I exploded. "That thing had to be six hundred pounds and the size of a grizzly bear!" If my nightmares weren't already crammed full of memories of drowning and my mother's fraudulent death, that wolf would stalk them.

With a sneer, Cal stared me in the eye. "Do you think I can't handle it?"

"I think I don't want to see someone I love ripped to pieces by that monster!"

That shot missed by a mile, Cal's eyes widening. He staggered back a step. "You think...he's a monster? What about Mark?"

"Do I need to point out the bruise again?"

"What about Eli?"

"He was...okay, he tried to kill me too, but he didn't know who I was at the time." *Jesus, how am I even able to function?*

Daniel must have shared in the thought as he hovered close and brushed his hand over the small of my back. I only felt a tingling cold from his touch, but it grounded my heart in a way I couldn't explain. I started to cup the locket around my neck that contained a piece of Daniel when Cal groaned.

"What about me?"

"Cal..."

"I'm no different than the rest of them. Same claws, same fangs, same...sire. We're all the same fucked-up monster you fear so much you'd steal my memory. Why not shove a tracker on me while you're at it? Seems easier."

"I'm. Not. Tracking. You!" *Why isn't he getting this?* It was a mistake, one I'd never intended, and wished I could take back. But if I did, it'd leave me in the dark, unable to help him if or when the wolf attacked. "What about you? Huh? You couldn't even text me that you were staying in the woods. That you were stalking the fucking compound!"

His righteous anger snapped for a second, Cal slamming his jaw shut. Tears of more than frustration rose in my eyes.

"What if you'd been hurt? They have guns, and I was so far away. I couldn't have...they might've... Aagh!" All I could do was scream in anger at the ever-looming fear that with one false step he might have been taken from me. And he'd had the audacity to tell me to keep my nose out of supernatural shit while he stalked around the army that had bayed for his blood.

"Layla..." He took a step forward, his expression unreadable. I moved for him, hoping we had finally reached the point of understanding, when a jabbering sound broke from above. I stared upward just as a dark shadow leaped off the roof and landed on Cal.

He reared back, trying to pitch off the jackal-like creature latched around his shoulders and waist. "What the fuck is this?" he cursed, swiping a clawed hand back, but the chittering thing hung tight.

"Hang on." I fumbled for my Sharpie to draw a spell on the attacker. Anything else could hit Cal by mistake. I had to be precise or—

"Layla!" Daniel called when the sky overhead went dark.

I had no time to move before fifty pounds of slathering, tittering monster smashed onto my back. I caught myself before hitting the ground and tried to reach around to find the cursed thing. It laughed like a hyena, then snapped canine-like jaws near my hand.

All the while, Cal was spinning in a circle chasing his nonexistent tail to try to shake the thing off. "There!" I shouted, pointing to a dumpster hidden behind a wall.

He met my eye and nodded once before rushing to scrape the damn thing off. I took a step to join him, only for its weight to increase exponentially. My legs bowed and my shoulders crumpled. I gritted my teeth and kept going, my whole body sinking as the monster grew heavier with each step.

"Cal!" I reached for him, but he too was crumpling under the similar weight-gaining jackal on his back.

"What…?" I sputtered, only for my legs to give out. My chest pounded against the concrete, knocking the wind from my lungs. I pulled in a breath just to hear the creak of ribs. Even pinned to the ground, the monster wouldn't stop. Pain spidered from my spine to every organ. What if it cracked my ribs and sent every jagged edge plunging into my lungs? What if it curved my vertebrae in until they pierced my heart?

Incoherent anatomy charts flashed before my eyes as I strained for Cal, who was at least still on one knee. The marker slipped from my fingers and Daniel batted at it as if he could kick it to me. "Layla, what do you need?"

"I need…" A knot lodged in my throat, blocking off my air. In a panic, I swung to the side, letting oxygen in before the creature grew to the weight of an elephant.

"Ahhh!" I screamed into the night, the bone of my cheek pressing so hard into the ground I feared it'd pierce through the flesh. "Daniel! Cal! Ink…" The stench of the back alley splashed through my sinuses. I fought against the cloying taste of spilled sewer water lingering in the puddles and thrashed my legs. But there was no fighting a monster that weighed hundreds and hundreds of pounds. All I could do was flail my arm around in agony in the hope someone might take it.

A hand wrapped around my hair and yanked my face up. Blissful oxygen rampaged down my choked-out lungs. I gasped, fighting to fill them even as my scalp screamed in agony. When my savior bent down and winked, I cried out in a strangled voice, "Ink?"

"Forgiveness for having to ravage you so abruptly, my bond. I promise next time to utilize the preferred safe word." Ink lashed a hand out and caught whatever the hell was on me by the jaw. It jerked around wildly even while keeping me pinned. I flailed and stared up at an unnervingly calm Ink.

The jackal bit down. Black demon ichor dripped down Ink's arm. He merely grunted in response and refused to let go. "Daniel, my book!" I shouted, directing the ghost to pick up the one thing he could.

He nodded and dashed for my purse. I stared helplessly at Cal, who was partially shifting under the same oppressive weight. Fur sprouted across his shoulders and back. I wanted to help him, but he was too far away.

Daniel floated above, clutching my book of spells. "What am I looking for?" he asked in a panic.

"What are these things?" I shouted, straining for Cal. My body felt like a stretched rubber band nearly at a breaking point. But I saw his paw, my fingers nearly touching him.

Ink released his grip on my hair, sending my face falling. But with his freed hand, he could cinch tight to the monster's throat. As he pulled, I heard a pop and some of the weight lifted off my shoulder. "They're off fuckers," he said calmly before crushing mine in the throat a second time.

"Cursing doesn't find them any faster," I snarled, though they were fuckers of the highest order. *Cal…*

"No, that is their name. They are aufhockers. Creatures who kill by leaping upon the backs of their victims. And have breath that would curdle the undead. What do you eat?" Ink asked the monster still clinging to me.

"Book! Find me a spell to get rid of aufhockers!"

The pages began to flip and Daniel hunched down so I could see it. They didn't move quick enough. A whimper broke the air. Nearly all of Cal was obscured by fur. I couldn't wait to find the spell.

Bundling my spell book in my hand, I twisted around and smashed the aufhocker right in the jaw. It shrieked, smoke spitting from its face. Two fangs tumbled free and I hit it again. Crying in pain, it wrenched its gouging fingers off my body. It felt like a suction cup had ripped off my skin, but I could take a full breath.

I turned to face it, ready to bash the thing's skull in, when it bit clean through Ink's hand and skittered away. Dark ichor stained its black skin where tufts of fur had torn. I didn't have time to chase it. Crawling over the disgusting ground, I wound up and smashed my trusty book into the aufhocker on Cal's back. This one had more sense and leaped away, taking the pressure off him.

"You goddamn fuckers!" I shouted, winding up for a harder smash against its jaw, when it jumped off him and skittered up the wall.

*I should chase after it before it kills anyone else.* A gasp of pain hurled that idea out the window. I collapsed to my knees and inched over to Cal. His wolf feet lay spread before him, his fur splotchy amid the pale skin. "Are you hurt?" I asked, readying my marker to heal him.

The ice-blue eyes I knew could only be him stared up at me and slowly he shook his wolf head.

Ink dashed out of the alleyway with his spurting hand. "It seems to be getting away," he said without a care in the world.

I was about to run my hand over Cal's head, but I paused before touching him and rose to my feet. "Fuck!" I cried. It felt like a gorilla had used me as a punching bag. Every rib ached, my stomach tender to the touch. I whispered the healing spell to myself while I walked over to Ink.

The orb of soothing ran through me, chasing away the pain just as I reached over and caught his arm. "Here," I said. "Let me fix it."

"Fix what?" he asked and raised the hand that'd been ripped in half by the aufhocker's teeth. As I watched, the skin warped over the wound, wiping away any evidence of his trauma.

"You…" I reached over to pat his shoulder while staring at the hand. A part of me expected the fresh skin to fall off, but it looked as solid as the rest of Ink. "You're terrifying sometimes."

Ink cocked an eyebrow. "Only some of the time?"

"Layla, sweet heavens. Are you okay?" Daniel crashed around me, his cold body setting off a tingle down the entirety of my left side. I wanted to reach over to drape my arm around him and pull him closer, but I had to settle for giving him a weak smile.

"Getting…ah." The spell worked its magic, un-bruising ribs and wiping away the punctures to my organs. "Right as rain."

"You were nearly crushed by those…"

"Aufhockers," Ink said. "They're quite popular in dark forests where villagers won't be missed." He kept staring in the direction of the escaped, bleeding one. I didn't have time to care about that.

Daniel was in dire straits, shaking his head and muttering, "You were so close to death, and I could do nothing but watch!"

"Don't be so down on yourself there, Daniel." A chipper Ink strangely cheered him on. "You weren't just incapable of doing but also of thinking. Quite useless in any fight."

"I was able to rescue her spell book while all you did was cling to the monster to, what, display your strength? Wow everyone with your prowess even as Layla was crushed below?"

Ink raised a shoulder as if he didn't care, but I knew why he had come running to my rescue. If I died, he went back to hell. It was a simple equation that at least kept me alive. But it didn't encourage him to protect the others.

Hobbling to his feet, a human Cal inspected his pants that remained and the shoes that were long gone. He sighed slowly, and I winced at the gasp of pain he couldn't hide. "Here." I whispered the healing spell, a small orb of light forming above my hand and held it out to him.

All he had to do was reach out to take it, but Cal tenderly wrapped his hand to his ribs and stared anywhere else. "I'm fine."

"You're panting," I argued back. "Let me take the pain away at least."

"No!" He slapped my hand, sending the healing spell flying through the air where it struck a section of wall and repaired the chipped paint.

I glared at my wasted gift, then him. "Why did you do that?"

Cal wouldn't look up. He ran a hand through his hair, his blond locks stained to a dark hay from the puddles. "Look, I…I need to get home. Before my feet freeze."

"My apartment is closer. It wouldn't take us more than a couple minutes—"

"No. I'm…I should go to my place. For a few days. I need time to…" Cal pulled in a breath as if he meant he needed the time to heal, but I knew what he wanted was space.

"Will I…?" *Oh god, not the tears.* I tightened my grip around my Sharpie, digging the pen cap into my palm. "Will I see you…?"

Cal pursed his lips and gave a noncommittal, "Mm-hmm." With that final half noise to me, he slunk away.

He paused beside Ink and the two whispered while I stood in shock.

Telling myself to not cry wasn't working, so I refused to look at them. Only the soothing sweep of Daniel's hand told me I wasn't alone.

"I am never far," Ink said loudly after their little conversation. I glanced up just as Cal limped out of the alley. "My bond, you're shivering."

The demon swept around me, rubbing my shoulders and staring as if he expected me to fall to his feet in gratitude. I hugged myself instead, incapable of not hearing every ragged breath of the man who'd rather suffer than let me heal him. Ink gathered up my purse and placed it on my arm, then he pointed to the book for Daniel.

They put me back together until I almost felt human. Daniel drifted beside me while Ink clasped me safe in his arms. They guided me out of the alley. *What am I going to do? How do I…can I make it up to Cal?*

"How interesting," Ink mused, shaking me from my slip into the depressive darkness. "The creature's blood trails to the empty land where the Animal Catcher's carriage was."

He wanted to distract me, but I wasn't in the mood. "Take me home," was all I said to my demon and ghost. My heart cried out for my stumbling werewolf.

# Chapter Five

*Layla*

For the first time in over six months, I woke alone. Not because my werewolf boyfriend was frying up a pan's worth of eggs. Or because he was locking together every extension cord in the place to warm up his truck's manifold. He was gone, and I had no idea if he'd ever be back.

I glared at my closet, half the clothes hung up, the rest scattered on the floor. Rather than pick from any of it, I wrapped my blanket around my shoulders and stumbled to my living room. My first glance was to the kitchen, where I'd normally find Ink concocting a terrifying breakfast out of things that were technically food. Nothing sat at the table save my new aloe plant that was already drooping. Had he abandoned this sinking ship too?

That had to be a record—*witch explodes her entire life in under an hour*. Didn't even require magic or rampaging beasts, just me and my fucked-up self. I moved to check the mail piling up on my kitchen passthrough, when a soft sound drew me to my living room.

It wasn't Ink watching his infomercials. The haze of the TV glowed not off the man perched on my couch, but through him. Daniel's hands dangled between his knees as if he didn't have the energy to raise them.

"What's on TV?" I asked, trying to act like everything was fine.

In a somber voice, he said, "I am."

*What?* Easing around, I sat beside him as the studio reporter switched to one in the field. More precisely, one standing behind a warehouse where police had taped off the shallow grave. I had dug it with help from Ink.

"Officers can finally release the name of the body discovered on Palomino Road. It's one Daniel Lu, a resident of Rockford who went missing over thirty years ago."

An old picture of Daniel appeared on-screen, not with the punk wardrobe and blue hair he'd worn when he died. This was a school picture of him with a blue and purple laser background. He'd stared skyward as if certain of a bright future. Instead, he was trapped in an undeath with only a worthless witch for company.

"Authorities are looking into the case at present..." The news said what it always did, trying to convince the public both that crime was always rampant and that the police would solve all those murders they'd never gotten around to. "If anyone has a lead in the murder of Daniel Lu..."

"Yeah," Daniel shouted at the TV, "you buried him with honors a week ago. Should be pretty easy to dig him back up!" We'd thought that would release him to whatever afterlife there was, but all the chase had led to was another grave. He'd seemed accepting of the outcome, but now his eyes blazed with a righteous fury I couldn't blame him for.

"Are you okay?" I asked and held my hand out.

He clung to his knees, hands flexing in rage as he hovered closer to the screen. "Bet they even draped an American flag over him. A real hero who died tragically. Who cares about how many people he stepped on to get there?"

"Daniel." I curled my hand and he finally glanced at it. With a sigh, he drew his fingers through mine. I felt them glance against the inside of my wrist before he took control. It was the only way we'd found to be able to hold hands, though this time it did little to calm him.

"I oughta march down there and go all poltergeist in the evidence room. Hurl a picture of the councilman onto the detective's desk. That a good enough clue for you?"

Before he could finish his tirade, the news switched from the discovery of a body to a cute cougar cub at the zoo. Umbrage railed through me from how quickly a tragedy that had ended a life was swept off in the blink of a segment, but I couldn't look away either. The cub was playing with a dandelion poof and it sneezed.

"They'll find nothing. Naught but rotted bones and grizzled flesh." He chuckled mirthlessly to himself, his eyes closed tight. I tried to cup my fingers, but they couldn't move. Daniel had full control. "I became accustomed to my voice unheard, my face unseen. Now that my bones are exposed to the light…this indifference is a thousand cuts deeper than thirty years in purgatory."

In his anger, he waved my hand up alongside his. Strain ran up my forearm and I couldn't hide the wince. He must have seen as he quickly turned away and calmed his motions. But he shifted closer, the chill of his body biting through the blanket. "Are you concerned about what they might find on my bones?"

"I'm sure if the councilman didn't wipe down anything incriminating, Samuke would have. Shit, he's probably the one running the investigation."

"I was thinking more that you were the one to dig them up."

I clenched tight around the locket that never left my chest. Technically it was haunted, but by a very friendly if not occasionally acrimonious spirit. His bone rested inside, the reason he could leave the library where he'd died and travel with me. The other piece I kept in a bowl of loose change in my apartment, though Ink often threatened to toss it out the window.

"Even with Samuke pushing it, there's no way to tie me to your murder. I wasn't even born yet," I said with a laugh, when the thought struck me hard. Probably hit both of us as Daniel stared away. If he hadn't died, he'd be in his late fifties. Then again, Ink was nearly two thousand years old. A thirty-year age difference meant nothing compared to that.

"My worry is what if Mr. White finds out you didn't fully die?" I asked. The others had laughed at my obsession with the strange man who was somehow involved in every problem that befell us. Or they had right up until Samuke revealed this threat was genuine. "Have you remembered anything about why—?"

"No," Daniel interrupted, shaking his head. "I've tried to piece it together, but my mind's blank. I remember the hotel room, a conversation with the band about…Bryan. Then the shot that struck me dead. I don't even know how I got to the library. It's all a fog."

I placed my palm to his cheek, feeling nothing but the cold air, but his smile lifted at my attempted touch. "We'll figure it out. Once I find a spell to bring you back, then it'll be easy as pie." Just a quick slip into his memory and I'd know the secret Mr. White feared enough to kill someone over. I prayed it wasn't his prize-winning butterscotch cake recipe.

Daniel laughed, causing me to shrink back. "You speak with such conviction, it's a wonder your enemies don't fall to their knees."

"That'd make my life easier," I muttered.

"Layla." He took control over both of my hands and clasped them together as if he cupped them. I gazed into his dark brown eyes, my heart skipping a beat at the intensity. "A ghost could not ask for a better champion."

With my thumb, Daniel swept his touch across my bottom lip. The gentle sway back and forth set off a buzzing that trickled down my tongue and throat. I was waiting for him to take my hand lower, when he said, "Only a fool would toss away your love."

"What?" My spine went rigid and I sat away from my own hands. Daniel held them before me, his hazy eyes sharpening.

"He was throwing such a fit over nothing. It's not like you meant to…"

"Don't." I ripped my hands back, Daniel letting them go from his haunting. "This isn't…you don't understand."

"I've seen plenty. The night he was off doing god knows what, which he still hasn't told you about, you were risking your life."

For him. For me. I didn't even know anymore. Cal had asked me to lie low, which should have been easy. But if I sat too long, my mind churned with who Mr. White was. It was an obsession without a face or reason. I couldn't explain it, the way poets couldn't rhyme purple.

Daniel was exasperated. "Why do you keep taking his side in all of this? You really think you walking around on eggshells to humor his messed-up mind was wrong?"

"Yes!" I shouted so loudly my upstairs neighbor banged on the floor. I didn't want someone to tell me Cal was wrong or he had overreacted. That I had just as much right to his secrets as he did to mine. I just wanted it gone.

Pain caught in my chest, and I stumbled back, knocking against the TV. "I..." I should have been in class, but Cal would be there, and Dana. Fuck, she'd know. She'd give me that pursed look that said, *"I told you you were gonna ruin it, now look at the mess we all have to deal with."*

A throbbing rose in my head and I raced about the room, grabbing my tattered jeans and a small T-shirt that strangled my breasts. "I'm going to try the witch's shop. See if they know a spell to get you a body. It's best if you don't come. Who knows what other witches would do to a ghost?"

I'd armed myself with only my purse and spell book, flip-flops on my feet for a late March jaunt. I looked a damn fool, but I didn't have the wherewithal to find socks for my boots. Putting on a smile, I said, "Sound good?"

"Layla...you should not go alone," Daniel said slowly, but I wasn't in the mood.

I wrenched open the door and came face to face with my wayward incubus. Ink smiled as if he were expecting me so I grabbed his arm and called back, "Come on. You can 'protect me' from myself."

"That sounds a tall order, but I shall endeavor," Ink said before I yanked him off his feet and down the hall.

# Chapter Six

*Ink*

Charms better for warding off good sense than evil dangled from a wire rack festooned with dried herbs. I risked leaning closer and pulling in a whiff, only for the scent of lavender and sage to fail to remove a single toxin from my inhuman soul. It did crawl up my nose, setting up shop where my inability to sneeze refused to dislodge it.

"My bond, do you perchance carry a kerchief in your bag?" I asked.

Layla kept her purse slung tight to her hip, as if she were protecting it. At my question she jumped, drawing my curiosity. Were we supposed to be in this den of cottage witchcraft? Or had she finally let loose and taken to a proper rogue life?

"You want a what?" she asked, no doubt all of her concern on the abrupt exit of the wolf.

I drew a finger beneath my nose and she blushed. "Right, that… Hang on." When a small plastic packet of disposable hankies emerged, the beaded portal to another room parted. "Here." Layla tossed the kerchiefs in my direction. Naturally, I caught the bundle.

With my nose and lower face shielded by the white tissue, I watched the noted purveyor of schlock and trinkets pause behind her shop's counter. She dressed like a woman who wanted to pretend to be a peasant, but not suffer the boils and arthritic hands. They called the style 'Bohemian', which confused me. My experience in Bohemia was fewer long skirts and linen blouses, more vampires and murderous old women in forests.

"Sybil, hi," Layla greeted her.

The woman, aged forty-three, though using a sheen of makeup to hide the more noticeable wrinkles, slipped on a patronizing smile. "The young witch without a coven. After our last encounter, I didn't think you'd visit again."

Layla coughed and I stared in curiosity. Had I missed my bond going vitriolic on this witch? Shame. I'd discovered the allure of drizzling caramel, whipped cream and mustard over popcorn—a tangy treat perfect for a magical showdown.

"Sorry about all of that. I…"

"Never you mind," the woman said with a wave of her hand, as if she were magnanimously forgiving the very thing she had brought up. I'd be impressed, if my skin weren't twitching. "How did the nail work out for you?"

"Nail?" I inquired, stepping from the land of incense and herbs into the crystals and scarves. "For what reason did you require a piece of iron? Had you encountered one of the fae folk?"

"Not that kind of nail. It's off a finger, from a…hung man," Layla said, her cheeks delightfully pink as she whispered.

"And you came to this store for such a thing when you could have asked me?" It was not a brag, merely fact I had control over, but the woman scoffed. "Or your werewolf mate."

The blush drained to ice, Layla grimacing at the mention of Calvin. How long would this ire last? Ten hours had already passed. I could never remember the lengths to which humans would elongate grudges. "I didn't wind up needing it," she said to the other witch before placing her spell book on the counter.

I had been created to answer the hedonistic desires of mortals, humans in particular, but even I could feel a wary hunger off the book. And it was increasing with each day. *Perhaps I shall mention that to Layla.* Though her shoulders seemed strained overmuch already. No rush.

"I need to ask you something," Layla said.

"First, dearie." The Sybil woman cupped her hand and a blue light rose from the skin of her palm. It solidified into a half-moon shaped glass which she pressed to Layla's forehead. I reached out to stop it, when the woman said, "Your aura is in dire straits."

She was an aura witch. Of course. Useless in the fight against the realms' spawn, even more pointless should nature or man pick up the sword. But they could make pretty butterflies, so most towns put up with them and their wagons of junk potions. I relaxed back on my heels, feeling a fake calm try to sweep through my bond's panic. It wouldn't do much, but some wanted the plaster while keeping the scar.

"Shall you balance her humors next? I believe that hair pin would work for bloodletting in a pinch."

The witch stared up at me, finally noticing that Layla had not come in alone. Her lip curled and she twisted her hands, casting out small bubbles of gold. They whooshed through the air, arcing to splatter on my face. I swept a hand through them, popping each one against my forearm.

Where they landed, the crimson shirt and tan flesh peeled away to reveal the black and red skin of the nether realm. It only lasted for a moment and caused no discomfort. Aura witches were, on the whole, pointless. Still, I watched the shirt stitch together over the exposed skin, hiding away my secret.

It was the Sybil woman who shrieked, "Demon!"

"He's not a demon," Layla said patiently.

"Incubus, at your service." I extended my hand in a friendly manner, before blanching at my overture. "Not your service, thank you. I do have standards."

She hustled over the counter and swept a protective hand around Layla. My poor bond looked like a cat being smothered in love, the whites of her eyes radiating confusion from between the woman's hands. "Get out of here, demon. Sin. Whatever you are! You're not wanted!"

Straining forward, Sybil reached for a yarn-woven god's eye. With it in hand, she thrust the rainbow yarn wound about four sticks in my face, and I cocked a brow. "I'm sorry, what is this meant to do?"

"It wards off demons," she said, as if she had sipped from her poisoned chalice by mistake.

"The most that is capable of doing is catching on fire when the villagers grow wise to your miracle elixirs." I batted it away with the back of my hand and watched the wily woman's certainty falter.

"He's fine," Layla said, shrugging her way out of the woman's embrace. "He's with me."

"You've raised a demon out of hell?" she gasped.

"As previously noted, I am not a demon. And she is right, I am bound to her. Even if I wished to entertain your desires—which, believe me, I have no intentions—I cannot." I clasped a hand to my bosom and stood taller. "My body belongs only to her."

Layla laughed awkwardly and shifted back. "Thanks…Ink. Look, I'm not here about him. He's not a problem. I need a spell."

"Not a problem? Incubi, all the sins, are created to pull the life force from their victims!"

"Ah, so you do know one thing. Color me impressed." I perked up, drawing the ire of the witch. Was it my fault if her wise woman façade faltered with a solitary question? Perhaps if she studied her ancient writings more and opened the windows in this oppressive, incense-laden shop, her mind wouldn't be that of a mule farmer who had bent too close to their animals' hooves.

"You are not wanted here!" The witch waved her hand as if casting me out. I cocked my hip to the side and met her eyes. She dug through the back of her counter and placed down her leather-bound spell book. This was an ivy green to Layla's blood red, and much thinner too. Not a strong line, not that I expected it.

Keeping one eye trained on me, Sybil flipped through her book before landing on a spell. I girded myself to be tossed through the walls, but when she spoke a familiar refrain I snickered. Upon finishing the string of old Latin, Sybil slammed her book shut and looked up to find my entire body awash in blue flame.

I, however, was not screaming nor writhing in pain. Calmly, I inspected my nails, perturbed to find a cuticle had torn at the base. At the dropped jaw from the aura witch, I smirked. "It tickles."

She wiped away the spell before the ethereal flames reached her tchotchkes. It was my bond who drew close, concern in her beautiful eyes. "Are you okay?"

"If I were a wandering corpse hellbent on destroying my creator, it would have been unpleasant. Alas, I am not. If this peacocking display is finished, my bond has a question to put to you. And I have a wonder about the price for this crystal goblet. How much iced cream do you think it can hold?"

Fully drained of her power, Sybil glared at the cup I held. It was only on Layla she focused, treating me like a moth among all the others circling her wares. "I will not help you until the demon is gone."

"How many times must I explain?" I muttered to myself. I returned the goblet—the only object of potential value—to the shelf and crooked my arm out for Layla.

My bond strode before me and said, "Ink, why don't you wait outside?"

I snickered at her playing along, keeping my feet rooted, when she added a "Please."

"You cannot be taking her side in this. She is little more than a charlatan masquerading as a witch."

"I am a powerful sorceress of the ninth order."

I stared at her boast. "Is that how many butterflies you can make flit from your fingers to the oohs of children?"

*Layla must see there is no validity in dealing with a woman such as this.* Her lack of skill and knowledge was obvious to even the lowliest of creatures. But my bond struck another arrow to my heart as she sided with the woman and crossed her arms. "I see. Well, it is your limited time to waste. Not mine."

Even with a smile and my head bowed, I railed inside. How could Layla be so easily bamboozled? How could she treat me like an inconvenient tissue tossed from her person? When her arm wrapped around mine, I leaned closer, ready to sweep her off her feet and to anywhere across the world—an opera in Rome, a snow-capped cabin in the Alps, a return to the erotic bathroom of Paris.

"Thank you," she said, patting me once like she was dismissing a dog.

Dumbstruck, I clattered down the stairs, shoved the whole of my body against the glass door and stumbled into the weak sunlight of this forgotten city. If she had so little use for me, then perhaps Lust was right. It was time to cut the strings that bound us. I had a whole world waiting for me.

# Chapter Seven

*Layla*

*Couldn't he be civil for once?* I shook the thought away as I faced down my only hope for a cure of sorts for Daniel. Sybil glared in Ink's direction as if he'd taken a shit in her petunias. It was my fault for bringing him in the first place.

"Look…" I began, but she spoke over me.

"I understand you are bereft of a coven or a mother witch for reasons beyond your fault." Without Ink cutting her down to size, the pompous language roared back tenfold. "But I am telling you, in professional and personal confidence, to sever whatever you've done to bind that demon to you."

Here it came. If people weren't snarling at me being a witch, they damn near leaped off a cliff upon learning Ink was a sex demon. "I don't really…"

"Demons are charming, slithering creatures that worm into your life and, seemingly without cause or care, destroy it."

I scoffed at the thought. "Ink's helped me. He's saved me."

She glared at me from above the moon specs perched on the tip of her nose. "Or has he created the danger in your life necessitating his rescue?"

No. Sure, he needed to keep me alive so he wouldn't go to hell. But he wasn't the one who… I ground my teeth at the memory of the flippant way Ink had revealed my secret about the red wolf and turned Cal against me. But he was always doing that. It couldn't have been on purpose. Right?

Sybil clasped her hand to my arm, causing the bangles on her wrist to clack. "While it is impressive for a witch of your young age to conjure a demon from hell…"

"I didn't." I interrupted her for once, and she frowned.

"What do you mean, you didn't?"

"He appeared one day in my living room, nearly naked and talking about how I was his bond." As the words left my mouth, my heart sank. I hadn't even looked into it, hadn't pried when I knew he was deflecting. We were busy trying to not die—I had to learn spells to fight off scroungers and werewolves and witch hunters and shark genies. If I had an incubus there by my side helping, who was I to question it?

But I had never asked Ink how he was bound to me. "Why do I have a bad feeling about this?" I asked, more to myself than the knowledgeable witch.

She twisted her head about, casting small magic birds from her hair. The tiny blue lights flew around the room, forming calming waves that did nothing to me. "A binding spell is… I've never cast one myself, but the way I understand it, it requires someone powerful and willful to tie two together."

"So you can't just wake up, and 'oh, you have a pet demon now'? Not that he's a pet. Okay, he's the most obstinate cat that breaks everything in the house then lays on your lap demanding attention. And I can't stop thinking about Ink with fur now!" My mouth ran away as panic zipped through me. If it wasn't me, then who had bound a demon to me and why?

*Mr. White?*

*Was he really sent to destroy my life?*

"Rid yourself of him as soon as possible before he wreaks more destruction." The conspiratorial whisper snapped away and she smiled. "Was that all you wished to ask?"

"No…" I started to lay my book on her counter, when the bell to her shop rung. Sybil stared up at whoever entered with a patient smile. But when a shadow in a suit passed behind me, her smile hardened as if she were baring her teeth behind her lips.

I ignored it and leaned closer to whisper, "Do you know of a spell that can bring someone back from the dead?"

"Why don't you join me in the back to look for that," she said and took my hand. Before I could argue, Sybil yanked me behind the counter and through her beaded curtains. Here was the magical land of storage bins and cracking labels. It felt less fantastical, and more like I had walked into the basement for a magic MLM. Most of the real potions were stored in mason jars with nary a twist of jute curled around the neck.

My book felt heavier, and I raised it in the hopes she'd fill it with my missing spell, but Sybil cupped a hand to mine and pushed it into my purse. "I don't know why you want to raise the dead…"

"I don't want an army. I just need to bring someone back. His body."

"You'd need a soul," she chastised me.

"That's not an issue."

She narrowed her eyes. "You keep most strange company, fledgling."

I hadn't even told her about the werewolf. The reminder of Cal caught my throat, and a burn rose up my heart as if the whole of my chest were on fire. *Put it away. This is about Daniel.*

"I'm sorry, but whatever you're hoping to accomplish cannot be done."

"But there's a mention of it, another witch who brought back her love." I started to flip through my book even though no one but me and my ghost could read it.

Sybil's easy-going nature slipped, and she eyed the pages with a calculating curiosity. "Regardless of whatever fanciful tale you found within your grimoire, I'm afraid I have no spell that can do as such."

"Any chance you know someone who would?" I asked, clinging to the hope there was a witch network out there.

She dashed that in an instant with a slow shake of her head. "If you will take my advice, dear sister—cut loose the demon, let the ghost fly free and join our coven. It is a welcoming place that would do well with you in our ranks."

"How so?" She'd been treating me like a dumb freshman. Why would anyone want that around?

The hunger snapped away, and the sweet Sybil returned. "We all learn better to hone our talents when teaching a new apprentice witch how to handle hers."

That made some sense. But abandon Ink? "I'll think about it," I said, committing to nothing.

She didn't lash out and chain me to the wall, but smiled kindly. "Whatever you think is best, dear."

Another bell rang, this time from the counter. Sybil snapped straight up and called out, "Be with you in a moment." Bustling, she softly pushed me out through the beads where I spotted a man in the kind of suit that screamed 'don't remember me.'

Stranger still, he wore a pair of sunglasses inside the darkened store. They hugged his impressively long and sharp nose, the black lenses hiding his eyes. Sybil placed her hands on the counter and asked, "What will you be needing?"

"Do you have these in blue?" the man asked in a carefully neutral voice. The accent was plain American, no drawl toppings added. He raised up a small pair of dreamcatcher earrings and focused his black lenses on Sybil.

"Excuse me," I muttered, slipping past him. He didn't move out of the way, causing my arm to strike his shoulder…and hit a brick. What the hell was he hiding under that black suit coat and skinny tie? I opened my mouth to make a cutting remark when an overpowering stench of eucalyptus rose from him.

It yanked my mind to anatomy and organs pickled in formaldehyde. My stomach danced at the thought even though I'd gotten rather good grades compared to pharmacology. Still, I placed a hand over my mouth, mumbled, "Goodbye" to the strange man and dashed for the door.

"Dear," Sybil called before I vanished. "Think upon what I said." Her eyes drifted to the man waiting patiently for his earrings. "The world is not a kind place for us."

*No shit.* I escaped into the street, which was casting off late spring for summer. The sun warmed my witch bones, which everyone hated as if they expected me to start hexing them right there. The only curse I had found in my book involved filling a person's garden with slugs, which didn't come in handy when most people lived in apartments.

"I need a vacation," I whispered to myself, staring at my bare toes that looked ready for a beach and not the wet streets.

"You only need say the word, and I will whisk you away for a fortnight of ravenous savagery beneath a canopy of stars." My demon swept from out of nowhere and clasped my shoulder.

His strong scent of brimstone and amber replaced the eucalyptus burning in my sinuses and I breathed deep. Thanks to Ink, I couldn't walk past open grills without getting wet. He must have sensed the thought as he swept a hand below my chin and plucked my head higher. Exhausted, I stared into his whiskey eyes.

Gently, he stroked across my chin while saying, "We can suckle wine and honey from each other's bodies while a bard delights us with his song."

"Would a bottle of three-dollar wine and a jar of Nutella while leaving Spotify on count?" I complained even while Ink's idea spun a web in my brain. *Say yes. Let him do what he does. Whisk me away to some deserted island, charm or steal whatever he wants and answer my every desire until I can't move.*

Or was it all part of his ruse?

"I can't," I said, my body collapsing in on itself. I only stayed on my feet by sheer willpower and the demon holding my chin.

Ink pulled me closer and placed a kiss on my weary lips. A jolt surged through me, trying to spark more. I raised my hands to hold him, but he had already backed off. A smile hung on his wet lips, though it wasn't his usual smirk. I'd daresay this one looked almost sad.

Despite being a sex demon, he listened to my words and let me go. "Perhaps another time, when the ghost has had his exorcise."

The pun wasn't subtle, but Ink had to add a wink in case I missed just how little use he had for Daniel or vice versa. Dealing with all that mess with Cal and yet another werewolf that wanted to rip my leg to shreds wasn't enough. I had a demon and ghost at each other's throats every time they shared a room. Maybe if they could finally come to blows, it'd work out whatever their issue was.

Ink crooked out an arm as if we were about to begin skipping down the street. "Now that your time with the aura witch has concluded, shall we abscond with a plate of breakfast donuts?"

I patted my stomach, which was already roiling at the idea of adding more fried dough to it, but watching Ink devour an entire box might be a good distraction. When I reached to take his arm, my phone beeped and I found two 'very disappointed' texts from Dana. Shit. She'd noticed I wasn't at class and wanted to talk to me. Now.

I hovered over the texts, trying to drum up an explanation. Pretending to be sick didn't work in a class of future nurses. The offered arm slipped away, and Ink stared sullenly at me. "Your attentions are directed elsewhere."

"It's Dana. I was supposed to be in class. I could still make the lab if I hurry." A half-assed explanation formed in my head about my car stalling, but she'd ask why I didn't come with Cal instead. Or she had already pressed him on my whereabouts and had sniffed out the whole mess in ten seconds. I had given a generic excuse about being there soon when the cool shadow of my incubus faded to a harsh burst of sunlight.

Blinking, I held my hand up to block it and stared at Ink. He gazed not at me, but toward the downtown cityscape in the distance. "Your time appears to be forever dividing. From this healing cloister, to the petulant wolf, to your time at the vegetable market, to the whims of the ghost."

Normally, I'd shrug him off. There was no turning on an incubus—their switches didn't come with an off and Ink was more than happy to wait until I wanted him. But the flippant tone of a demon with time to kill turning careful and guarded drew me to speak softly. "I'm busy. With a lot. What of it?"

"It leaves little time for…your witchcraft." He abandoned the horizon to glare at Sybil's door, the sunlight glinting off a rainbow pentagram in the window. "Perhaps it is time we dissolve our partnership."

"What?" My mind reeled and heart raced at the thought when I took a moment. Ink pretended he didn't care, but it was as obvious as when a puppy pretended it didn't want to leap onto a counter and steal all the food. "Look, I just needed to ask her a few questions…"

"The witch pressed upon you to join her coven." He said it with such authority I couldn't argue.

"Well…yes. But I wasn't gonna—"

"You should consider the offer. After all, I am but a simple demon of hell who cannot teach you much past the few tricks and spells I've acquired. A witch would have intimate knowledge, and you have your pet spirit to read over your shoulder. It appears that I am redundant in such matters."

Why did he sound so damn cheerful about the idea? As if he already had one foot out the door and the last thing on his to-do list was telling me. "Are you serious right now? Are you standing here telling me, right after Cal fucking…" My throat clutched at the gaping wound left in my heart and the unvoiced fear that I'd lost him. "You're telling me you want out? Why?"

"Your life is forever at risk, at your choosing, and I am of no mood to return to the desolate hell I fled." He was so cold, as if he'd decided everything by filling out a pro or con list.

In the five months I'd known him, Ink had been infuriating, temperamental, vague, gregarious, charming and licentious, but never cold. At least not to me. "Why?" I sputtered, near tears. I shook them down and came at him hard. "Why now? You didn't pitch a fit when the werewolves nearly killed me?"

"It seemed a mere trifle to me. I'd forgotten how frail human bodies are."

"Or just last week with the Marid. You went along with every plan to stop it."

"Do you not see the pattern arising? With each moment, you grow bolder, riskier. It is not only your life in your hands, but mine as well."

I didn't walk into danger on purpose—shit kept finding me. I opened my mouth to argue, when the dissociated Ink slipped away and his magnanimous smile returned. "There is an entire world of fresh-faced mortals waiting for me and my many talents."

That son of a bitch. "Are you serious? You'd…you want to leave me, break our deal just so you can go out and…and kill people?"

His smile crashed and he said, "I never made mention of killing."

"But that's what you do. Everyone else who's not a…not like me dies if they fuck you. That's how it works."

"And who informed you of such an end? The ghost? The wolf? The aura witch who told you to rid yourself of me?" He stood proud and tall, as if he were already above the discussion we hadn't even had.

"You think I should just let you go? Like that? Let you run around free…hurting anyone you want?" Even with every warning from damn near every person about Ink, I couldn't picture him as a killer. A sneaky schemer who cared only for himself, yes, but not a killer. Not the way the other monsters I fought were.

"I see." Ink shook his head and he turned from me. "Your solitary reason to keep me in your life was to restrain me because you believed me a danger to the world at large."

"That's not it."

"No? Do you not keep your human friends away from me? Have you not feared that I will visit them in the night?"

"That…" I began to argue it was stupid, when he cast his gaze back to me and I remembered pushing him away and fighting to keep my human life separate from this magic stuff. A lot of it was to protect Dana and Fariah, and anyone else I feared the demon in my bed might eye up. My jaw dropped, any excuse I could think of fading to a soft whimper.

Ink sighed to himself. "You need not throw yourself upon this grenade any longer. The witch's coven can teach you, even protect you from the death you cannot cease chasing."

I reached for him, trying to pull him back from this madness. "Ink…"

He dodged my touch. "I believe you had a lab to attend. Good day." Before I could get another word in, he vanished to god knew where.

Denial struck first. He wasn't serious. This was some game with him. Maybe he was toying to see if I'd reject Sybil's offer and prove that I needed him.

After that, I slipped straight to anger. How could he fucking do this now? First Cal, now Ink? The only reason Daniel didn't abandon me was because I carried a piece of his finger around my neck.

He'd get tired of me too, just like my mother.

"Ahhh!" I swung my foot out and kicked a parking meter, hard. The sound clanged up the street, drawing everyone who'd watched my breakup to stare harder. Pain crumpled up two of my toes, sending me hobbling away from the site of the crime. Why did I even want to keep some stupid sexy incubus around?

Sure, he could vibrate his tongue at the speed of a Hitachi and he believed I came first, second and third. But he never turned it off for even a minute. Middle of the fight of our lives, there was Ink making some jerking-off motion and trying to pull my pants off. And fine, he'd saved my life a few times. But how many times did he put me into danger? Not to mention his teaching…!

What teaching? Every time he'd tell me to practice a spell or question me on a monster, it'd end with him ripping off my clothes and raw-dogging it on the couch. An image of Ink, naked and inviting across my kitchen table, tried to invade my mind. He'd glistened from the rising heat of the radiator in winter, not sweated like me. No, the whole of his perfect tan had glowed, highlighting the edges of his newest tattoos. Tousled hair, his lips slightly parted, he had crooked a finger at me and held out a strawberry. The last one left in the package after he'd downed the rest with a pint of sour cream.

*It's just the sex. Fine ass, great arms, perfect cock. Nothing more. If he wants to be free, then…*

A scrabbling sound caught my attention, yanking me straight out of my abyss of man problems. Leading around the corner was a black set of footprints shaped like a very large dog's paws. Spots tumbled between the prints, as if the owner had been leaking black ink…or blood. The off fucker!

I yanked out my spell book and hardened my spine. Beating the shit out of something that had tried to kill me was the only thing I wanted in that moment. Armed and ready, I turned the corner, raised my book to shatter a jaw…and found three men in suits. They stood around the netted aufhocker whimpering from where it was pinned to the ground.

Witch hunters! I took a step back, fighting to keep from screaming for Ink. A squeal must have slipped out as they looked up as one. They were too far back to catch me.

I turned on my heel, ready to break into a run for my car, and I came face to face with a man in sunglasses. "Hello, Miss Leeland," he said. Lightning burst from his hand and struck through me.

My hand opened, sending my spell book crashing to the ground. I fought to keep upright, to run. A spell drifted through my mind, but my jaw locked at the electricity pulsing through me from a taser. Darkness swept in around me. I gritted my teeth, refusing to fall, when strong hands caught my shoulders and pushed me to my knees.

I stared up the long nose of the bastard tasing me and spotted emerald-green eyes peeking out from behind his shades. "I know…" I began, when a bag slipped over my head and all was lost.

# Chapter Eight

*Ink*

"That will look atrocious upon your body. Here..." Before the woman had a chance to ruminate upon my words, I extracted a garment of less-than-stellar qualities. With a frown, I inverted it and pinned the sides. "That shall emphasize your voluminous buttocks better."

She glared at my declaration but accepted the cheap frock before slipping into the back of the store with both. I'd found my way to the local market, as had been my wont whenever unsettled since the days of Alexandria. There were fewer calls for amphoras of oil or displays of Persian spoils, but the cacophony and energy remained the same. Desires answered with a flick of a wrist radiated from the throngs, slipping out of one stall to another, bags dangling across their arms. It was not as lively as I'd hoped, the open air of the market only containing at best a half dozen people.

Though I felt a tingle in the air of excitement and traced the line.

Wherever excitement led, desire was soon to follow. I found the mortals not entranced by a water wheel or Frankish fork but gathering around an open stage, their hands clasped together, shaking their purchases as a woman strode onto the stage. Her white-blonde hair was pulled back into a ponytail tight enough to raise the whole of her face. She wore little, a scrap of fabric reminiscent of a bandeau across the top, and small shorts I'd thought only meant for children over the bottom. All the better to display the chiseled abs in a full two rows and the cut of her arms as she waved them in a half circle to enliven the crowd.

It wasn't until she approached the microphone to speak that I crossed my arms and smiled. "Gluttony."

"Is everyone ready to learn the secret to your best body?" Gluttony shouted to the crowd. They didn't politely clap but broke into near riotous applause at the idea. Encouraged by the sound, Gluttony hefted up a stand of gray-green drinks and raised them above her head.

The rest of the presentation was of little merit. By the time she'd finished, I had to press through the crowds bleating on about her every nonsense word. They seemed to be under the delusion they too could mimic a body Gluttony sculpted with magic and will. One woman clung to her hand and cried out, "You're an inspiration."

"No, you are! For the journey you're about to undertake." Gluttony sounded about to explode with energy when she glanced up and the pep shifted to a slow laugh. "So it's true, you're back."

I snickered. "Is there an entire network of sins crowing about my ascent to earth?"

Gluttony shrugged. "Heard it from Lilith." She extended a hand to me which I took to join her on the stage. The slathering hordes were forgotten as we convened for a private sin conference.

"You mean Lust," I prompted, but Gluttony held her hands up in surrender.

"Only you can call her that. What does she call you again, Lust?"

I frowned for a brief moment. Out of respect for the hustle, we never used our names, only referring to each other by our sin demarcation. A name was power, a fact Lust—Lilith—knew how to use to her advantage. "A foolish word that means little. But I must ask, Gluttony, what has become of you?"

She laughed and twisted on her heel.

"You're far more spry than I remember."

"The world changed. No more feasting for all hours of the day in the homes of wealthy Jacobians. Did you know they don't even consider gout to be a kingly disease? I do miss those days."

I glanced back to the people who'd handed over a goodly amount of their paper for the consumption of the gray-green goo promised to bring them vitality and happiness. They were happily guzzling it down, no doubt feeding Gluttony, but there'd also been talk of restraining oneself to the point of fasting. "And now you preach of dieting to the masses?"

Gluttony chuckled. "I'd been starving, Lust. My arms turned to dust in the famine. The elite shifted, preferring body sizes that'd slip through the cracks in a wall and taking to refusing food for days on end in pursuit of some holy calling. It didn't sustain them, never mind me."

I walked beside Gluttony toward a stack of boxes of the liquid where another woman wearing the same logo sold them off. "You've always had it good. No matter how the norms change, there's always some lecherous bastard out there. I had to change my hunt and I've hit gold. How are we doing, Sara?"

The Sara in question shouted, "Ten sign-ups for the whole course already!"

Gluttony gave her a thumbs-up, then whispered in an aside to me, "I took your advice to heart. Do not pursue the fat fucks who delight in duck livers and wren's tongues. No, you go after the chaste and pure, and wait for them to debauch themselves."

"It always worked for me," I said. Any common vagabond could find release in a bordello or on the street corner. A proper connoisseur courted from the sisterly cloisters or behind the doors of abandoned spinsters.

"All those people out there have pledged to abstain from solid food for a week in the name of health, beauty, whatever I say. And once that week is up…"

"They will be ravenous," I said, causing Gluttony to snap her fingers and laugh.

A noise broke from her phone and she raised it up. Turning to the side, she willed her abs to appear more pronounced and said, "Hey, Cincinnati! I'm going to be there in two days! Can't wait to teach you the secret to owning your best you!"

While she pressed buttons on the phone, I twirled my pinkie in my ear. "The overabundance of enthusiasm must drain upon you."

Gluttony's high-pitched girlish chuckle dropped to a low rumble. "It's all part of the show. You play the demure gentleman."

"Only if that is what they wish…"

"I am the peppy, happy, perfect guru they wish to be. This world is starving for validation, and it is a delicious delicacy." Gluttony hunched over her phone, no doubt sharing more suggestions of starvation. I'd thought I had understood these lost four centuries in hell with research and general human watching. But Gluttony becoming the complete inverse of the sin I once knew walloped me with every lost year. Was I going about this all wrong?

She finished and stared at me. "Oh…open your shirt." Before I could agree or not, she ripped apart the buttons, revealing the body my bond had desired when we met.

"Everyone, this is my old friend…" She stopped pushing a red button on the screen displaying my body ready for consumption and whispered to me, "What name are you using?"

"Ink."

Gluttony blinked slowly. "Never were one to think outside the box, huh?" She pressed the button again and shouted, "Ink! Just look at those abs." Gluttony placed her palm to my stomach and traced down it with the phone.

In my long years of existence, I'd never once cared who pawed at, toyed with or enjoyed the fruits of this flesh carriage. But a sensation prickled over my skin at her touch as if I were in the wrong. I began to rear back just as Gluttony pulled away to message her acolytes.

*What was that?* Not Gluttony's manhandling—sins thought nothing of utilizing other sins on the hunt. *Why did my body react so negatively?* I cinched up my shirt, hoping to silence the sour note singing in my mind.

"That thirst trap ought to get me at least a couple hundred bites," Gluttony said. "You need to get on social, Ink. Face like that…good one by the way. There's a bad boy edge with a touch of mystery to it that'll drive bored housewives wild."

"This is what my bond prefers," I said, dumbstruck.

I pressed a finger to my long nose, then trailed it down to the full lip below. While the face never changed, the presentation did. If someone preferred the full lips and a short nose on a man, they would only see my lips and skip past the nose. I cared little for what the mirror told me, as it was always a lie. All that mattered was Layla's happiness with my features.

"Ah, right. Lilith said something about a witch."

"Lust spoke to you about her?" The hairs at the nape of my neck stood at attention. What purpose could she find in sharing that news with the others? Who else was she telling?

Gluttony shrugged and twirled her phone through the air without a care. "I don't know what you're thinking, binding yourself to one mortal. They die from eating the wrong mushrooms. It's a precarious perch I'd never sit on."

"You've never been to hell," I said.

"And I have no intention of visiting. Though I am curious how you got out. Lilith didn't mention."

Because she didn't know. I smiled brightly and waved a hand. "There are some secrets an incubus never reveals."

"Well…" Gluttony began to walk away, preparing for a second presentation on her lifestyle. "If you ever get tired of the witch's warts, hit me up. We can feast like kings from your pictures alone!" With that, she turned to face her crowd.

Spending my days taking erotic photographs and posting them across the world did not entice me. But I would need a plan of attack once Layla…once my bond accepted my request to sever our arrangement. She would be free to frolic with other witches and I could travel with whomever I wished as well.

Layla had no use for an incubus to share her bed or life any longer.

# Chapter Nine

*Layla*

"Are the defenses in place?"

The voice drifted in and out, like having only one ear bud in. I struggled to get up off my stomach only to find my arms were chained to the floor and my legs strapped to a… *Is that a fucking spreader bar? What the hell is this?*

Fear should have been rolling through me. I had just been kidnapped in broad daylight by a squad of weird men in black suits who kept spreader bars and chains in their van. But I'd save it for another screaming nightmare later. All that bubbled through me was a growing rage that they had kept me from my lab. If I missed it, I'd have to make the entire three hours up later.

"This isn't our first rodeo, Stone," a man, cocksure and in need of a facial rearrangement, said. He spoke close to my left hand and I tried to listen without shifting. Let them think I was still knocked out while I planned.

The ground rocked again, and I realized we were moving at an angle. My body didn't slip far thanks to the incredibly creepy bar between my legs, but I felt the dip in gravity thanks to my hair swinging forward. Good thing I had skipped breakfast, or the rumbling metal against my stomach would have sent all those donuts into the bag over my head.

*Where is Ink?* We were still bound… If these guys killed me… Oh fuck, they were going to kill me. A wheel smashed into something, causing my chest to compress against the ground, and I gasped, all the air fleeing my lungs. I started to panic, drawing the bag into my mouth instead of air. It tasted like old socks days out of the dryer and I tried to spit it out, only clogging it more.

A hand clutched my shoulder, raising me off the ground, and fingers pinched through the darkness to pull the soggy bag out. For some stupid reason, I almost said, "thank you" to the bastard that had kidnapped me. He reached under the collar locked around my throat and tugged the bag out so the wet spot clung to my forehead instead. *Great. Much improved.*

"There are reports of a werewolf and demon trailing her." This came from the man that'd yanked out my bag. I grew more aware of his foot pressing next to my chest—more specifically, the ankle, less than innocently nudging against my breast. *Urge to kill rising.*

*I could set him on fire by twisting my hands around.* Which wouldn't do much more than panic the drivers, who'd probably careen this van straight off the cliff we'd been going down for a half hour. And even if they all burned up, I'd be left chained up in a flaming van. *Okay, new plan. What if I…?*

"Stop worrying so much, Stone. It's covered. We read your damn report."

*Report? Has he been stalking me?*

*It wasn't an accident.* I hadn't walked into them capturing the aufhocker. They had set it up on purpose to catch me. The man with the sunglasses…

A groan slipped from my mouth. I was in a van surrounded by witch hunters.

"She's waking up," the front seat said. "You wanna shock her again?"

*Fuck.* I flinched away, rattling the chains and causing the driver to laugh.

"There's no need," this Stone guy said. God knew his voice matched his name, dead of all emotion like he didn't give a flying shit about kidnapping a woman and chucking her into a van. How often did they do this?

All the stomach lurching came to a halt. I felt like I was hanging on the edge of a cliff, my legs crying at the strain and my hair dangling above my head from the incline. Where the hell were we?

The sound of doors opening and the bong of the ajar alarm told me they'd exited. What if it was a boat ramp? What if they were going to send the van into the lake and drown me like those witches of old? *Ink!*

Warm hands cupped my ankle almost innocently. Whoever was touching me winced with his words. "You're not wearing any socks. The cuffs have reddened your skin."

"Sorry, I didn't plan on being kidnapped when I got dressed," I said before biting my tongue. So much for silently watching them.

He chuckled, and sweet relief broke from my ankle, then the sting of air hit the raw skin the metal had worn down. I gasped at the cold of the van's stripped bottom striking my bare foot. In the scuffle I'd lost one of my flip-flops, so I clenched my toes around the other.

My heart lurched at the presence of a shadow above me. Those damn feet stood astride my waist and I felt the man lean down. I locked up, my mind running rampant with what he intended to do up there. Meticulous fingers unwound the chains that'd bound my wrists.

As he worked, I felt his breath ruffle across the nape of my neck. "I believe we have a salve that can heal your injury."

I nearly laughed at the idea of my kidnapper giving a shit. "Or maybe you'll listen to the safe word next time. It's… Help!" I screamed at the top of my lungs and tried to crawl forward. A hand pressed to my back, pinning me to the van floor.

"Cute," was all this Stone said. He pushed harder, digging my bra's hooks into my skin. I tried to squirm, to do anything to fight him off, when he bent down and whispered in my ear. "Try to conjure any spell and I'll know before you can form the first syllable."

He released the pressure and I finally got my throbbing hands under me. I pressed up and whipped my bagged head to glare in the direction of the man still straddling me. "And if I set your ass on fire?"

"River will put a bullet in your brain," Stone said, like water was wet. He grabbed my shoulder and dragged me out of the van. My foot landed on cold, ridged cement and a heartless wind tugged on the bag. "I'd also be quite put off. These are my favorite boxers."

"You think I give a shit—"

"Move." River, or the other guy, shoved his overcompensating barrel into me. I had no choice but to shuffle forward very slowly. I brushed my foot over the ground, trying to get a feel for the terrain, and held a hand out to find a wall for balance. As I did, I felt something metal and hanging nearly free.

"Ah!" I cried, faking a fall. With all the momentum I had, I yanked hard on the metal ring. Cement cracked from inside and I took on the weight. *Yes! I* swung wildly, trying to bash in a face that got too close. "You sick, twisted son of a…" It connected once, hard.

A man cried out in pain and I felt the spray of his blood over the back of my hand. Good. Only two more to find in this darkness. *This is so stupid. They could just shoot me while I'm swinging blind.*

But in the back of my mind, I knew if any of them dared to pull the trigger, Ink would be there. Ink was always there, waiting to see what I would do before he stepped in to rescue me. "You're all going down!" I shouted, giving my best warrior cry.

I raised the metal ring above my head, ready to smash it on the shadow before me, when a hand clamped onto my wrist. Fuck! He twisted my arm back, pain from not only the hold, but also how he pinched where the cuffs had worn seized my whole side. The ring slipped and landed right next to my bare foot.

"Fucking green skins," the man I'd bashed in cursed. I tried to bare my teeth, but as they were behind a bag and I couldn't see him, it didn't mean much. But I felt it in my soul.

A low chuckle rumbled from behind me. Whoever it was caught my other hand and pinned both with his single palm. "You planned for all contingencies, Drake?"

Only a snarl from the Drake I'd bloodied broke through the darkness. Stone pushed me forward, using his knee to press on the back of my leg. It caused me to slip and I nearly planted my ass on his crotch. Funny. So fucking hilarious. The last guy, River, was cracking up the whole time.

*Okay, Ink. You made your point. I need you. I'll stop chasing after random creatures down dark alleys. Ink?*

The sound of cement dragged over a road burst before me. I blinked, staring down a deeper darkness ahead of me? Hands pushed me forward and I could do nothing but obey.

*Ink!*

* * * *

*Ink*

I rolled my tongue around the straw on Gluttony's green concoction and pulled in a hefty sip. It tasted of a rotted whale carcass left to explode, then gathered up along with a bed of seaweed and ground up into a slurry that had been passed to the masses. Could use a drizzle of caramel to really bring out the haunting death within, or some cinnamon. There was an emperor's worth in my bond's cupboard.

I squared my shoulders, prepared to take a step into the realm between realms, when a woman's exuberant squeal twisted my attention. My history with that particular mouth arrangement typically occurred in the darkened bedroom or behind the castle's tapestries. I cocked an eyebrow, gazing at the denizens who weren't scandalized by any thrusting of body parts into orifices. Shame.

"Mr.…whoever you are!" The woman rushed over and clasped a hand to my shoulder. I stared a moment, then slurped up my whale slurry. "You're so right. This fits perfect. I've never looked better."

Ah, the woman from the store who'd been about to drape her curves in pulled and poorly-composed fabric that had shimmered like an oil slick. I smiled wider and raised my glass. "Any form can be perfect provided the clothes do their duty and not the other way around."

She gasped as if I had spoken a wisdom gathered from the peak of a mount and took my hand. "I need you," she shouted aloud, and I smirked.

"I'm afraid my body is spoken for," I said, causing her cheeks to pink below the false rouge.

"No, that's…not what I meant."

Liar. Her desires shrieked through the air sharper than her mouth. I didn't even need to trace the dip of her eyes canvassing my form to know how hard she wanted me to pull her hair and slap her buttocks. Instead, I took a deeper drink of my green slurry.

"I run a boutique for the full-figured woman," she said, extending a card embossed with gold.

While I took it, reading over the name, I exclaimed, "There are shops who cater to women lacking a corporeal form?"

"What? No, it means…plus-sized." She whispered the word as if it were cursed.

"Women shaped like a cross?" And here I thought the church had its power divided like a king with too many sons. I glanced around the throngs, hoping to spot a woman with her arms spread out wide.

The lady, a Ms. Desdemona to guess by the card, laughed as if I'd told a grand joke. It was a delightful quirk of humans to treat anything they did not understand or found unpleasant as humor. No wonder most of them had no idea monsters that wanted to eat their spleens walked among them. Happening upon the mailman devouring Mrs. Johnson would send the whole neighborhood into a fit of giggles.

"I have to go, but call that number." She pressed an acrylic nail to the card. "Your talents should not be wasted on snake oil."

Oh, it was an offer of employment and not vigorous thrusting. How many times over the years had men tried to entrust me with their companies, ships, smithies or pubs? It seemed that showing an ounce of competency, while a potent aphrodisiac, also brought all the employers to the yard. I twisted the card around, watching it catch the light.

Still… Gluttony directed one of her minions to gather up the boxes. She'd never looked stronger, not even during the gout days. Whatever this thirst trap she had concocted to guilt the humans into gladly feeding her their sins was seemed to be the hunting trick of this new world. Perhaps a vivacious man of needle and thread would be a good hole to hide in to begin my hunting anew.

I pocketed the card and took the last sip of the brew. It hit my stomach about on par with a slice of cheesecake slathered in barbecue sauce. The humans who'd been praising Gluttony's every word glared glumly ahead as they sucked down their cultish brew. Instead of pleasure and delight in breaking morality's shackles, did they only languish in a moment of climactic ecstasy swallowed by despair? What had happened to them?

The heart I suspected I had beat faster. My bond must be in some straits of her own making. Perhaps she had properly confronted the wolf, or that cursed ghost had talked her into another trap. Soon I'd be free of that tingle that ran down my arms every time Layla…

Her voice rang in my ears, calling out to me.

I nearly ran to her side, but if we were to uncouple, then it would be in her best interest if I refrained. Let her grow under the tutelage of witches and their codes. Or be adopted into the pack of wolves. I'd be a fool to think our business relationship would have lasted as long as my previous one. Though, that was more slave and master than I'd typically enjoy. At least Layla let me roam freely as long as I returned to her bed each night.

A conflict I could not put words to tumbled in my heart. It was a disquieting sensation. Being a creature of sin meant I was hyper vigilant with all my emotions, finding no use in squashing or avoiding them. This tasted of worry and loss, two concepts I had no use for.

It was a lingering fear of hell. Nothing more.

"Ink!" Her voice screeched through the space between us, bursting with terror.

Without pause, I ripped open the tatters in the realms between realms. Unquenchable fire roiled below my feet, the abyss ever lengthening the longer it was stared into. I kept my head level as I clenched to the chain around my wrist. Locking one hand to it, I guided myself link by link at a run. Within this in-between realm, time did not exist. I could take five weeks and still arrive where I needed the moment I entered.

Yet my mind reeled with Layla's cry. I'd heard her inquire upon me, desire for me, even panic in the face of near death. This stung deeper than all, striking past my mind and muscles straight to the heart. It sang of abandonment.

I picked up the pace, running at breakneck speeds atop the lava fields. The chain between us shortened, each link sucking into the one before. Ahead, I spotted her silhouette bathed in a white light. It was only a few more feet. I could pop out and slash the throat of whoever dared to hurt her. Carry her in my arms to safety and watch over her until she was well.

Everything was going perfectly to plan.

I tugged on the last link, expecting Layla to turn even if she did not understand why, when my body jerked to a halt. She stood beyond my reach, nothing of her visible to me through the light. *What is happening?*

Without pause, I yanked into the earth realm and stared down a car barreling toward me. It laid on its horn, the driver so frozen in fear, he didn't even swivel the wheel. I lashed my arm forward, and sunk my claws into the steaming manifold of his vehicle. The bumper crumpled, wrapping into a ball like tinfoil as the whole of the engine thudded to the ground.

Steam buffeted around me, my skin crackling in ichor from where the metal shrapnel cut into the flesh. If there was any pain, I couldn't feel it. My heart pounded in abject terror, my tongue struck dumb in defiance. Vehicles piled up at the site of the carnage, and nary a single one of them was Layla.

*My bond…*

I tugged on the link keeping me tethered to her until the spell was broken, and I heard a crack. Where was she?

"Layla!"

# Chapter Ten

*Ink*

"Wolf!"

I stumbled into an enclosed drinking hall, flames belching from ovens of brick and the overpowering scent of nightshade in the air. The wolf glared at me as if I walked in upon him attempting to lick his own genitals. Instead of what would be a far more appreciable sight, he sat between two humans whose muzzles were coated in a red sauce and cheese. They seemed to care little for my flustered approach, a tournament on the television far more to their liking.

Crossing faster than the eye could carry, I stopped beside the werewolf just as he rose to his feet. "Don't call me that," he growled.

"For what purpose?" I inquired, confused as to why he'd care what I named him.

"You know this guy, Cal?" one of the men asked. He wore a red cap while the second wore a blue. Ah, clan colors. No doubt a duel was about to commence.

The wolf stared harder at me, then he clasped his fingers to my wrist and pulled. "No," he said, confounding me even more.

"That is a…" I gave in to his tug, not because he used all of his werewolf muscles, but because it seemed more prudent.

Tucked in a back corner beside a machine pulsing with light and tempting us to roll the digital bones, the wolf pushed me against the wall via his human digit. I rebounded quickly but held my hands up in mock defeat. "Why did you lie to them?"

"Why are you here? Are you following me?"

"Yes, my time is of so little interest, I spend my days trailing from one drunken den of debauchery to an ether-filled symposium."

He shook his head as if a buzzing clung to his ear. I would not put it past a werewolf to attempt to devour a bee out of curiosity. "You're not supposed to be here."

"I did not see a 'No Demons Allowed' sign on the door. Though I must say the shirt prohibition is rather restrictive in the event of alcoholic coitus."

"Don't…" He pressed me tighter to the wall then glared back at his friends. The two waved their arms through the air as if they could have an effect on the teams miles away. "I am not in the mood to put up with your incubus bullshit."

I snickered at the idea any of my skills could ever be on the level of bull feces. "And, pray tell, what mood are you in? Is it the wallowing in self-pity and hot wings mood? Or perchance the 'woe is me, I will drown my sorrows in beer until a warm smile catches my eye'?"

The dodging gaze sharpened to one of death and he slammed both of his paws onto my shoulders. "I put up with a lot of your tongue, Ink."

"Hardly. It's never even touched your lips, much less..." I drew my eyes lower and jerked my brows once.

Instead of recoiling, the wolf rolled his eyes. "If that bothered me, I'd have run from her place after the first night."

"Yes, that is the topic of conversation..." I began, but the wolf wasn't done manhandling me. Given how he seemed unable to stop touching me, it appeared his protestations might be in vain.

"No," Cal repeated. "I'm not dealing with this now."

"Then when? Shall you run, as is your wont, until your paws become bloody stumps and the fleas have chewed off your fur?"

He finally retracted his grip, allowing me to adjust my shirt. Cal glared at his hands, as soft and smooth as any middle-class human's could be. But I knew his desires nearly as well as my bond's. Rarely sharp, lest the moon was high, but forever throbbing in the background. A sliver of white would send him chasing after her until he dragged her back to his nest. It was the black, forever circling him, that pushed him deeper and deeper into the forest. What he was chasing, I didn't much care.

"You don't know what you're talking about," the wolf said, clenching his fists tight.

"So people keep surmising, despite the evidence."

"Did she send you? Why you of all people? I don't want to talk to you. I'm not...I don't want to talk to her."

Petty drama between conflicting hearts was not what I needed. "Well, that's a delightful turn for you, because she's gone."

All of his posturing snapped away. The gruff, closed-off werewolf transformed into the panicking boyfriend. "What are you talking about? Gone? How can Layla...?" His voice peaked to rockslide levels, directing eyes to us. Dropping it lower, he whispered against my face, "Even if she left...you'd find her. You always find her."

"Yet I cannot," I said, waiting for his feeble mind to catch up.

He twisted on his heels, keeping his feet planted while trying to pace with only his hips. The fangs elongated and he spat out, "How can she be gone? How can't you find her? Did you even try?"

"Do you take me for an imbecile? Of course I tried. I pulled myself to her location, sliced apart three cars, and each time I found nothing."

Cal wrapped his hands to my collar and raised me off my feet. In a great growl, he snarled, "Where is she?"

"Why do you think I came to find you?" I asked, swaying my feet through the air.

"Are you okay?" a soft-spoken woman asked from near the front door. She stared past the animal nearly sprouting fur to me dangling off the floor.

I gave a little wave to assure her I had this under control. "No problem," I said. "Merely a lover's tiff."

Cal snorted, but he placed me back on the ground. "Is she hurt? Or worse… Who could keep her from you? I can't even get two minutes alone with Layla."

Hyperbole. I'd left them alone for a good half hour at a time. More than enough for him to finish his dance. Confronting the wayward boyfriend had cooled my temper and distracted me. But now, with him in agreement, the panic in my soul returned. I spoke in a dark voice. "Someone who knows how to ward off demons."

He ceased tugging on his hair and turned his glare upon me. "You don't mean…?"

"I think we need to find her fast, before they prepare the kindling."

* * * *

"Well…"

I pulled the werewolf to the exact spot where I had last left Layla. The impudence of rush hour whooshed past, casting smog into the damp air as Cal crossed his arms and stared.

"Well what?" he asked incredulously.

I held a hand out to the ground. "Sniff her out."

Rather than fall to the ground and take in a deep whiff of the personal scent for every person who'd passed by, he sighed, "That isn't how it works."

For a beat, I looked to the witch's shop. It boldly declared the danger of the owner inside, yet she seemed to have nothing to fear from the hunters. How?

The chances of her helping seemed negligible. All she could do was toss a fistful of glittery butterflies my way. I steadied my shoulders, growing more perturbed by the slow beat of my bond's heart. "Why are you not in a panic over this? Have you shed all care you once proclaimed for her?"

Cal lifted the edge of his lip. "Far as I can see, you're pulling my tail."

"I assure you, if I were to pull your tail, you'd enjoy it immensely."

"That. That's why I know this is all a trick, whether by Layla or just you pulling some long con. If she was really in danger, you'd be freaking out."

I snorted at the idea of me ever dipping into a panicked state. Centuries had a way of cooling even the hottest of heads. Instead, I approached him and whispered near his cheek, "So you no longer love her."

I missed the hand flying through the air until it clenched my throat. He was getting quicker. The wolf railed in heart-wrenching agony. "That is none of your fucking business."

"My business is keeping her safe, a state you only laugh off. But if it requires me pressing your nose to the ground until you breathe in her trail…" I shook off his grip and locked a palm to the nape of his neck. With little force, I pulled his head lower, bending the man to the sidewalk. "I will not hesitate."

"You think I can't take you out," he grumbled, despite being folded over with his white-blond hair nearly dragging on the mud-strewn sidewalk.

I answered by pushing him further. His desires raged through me to release him, but I ignored each one with smug satisfaction. The wolf began to shift, and he swiped a full set of claws across my stomach. It was not a raking, but an attempted disemboweling. Still, it only tickled a trifle, so I continued my press.

"Find her. Now!"

"You twisted sonofa…" His wild swiping froze and he took a knee while staring intently at the sidewalk.

I released him, leaving the wolf to breathe in where Layla and I had had a mutual discussion on our partnership. No reason to tell him of my declaration, not until she was safe. After a moment, Cal stared up at me, his sarcasm and defiance drained to concern. "She was here."

I parted a hand through the air at the obvious realization.

"Doesn't mean she's been taken though," he grumbled even while inching along the sidewalk. Rather than fall to all fours, he hunched over, one knee to the ground while his second leg slapped against the dirt. "Something else is here. Something strong."

"What is it?"

"I can't tell, okay? There!" He pointed to an alley and my heart sank. *Why could she not stop going down them?* If it weren't a woman diced to ribbons by a wolf, it was a murderous kelpie. One day we'd stumble upon a unicorn with three non-virgins skewered on its horn like kabob. I didn't know how I hadn't gone fully gray in the last six months.

Calvin rose to his feet and took off. I investigated down the street, growing more aware of eyes on us that came not from a mortal. "Fuck!" he howled, directing me to his side. Fallen to his knees, he held a small pink sandal clutched in his hands. Layla had begun the day with it.

His voice was near tears as he delicately presented the shoe to me. "I wanted you to be lying. Why weren't you with her?"

"Why weren't you?" I volleyed back.

"Damn it!" He sponged away the water before it could fall, wiping the evidence on his jeans. "All this bullshit over… It's his fault for fucking me up." Cal swung a foot wide, thunking into an abandoned stand of soggy cardboard. It did little beyond flattening the box.

I folded my arms, watching his tantrum. "Yes, more werewolf politics, woe is me, my childhood was also not roses and sunshine. Could you focus? We can still find her."

"How do you know?" It wasn't an accusation assuming I was behind her abduction, but a plea for me to provide proof.

I did so by patting my chest. "I yet remain in this realm, so my bond must still be breathing. Now…" Forgetting my place in the world, I clasped a comforting hand to his shoulder. "Put aside your self-loathing and use the part you hate to find what you love."

He pulled in a deep breath, and the whole of his face crumpled. "Shit! It stinks of that stuff you rub on your chest."

"Body oils?"

I was graced with the steel-eyed death glare. "Can you stop thinking about sex for a minute? It's something common…eucalyptus!"

"A plant from the forgotten continent? Has she been taken by a Malingee? Look for stone knife cuts!"

The way he stared caught my tongue and pinned it up. "No, it's not a stone-knife-wielding whatever. It's a person, someone probably with a backache or…" He breathed deeper, then pawed at his nose. "Damn it, I can't find Layla. Her scent is strong here, then it's overpowered by the eucalyptus."

"If not a Malingee, then perhaps someone who knew to shield himself from a werewolf's nose," I said slowly.

The wolf clenched a hand tighter to the shoe and began to rock on his heels. "I thought we killed all of them."

"I wish. I've been trying for two thousand years, and they keep popping up like poisonous mushrooms after the rain." I would gladly paint the streets with the blood of hunters. The challenge was finding them hiding amongst the rest of the humans. They did not have backwards feet, nor leave watery footprints nor tuck horns below their hair. They could vanish into the crowd because, in the end, they were nothing more than the crowd given a weapon and purpose to destroy.

All the panic I'd pushed onto the wolf reverberated back through me tenfold. If he couldn't smell her, if we couldn't track her, then they'd… No. There had to be another answer. I was not falling back to the realm of mist.

Strange. Even in a rage approaching apoplectic, my mind twisted not to the entrails of the hunters dangling off my mantle but a moment with Layla. She'd been hunched over at her table, books of medicine scattered across it, when a pain rose in her neck. I'd pulled her hair aside and kneaded the wayward muscle. There had been no heat in the touch, nor had her desire tripped to ravaging me in the bedroom. Instead, she had placed her fingers atop mine and smiled so sweetly I had returned it.

*If they hurt a single hair on her head, I will tear every finger and toe from their bodies, then their limbs, crush their ribs, rip out their hearts and stuff them in their mouths.*

"I've got something," the wolf said, plucking me from my dark fantasy. I joined his side as he bent over a black stain on the ground.

"Oil?"

"No, it's ichor. Strong. Stronger than even the eucalyptus. Wanna bet they tried to lure Layla into the alley via an injured creature?"

It sounded precisely like what the hunters would do. "They would never leave any monster unturned. No doubt their hands are stained with its ichor. If you can track that…?"

"I'll find Layla," he sputtered before passing me the shoe.

"What do I do with this?" I asked.

"She's gonna need it back when we find her," he said and turned around. The man made quick work of disrobing, removing the shirt that'd loosely hidden away thoracic muscles that'd make Adonis homicidal. His jeans and undergarments vanished in one tug, and I frowned at these modern fashions. A man such as that would shine in tights suckered to his calves, and breeches that clung to his bulging thighs. Alas, they had to be covered as most men seemed to move through this world in bland sacks.

Once naked as the day he was born, the wolf began to shift. He kept his back to me, as if I would be incapable of appreciating the male form from behind. The crunching of the bones was disquieting. I did often wonder how the sensation of a bone solidifying around the penis felt. Perhaps as strange as fur sprouting from his testicles.

The blue eyes of the gray wolf glared up at me as if he'd caught me staring. Did he think I would ever stop? With a snort, Cal dipped his head down to the ichor stain. The hair on his back stood and he broke into a loping run out of the alley and to the road. I gave pursuit, leaving his clothing behind.

In my impressive lifespan, I'd been privileged to swim with a mermaid, tussle with a manticore and do things with a minotaur that'd make Poseidon blush. But this was my first time in over two thousand years trailing behind a werewolf on the hunt. It took everything in my nature to not toss him a biscuit when he picked up the scent.

"Come on, boy, find it!" I called, when Cal's head twisted from the south to the north. He paused in his search to glare at me and snort, but it must have been enough as he resumed his run. We dashed across the street and closer to the lake. Here, the denizens grew more cultured, with scarfs of the infinity variety and cups plastered with the green mermaid in play. They all gasped at the monstrous wolf trotting past, his tail dangling low.

"Good morning," I called to a couple, touching my forelock.

Rather than greet me, they yanked out their cellular mobiles and thumbed the screen with wild abandon.

*Why didn't I try calling her?*

"It would not work," I said aloud and fished out Layla's phone that'd been in my pocket since the morning. A low growl broke from the wolf. I couldn't guess whether it was from me possessing her contact device, or because I had read his thoughts. "If you would be so kind..." I directed him to keep on the path, when a sound blipped from behind.

It was a heart-wrenching noise designed to unnerve and startle the most stalwart of souls. I half expected to find it the work of an imp or even elf, but alas, it was only a mortal in a blue shirt and pants who emerged from the car trailing us. "Excuse me, sir," he said, not in greeting but demanding attention.

I had no choice but to pause in my quest and face him. "Yes?"

"You're gonna have to leash your dog," he continued, refusing to draw close to the 'dog' that stared death through him.

"I assure you, my good man." I draped an arm around Cal's neck and rubbed my cheek against the fur atop his head. He tightened in my arms, wishing to rip me to pieces, but I held firm and smiled. "He is a mere pussy cat, if you will forgive the pun."

"Don't care what that…thing is. It has to be on a leash."

I was tempted to inquire what precisely he would do to me if I disobeyed. But there was no time for me to make use of his handcuffs. "Very well." I extended my hand to him and he stared blankly at me. "So you require me to do a task without providing the tools to accomplish it. Guards never change. Give me a moment."

Turning away from him, I spotted a line of rope left dangling off the bridge overlooking the lake. A bit of luck, for once. Unknotting it, I tugged a good six feet free, then sliced off the anchor on the other end. Let it enjoy the depths of its watery grave in peace.

With a great show for the guardsman, I wound the rope around Cal's neck. His hackles stood at attention, but he didn't spin around and bite me. It wouldn't have stopped my actions, but it might have given the policeman pause. "There," I declared, standing with the bit of rope in my hand. It was fraying along the fibrous edges, barely more than an inconvenience to someone of Cal's girth, but it gave the illusion of safety and that was enough.

"Thank you. That monster had better be registered," he commented quickly while slipping back into his car. Strange how no one wanted to draw near the four-hundred-pound enraged wolf.

I drew my hand across Cal's head and called out, "I shall have him properly neutered as well."

The head slipped away fast from below my palm and teeth pressed against my wrist. The cop froze in pulling out, staring at where the wolf was trying to scissor through my bones. "Just a fun game we play together. He's really gentle when you rub his belly right."

Cal opened his mouth and spat me free.

I whispered to him while waving the cop away, "Do not act as if you don't melt like a marshmallow when Layla toys with your stomach and lower parts."

Tugging on the lead knotted to his throat, I directed Cal to resume the trail. He had no choice but to trot alongside me, the rope too short for him to take much slack. "Don't worry, I promise…I am greatly enjoying this."

*Fucking demon,* he cursed inside his head even while pulling in a scent and charging ahead.

"As if you don't harden at the thought of your neck collared by a piece of black leather."

*I don't want you holding the other end.*

His desires, which had been nothing more than a sharp black in the hunt, shifted to a throbbing red. Layla with a leather strap wound about her palm so tight her hand pulsed pink as she tugged on it, pulling the willing and happy Cal to his naked knees. I'd been asked to politely vacate the premises when they'd toyed with that new play, but even I felt a pang of loss at them only having a moment to enjoy it before she was taken. When we rescued her, she could bring us both to our knees.

"Believe me, mutt. I don't want to be the one holding it either."

At that he spun around, glaring over his shoulder like a wolf in the forest that spotted a helpless fawn. *Can he hear me?*

"Of course," I said with a laugh.

*The whole fucking time?*

Ah, there was that crutch of privacy he couldn't break free of. "Yes, I could read your mind whenever I wished, but frankly I prefer not to. Humans, on the whole, have the attention span of a flea at a canine buffet. I am only bothering now because I have need of you. Once Layla is in my arms, I assure you, I will return to ignoring every tiny thought in your head."

He snorted, but seemed to accept my offer. Though, as he turned to break into a run, he thought, *She'll be in my arms first.*

*No. Because the moment he finds her, I will rip through their lair, obliterating every hunter in sight, then pull Layla into my embrace and run both of us to freedom.*

My sniffing-nose dog reached the end of a bridge, whimpered, then turned back around. He kept circling, pulling us from one side of the narrow waterway to the other. "Have you lost the scent?" I inquired even as my heart lurched at the idea. Why did I even invest such hope in the wolf's nose?

He shook his head, and the once silent mind lit up. *Something's not right. It's here, but not. Almost like it...* The wolf leaped up onto the railing protecting citizens from a watery death. He placed his nose to the metal, breathed deep, and his tail began to wag.

*They went over this and into the water.*

I peered over the edge, finding only dead leaves and garbage sloshing against the light waves. Grass peered out from between the human's debris, revealing a shallow bottom—which was an incubus' nightmare. "We require a way down to…"

The wolf dropped to its haunches, then sprang up, clearing the barrier and falling with all four legs out. He struck the water with his belly, the slap echoing back to me. But it barely slowed the wolf down, as he turned and paddled for a mesh screen.

I certainly couldn't let him show me up. Jumping four feet from a standstill, I perched upon the banister and stared down. A voice called to me, asking what I was doing. I turned to face them, gave a smile and dove backwards. Before I tumbled, I unfurled my wings and inverted myself, harmlessly gliding beneath the bridge and out of any gawker's view.

While the soggy dog paddled up the cement embankment, I landed dry as a bone beside him…until he shook his fur, splattering me with dysentery. The rope smacked against my leg and I caught it, holding his leash loosely as we approached a grate.

I stared through the darkness. Only filthy water sluiced past. The rest of the passage was a cement pipe, narrowing the further it went. How were we to get inside?

"They took it into there."

I nearly jumped at the voice no longer in his head. A bedraggled and naked Calvin stood behind me. He wrapped his hands around the small bars and pulled in a breath. "I don't know how, but if they got through, we can too."

I nodded to him, prepared to rip the grate out by bare strength alone should it come to it. "We're coming, Layla."

Cal nodded to share in the sentiment, causing the rope yet around his neck to bounce. I smiled at him and said, "I wish to retract my previous statement. This is quite enjoyable." I pulled slightly on the rope then glanced to his crotch. "For both of us."

The wolf snarled and cupped his loins, despite his desires giving him away.

# Chapter Eleven

*Layla*

When the bastard pushed me over the low-slung bar and ducked my head, a tingle ran across my skin. I recognized it as magic, but nothing else. We'd been trudging through these open drainage pipes forever at a snail's pace. I struggled to keep upright in the slimy water, my only remaining sandal having no tread to help. It left the fucking hunter to keep one hand wrapped around my shoulder. Not gripped to my arm—no, he had the whole of his arm traversing across my body like we were 'friends' about to head into the tunnel of love.

I wanted to shove him into the cement wall and run, but if I took a step without his help, my foot would slip and I'd only face a bleeding nose. *Play along, wait for an opportunity.* There had to be a time when these assholes would turn their backs. "We're getting close," he whispered near the canvas over my ear. "I think we can lose this."

Darkness invaded first, then a pinprick of light. I squinted, fearing they were about to blind me with a megawatt bulb. But all I stared at were the black lenses perched on the narrow bridge of Stone's nose. "Better?" he asked, delicately folding up his kidnapping bag and putting it in his pocket for the next assault. My nose began to itch, but I couldn't do anything. My hands were once again cinched behind my back, this time courtesy of a zip tie. If I pulled too far to the left or right, pain shot through my arms. I had to settle for turning and dipping my nose against my shoulder in the hope of scratching it.

"Here." Stone drew the edge of his nail against my skin, mercifully alleviating the itch. An infuriating sense of gratitude washed over me, which I stamped down with fervor.

"I could have done it myself," I said, and lifted up my binds in the hope he'd cut them.

"Nice try, but after Drake's bloody nose, those are staying on."

Drake growled from behind Stone's shoulder. His face was already shifting black from where I had smashed in his nose, most of the capillaries popped. He had a bulging tampon shoved up his nostril to stop the blood flow. With a smirk, I said to him, "Might want to change that soon before you leak all over your white pants."

The last guy, Detective River, approached a small fuse box and tugged open the catch with his pocketknife because he was a total tool. Instead of a nest of wires, a soft blue LED screen rested inside.

He plugged in a handful of numbers, his finger hovering near the four first, then up to the top right corner for a three. After that I couldn't see, Detective Stone pressing me tighter to his chest as if I were a long-lost friend he couldn't wait to embrace. "Will you stop fucking…"

Drake shoved both of his bloody hands against the back of my shirt, sending me tumbling for the wall. I turned my cheek, not in the biblical but literal sense, and tensed for smashing against concrete. But I passed straight through thick concrete and steel rebar. It wasn't an illusion. I could see the inside of the wall, count the steel bars as I went.

With my hands tied behind my back, however, I couldn't control my fall. I tried to swing a foot out to stop the shock, when something grabbed my wrist. "Gah!" fell from my lips at the tug and I cursed myself for the first slip of pain.

"Sorry," Stone whispered, and he placed his hand around my waist to help me to my feet. It clung there, pressing to my soft belly that Cal would knead and Ink would lick. "She is a guest in our halls, Drake."

Drake grumbled in a rising eastern European accent. It'd been a flat American one before. "Didn't think most people called the maggots growing in their flour 'guests'."

I opened my mouth, a good retort just waiting to fall from my brain to my tongue, when Stone turned to order his fellow hunter, "Go and get yourself cleaned up. I can handle this part."

"Sure you can, Stone." Drake leaned so close I could count the number of contusions. I bet I had shattered his septum. *Hope he was wanting a nose job.* "And when you're done with her, we all get to have some fun."

I crinkled my nose at his threat and turned away. "Stop getting your lunch out of dumpsters behind the discount sushi."

The grown man, easily in his early forties, snarled and leaned away. He shook his head and stomped to the left, but I caught him checking his breath from the corner of my eye. *What's the first rule of kidnapping? Antagonize every one of your kidnappers until they all want to murder you? If so, I'm off to a great start.*

Rather than stare down Drake, I dropped my head to focus on the hand still stuck to my stomach. It took a moment before Stone seemed to realize, his stupid smile dimming as he wrenched it away…only to once again pin a hand to my shoulders. He guided me down the new pipe that'd been hidden by the magic wall and it hit me—my foot wasn't splattering into fetid water. If anything, the floor hummed in a familiar sound, an unnatural chill rising from the stone.

Fog seeped in, wicking away the ability for me to see much even as lights appeared overhead. The whole of the pipe faded into a dank hallway so gradually I couldn't point to where it happened. Mist drizzled down from an invisible pipe above me. I frowned at the mess it would make of my hair, but I couldn't feel it building up and pulling back my head. *What is that stuff?*

*Oh god, are they going to gas me?*

I tried to dig my chin in under my shirt's neckline in the hopes the T-shirt could act as a mask, when I noticed the other two humans weren't wearing anything special. As we traveled deeper at a slight decline, the light shifted. A faint haze radiated overhead, but another rectangular shape appeared to both sides of me in the fog. It disseminated through the mist, leaving what looked like dark doors between the shafts of light.

Almost exactly like doors...with no way for the person inside to get out.

"Where are we?" I gasped, losing the chill I'd managed through the last hour of my kidnapping.

Bloody handprints slapped against the wall, sending me leaping back. A face without a face pressed against the glass, a giant tongue trailing behind as it licked up the red stains. It jabbered, not in anything approaching a language, but like a giant angry squirrel about to rip a throat out.

Stone reached over to press a button, and the lights rose upon an endless hallway packed with cells. "Processing," he said.

"Processing for what?" I asked even as he pulled me past the cells struggling to contain the pacing creatures. Some I couldn't see into because a dark cloud was roiling inside. One held a pile of imps, their plump queen sitting in the middle while the rest served as her chair. In another, I spotted a small bird the size of a wren perched on a branch. It opened its beak and a beautiful song filled the air.

"Aw." I inched closer, when the whole thing burst into flames. "Holy shit!"

Fire retardant shot from above, drenching the poor little bird in white foam and putting out the fire. But it kept singing as if it didn't even notice.

"This is where we keep the creatures too dangerous for this world," Stone said.

The mists parted to reveal the hazy back end of a horse standing inside one of the cells. I snorted at the grown men scared of a horse. "Dangerous...?" It turned at my voice to reveal eyes of darkest red and a serrated horn protruding from its forehead. What stuck my tongue was the blood staining its white hair down the nose and across the head of the animal.

"You don't want to stumble across a unicorn unarmed," Stone whispered. "Unless, of course, you're a virgin?"

I snorted and choked on his question. If I were a virgin, Ink would have blue balls the size of Uranus.

"Are you going to give away all of our secrets?" the man named River asked and I jumped. Unlike Drake, he'd kept so quiet I had almost forgotten about him.

"There's no reason to hide it anymore. And from what I've seen, she's been doing our work for us," Stone answered as if he were proud.

"That's why the boss put a 93-W on her. As thanks for all that freelance work," River said back. I shivered not just from the tone but the use of a case number. Nothing good had ever come from my life being reduced down to a file in someone's cabinet. A person ceased to be that when they had a serial number attached.

Stone did not respond, but only pursed his lips tighter and marched me on. Fists that ranged from nearly human, to animalistic, to not of this world, banged on the glass as we passed. I couldn't hear it, but I saw the mist warp as they fought against their jail cells. And I had thought I was a badass for taking down the kelpie. That had been a minnow compared to what lurked in here.

The mists gave way to an office from the nineties, hidden underground in a high-tech sewer. Plain desks sat two to a row across a room where boxy monitors and their ancient computers took up most of the space. A long table with white coffee cups and an old stainless-steel pot sat at the far end. I drew my bare foot across square-patterned carpet, then froze, remembering all the blood that had to have been shed there.

If it weren't for the chains dangling from the ceiling beside each desk, or the wires hooked up to a chair beside them, it'd almost look like a nice place to work.

"You finally got her."

I was turned around to face a woman with frizzing brown hair and a painfully familiar face. An ache formed in my back as I stared harder and it hit me at once. "You!" I shouted, stabbing my shoulder at the woman in the black suit.

Eve—at least that was what my last kidnappers had called her—crossed her arms and raised her chin as if she were impressed. Or was enjoying seeing me tied up.

"Aren't you supposed to be squished to a brick in the desert?"

She smiled with her thin lips pressed so tightly they vanished. "We're more resourceful than you believe, Witch."

"Big talk for someone who got her ass soundly whooped by a flock of nymphs."

Eve's eye twitched, her smile going full sneer as she lost control. "Well, who's the one in chains now?" She reached behind and latched onto the cuffs, yanking both them and my arms down until I heard a pop.

"Is that necessary?" Stone asked.

"I watched two good men get mutilated because of her." Eve cursed at my face. "And her nymphs."

I stared her dead in the eye. "I'd do it again."

Rage overtook her, eyes bulging, cheeks red, but Detective Eve shook it all off. She released me and I staggered while she calmly tried to push back her hair.

"The 93-W will be processed in holding tank three. Where is the book?"

I felt the panic before I saw Stone pluck my spell book from my purse. *When did he grab it? How dare he touch it!* I tried to lunge for it, but Eve snatched it up in her filthy hands. She flipped through the pages even though it was blank to her.

A snarl built in my lungs, feral magic demanding I leap on her chest and slash at her throat until she dropped my book. I tugged harder on my wrists, but only got pain and exhausted sweat for my efforts. Eve watched with a single raised eyebrow and laughed. "Calm your cold teats, witch. We know destroying your book will only doom you a life of a madness."

*It'd do the what now?* No one, not even butterfly Sybil, had told me that could happen.

"But…" Eve snapped my book shut hard and glared me down. Dropping her voice to a whisper, she said, "If you step one toe out of line, I will pitch it straight into the woodchipper. Rules be damned."

A low cough from Stone told me that not only had he heard her, he disapproved but wasn't going to do anything to stop it. So he was either weak or she outranked him. My skin bristled at another living hand carrying my book, but I could do nothing. I fought to level my voice, watching Eve run a measuring tape over my book and jot down the numbers.

She once again tried to calm her frizzy hair and I laughed. "You know, if you're going to manically destroy people's lives, you could at least use some conditioner once in a while."

Eve glared, telling me I had struck a nerve, when a disinterested voice announced over the loudspeaker, "Code Blue. Please utilize glasses."

*What the hell does that…?* I caught Eve unearthing her sunglasses and Stone checking his. Suddenly, a bright flash struck across the whole of the room. The explosion came after, sending me toppling to the ground.

A chunk of cement fell from the sky and a rope fell after. Rappelling down it came my heroes. Cal leaped down first and I tried to run to him. Stone snatched my hands, pulling me back. Before I could blink, Ink leaped over both me and Cal, and landed on Stone.

I only heard a crack of bone as I rolled away. Cal was there to catch me. With his claws, he cut my bonds and held my grateful cheeks in his hands.

"Thank you!" I sputtered, tears springing freely. He had come for me.

He guided my hair back behind my ear. "I love you," he whispered, before kissing me with a heat that'd curl the whole of my legs. Cal took me by the waist, hefting me up into his arms as Ink rose from finishing off Stone. I felt his nose breathing in my scent, his hands tightening to cup my ass as a prominent figure rose in his pants. We were going to fuck for hours after this.

Ink joined me, first kissing the tip of my nose tenderly, then my lips. "I never want to lose you," he said breathlessly and clung to the rope dangling through the hole.

Cal wrapped his hand around it and tugged. We both began to lift to the heavens, when I gasped. "My book!"

"Yes!" The mad Eve stood to her feet, clutching her talons to my grimoire. Suddenly, a handsome man flew through her and wrapped his ghostly fingers around my book.

"I have it, Layla!" Daniel called, lifting up the only thing he could carry in this world.

Eve lunged for it, but Ink punched her in the face, sending her toppling to the ground beside Stone. Daniel floated to me and placed my book in my arms. I nestled it safe to my heart and reached to run my fingers through his cheek but as I did, my palm pressed to him instead.

How?

They sank in, a chill rising, but I'd felt him. I'd touched him. *Can I touch him again?* Daniel smirked as if he'd read my mind and I blushed hard.

Safe in the arms of my boyfriend and my ghostly love floating beside us, I called to the third in this steady square. "Ink?"

He paused in his retribution against the hunters, fires raging through the office and people screaming. A sweet smile swept across his sharp features and I held a hand out to him. He took it, joining us on the rope. "Let's go home," I said.

All three men smiled at me and we began to rise. The cruel hunters' lair was exposed and beaten. We could return and finish the job. I tried to ignore the lingering threat in favor of the promise of a bright future, when a face drifted through the mists. Thin and long, it hovered just at the edge of my eye, like a grain of sand after a long night of sleep.

It didn't matter. "Cal, Ink, Daniel," I said to them as the light of day burst around us, "we need a foursome when we get home." Ink laughed, Daniel grinned and Cal caressed my cheek, pulling me to him for a kiss.

A hand landed hard on my shoulder and pain snapped through my brain. It was the ice-cream headache from hell, upending my stomach and twisting my heart into knots. Instead of the blue eyes and guy-next-door looks of my boyfriend, I stared at the blackened lenses and hungry face of Detective Stone.

*No!* "You…how are you alive?" I sputtered. Ink would never let a hunter live. Worse, I was still in the zip tie, and that bitch had my book. *What happened?*

"Got it in the collar!" another man in the same black suit and skinny tie called from the end of the hall. He held up a thumb, and both Eve and Stone removed their sunglasses. His green eyes glowed under the misty lights almost as if they were radioactive.

"Did you fall under the sway of the siren?" Stone asked earnestly while Eve laughed…hard.

My skin burned as the two needlessly explained that the siren projected a victim's greatest desires. I stared at what had put that vision of escape into my head. It wasn't very tall, at most three and a half feet, with skin so pale it was nearly translucent. An opal sheen ran across the bald head and spindly limbs. The head was huge and stretched at the chin like a poorly blown balloon while the neck looked as thick as a bundle of spaghetti. *I bet it can snap as easy too.*

"I've had enough of this green skin," Eve grumbled. She hurled my book back to Stone, who caught it and slid it into the bag he took from me. "Take her to the chamber already so we can get this over with."

"Wait. We have yet to…administer the potion."

"You didn't in the field?" Eve asked.

"I feared it wouldn't be strong enough in dart form," he said. Whatever they were talking about couldn't be good.

Eve's face split into a maniacal grin. "You do live dangerously, Stone. Shame they've got you here. We could use someone like you out in the southwest."

Rather than answering her, Stone gripped my arm. I tried to shake him off, straining against the bonds. My arms slicked up with sweat or blood—either way, it made my wrists slippery. If I just pulled harder… *Fight through the pain.*

Eve opened up a safe on a desk where screw-top vials filled with a pale pink liquid were clasped into a velvet case. She slowly undid the lid while staring at me.

"I am not fucking drinking that," I said, and locked my jaws tight.

Eve dug her fingers into my cheeks, trying to pry them open while I struggled. *Yes!* The plastic around my wrist was slipping. *Just a little bit more…*

"Good," she said, startling me to stare at her. "Because it goes in the ear." She yanked my head to the side and, before I could move, dumped the whole of the vial into my ear.

It slithered through the canal, freezing cold, then boiling hot. In my anger, I finally ripped my arm free and hurled Stone to the side. Eve let me go and stepped back. I whipped my head around, trying to dislodge whatever she had put in there, but it wasn't coming out. It was crawling deeper inside my head, nestling in my brain with no way out.

# Chapter Twelve

*Ink*

*This is disconcerting.*

Wards in the blood of lambs and ocelots covered the whole of the walls. We'd walked through filthy waters for an eternity before turning a corner and discovering every protective spell I'd seen—and some that were new even to me. A circle carved into the stone sported an eye in the middle. Trying to avert an evil one's gaze was standard. However, the outside was swarmed not in runes but those little symbols humans send to each other on their scrying devices. I did not know what the winking one had in store, but the scat pile had me concerned what crossing that ward would do to the bowels.

"I'm going to risk it," the wolf said and he took a step forward. One of the runes lit up ruby red and a cacophony of pain burst from the stones. I gritted my teeth at the sound. The wolf slapped his palms to his ears and collapsed to his knees. That only encouraged a second rune, which lit up white-hot and sent a beam of fire dancing after us.

I latched onto Calvin's shoulder and pulled him across the stones. The noise ended, but the fireball shot over my head. I stared skyward at the wisps of smoke puffing from where a handful of my hair had burned to a crisp. That would take a moment to repair.

"Perhaps we should try using our heads"—I tapped mine right below the burn spot—"before we fall back to muscle-bound dolts rushing straight into a trap."

He glared at me, probably failing to hear a single word I said due to his over-eagerness. However, he could do nothing but accept my worldly advice. I approached the warded hall with more care than the furry one. "A noise alarm is a perfect way to turn back a wolf or a boggart. That is one that melts away illusions, calling out any changelings or other such. Some of these are simply crude elementals, I assume for humans that enjoy the taste of sewage."

"I know that one," the wolf chimed in. He was shouting at the top of his lungs and had one hand placed to his head, but seemed none the worse for the wear. With his free finger, he gestured to the last ward far at the end of the hall. "That keeps demons out."

I laughed at his knowing glare. "No, that would keep a demon pinned in place. The only thing that keeps demons out is liver and onion night."

"Two traps just for us. You think they knew?"

There were numerous others, but one at the front to turn back a wolf, and another at the back to trap an incubus like a fly stuck to paper... It felt less and less like a coincidence the longer I stared.

The wolf gasped to himself and I stared askance at him. His shoulders dropped and he groaned. "Mikki."

"We did seem to overplay our hand in that rescue," I admitted, as if I hadn't been the one pushing us to save her before they'd arrived at their lair. Though, whatever happened with the nymph was beyond my caring.

"But if we hadn't saved her, they'd have trapped her behind this same fucking gauntlet. Shit, I cannot stop cursing." He paced arrhythmically in a circle, on occasion dragging his claws against the cement bricks trapping us in place. "It's my fault. All of it. If I hadn't...they wouldn't even have known about Layla if it weren't for Mikki. If I didn't drag her along to Santa Fe. If I'd told her to stay back home because it was too dangerous."

"Will you cease your self-flagellation, or utilize this to make it entertaining?" I extended the rope he'd taken off his neck, letting the hefty knot dangle against my thigh. Rather than take me up on my offer, the wolf snarled, though the blame wouldn't stop running through his mind. It did me no good. Ruminating upon the failure did not solve the current problem.

"When Layla is returned to us, and you are holding her in your arms safe in the warm confines of the apartment, then you can tell her that she belongs in the kitchen lest your manhood sting."

"I would never...!"

"For now, we must discern how best to dismantle these wards. I know a trick for some of them, but it will take time." I dropped to my haunches and carefully rolled up my sleeves. There was always a gap between wards, because if they touched, they'd set each other off—a roiling mess of sound and fury, attacking no one.

Rubbing my chin, I inspected the casting lines of the noise blast. They were chalkier than the others, some of which had been carved into the walls. The wolf was right—they had put this here recently to stop us. Had they known we could track the aufhocker's blood and taken a calculated risk, or was it all a happy accident for them?

"How are you being so calm?" the wolf asked, a whimper in his voice. His desires teetered between ripping out throats and tying Layla to the bed, leaving a most confounding taste on my tongue.

"Because panicking will do nothing to help us help her. Besides…" I tossed a small pebble into the hallway. The sound didn't blare, nor did a fireball burst from down the corridor. It was a start.

Extending out my arm, I felt the chain around my wrist and let that weight bring it into focus for him. "I have definitive proof that Layla…"

Emptiness struck me. I could yet hear the drip of water, the rumble of cars overhead and the gurgle of the wolf's ravenous stomach. But another voice, one I had come to know as intimately as my own, had been severed. I yanked up my arm and reached for the chains dangling there, only for my fingers to cut through.

"No! No, no, no!"

"What is it? What's happening?"

The chain phased back and forth, sometimes being solid enough I could pull another link. Others vanished entirely and I feared it was lost forever. "They've broken the bond," I sputtered in complete shock. The only time I'd felt such desecration was right before the ground had split in half and I had tumbled through the realms into hell.

I stared at my toes, waiting for the inevitable even as I dug my claws into the wall. I would never go without a proper fight. They'd have to send Lucifer itself to pull me down this time. "If you want to claim me, then do your best!" I shouted, but the cement remained firm.

If hell had not opened, then what evils had the hunters wrought upon her? "My bond!" I shrieked down the hall and unrolled the rope. With a snap of my wrist, I whipped one of the wards. White light beamed from the end, igniting the rope's knot. Still, I wouldn't stop, swinging the burning holy fire around like a mad cowboy hoping to strike apart every ward within reach.

The sound resumed, blanketing away my hearing. Shards of ice and a green mist buffeted from between the bricks. But all I could hear was the emptiness inside, as if someone had ripped out every organ in my body save the worthless heart beating alone.

"What are you doing?" the wolf shouted into my ear.

Even with the flames licking up my fingers, I wouldn't stop, using the ash of the rope to dismantle the wards. "Saving her!"

A hand slammed into my shoulder, pinning my arm to the side. The remains of the rope fell from my fingers and I stared at Calvin, who'd used his might to push me against the wall. "Will you calm the hell down?" he sputtered. "You keep that up and they're going to send an entire squad down to kill us. I don't even have pants on."

"Who cares about the state of your genitals!" I screamed at him. "I can't feel her!"

"What are you talking about? You always hear her desires, or whatever. You know she's alive. She's alive…right?" The same panic I'd chastised him for earlier passed from me back to the wolf.

"I do not know," I said, unable to lie. "The bond is not yet fully cleaved, but it is weak and fading, which means Layla could be—"

"Don't!" He clamped a hand over my mouth, severing my words. "Don't even… I can't. She's fine. She will be fine once we get to her."

"And how do you propose we do that?" I asked, extending a hand to the magic still exploding from my attempt. Rushing headlong would mean utter destruction, but wiping the wards would take time we no longer had.

Deep thought crossed the wolf's brow and, for a moment, I could almost understand why my bond put up with him. "Daniel," he exclaimed. "She's still got the necklace. He can find her. Talk to her."

"The ghost is our only hope?" I muttered, giving in to the madness. The wolf glared at me as if I'd dare refuse such an option. But I'd seen the work of witch hunters up close, sometimes at my own machinations in my wilder days of youth. I would swallow the bitterest of pills to save her.

"I know how to conjure him, but we have to return to the apartment."

For a beat, we both stared down the murder tunnel. Layla was somewhere beyond it, completely unreachable. Neither of us moved, Cal the first to say, "I don't know if I can leave her."

I nodded in agreement, but said, "It's the only way to save her." Before he could argue, I tugged him into the realms between realms, and ran for her apartment. Our only hope remained in the cooperation of the dead.

# Chapter Thirteen

*Layla*

Stone pushed me in front of a door with glowing pentagrams etched into the frosted glass. He pressed a handful of buttons on the side, causing strange sounds to play with every change of color. The door shifted from a calming blue, to a ravaged red, a hostile green and finally a stark white. Locks appeared before the white glass, then pulled apart. The door swung inward to reveal…an IKEA desk on a beige carpet.

All that drama for a conference room. A hand pressed the small of my back, pushing me through the door. As I went, a tingle sparked across my hands and up my arms…before it stopped entirely. My flip-flop caught on the carpet from energy seeping down my knotted shoulders and out my fingers. I clenched my hands, trying to catch whatever it was, but that was foolish. I was exhausted and not thinking clearly.

That damn clinging hand caught my arm and kept me upright. "Here," he said. I felt the cold knife against my skin just before it slit my bonds. It happened so fast that panic lanced my heart even while I tried to rub my wrists.

A red ring had dug deep into my skin while a blue bruise pulsed outside the raw wound. I winced, trying to fight off the pain, when Stone stared closer. From his pocket, he pulled out a small nondescript bottle, which also caused a mess of pens and papers to fall out and scatter across the table.

Opening the bottle, he said, "This should help." After squeezing out a quarter-sized drop, he rubbed the oatmeal-like compound between his palms. Delicately, he swept them around my wrists, taking care to cover the whole area.

As he went, a cooling sensation numbed my skin. I couldn't stop a sigh from the building, pain vanishing. Stone looked up at me, his green eyes cutting from over the top of his fallen sunglasses. The intimacy of him tenderly healing my skin and caressing my wrists struck me hard. My cheeks started to burn, but I clenched my jaw and reminded myself who had put the cuffs on in the first place.

"Better?" he asked, drawing his fingers down the back of my hands so the last of the unguent trailed after.

I swallowed deep and in a fake snarl, said, "I could boil your skull until your eyeballs popped."

Rather than show an ounce of panic, the asshole chuckled. "We'll see." He gave one last caress around my wrists before letting me take them back.

I rubbed my hands, unable to shake off a tingling from his touch. No, from the ointment. Who knew what the hell was even in it?

"Do not worry," he said turning away from me to pick up a towel off a cart. "It is gluten-free, vegan and has only been tested on creatures who don't like to talk. Until they must."

He was trying to scare me. That might have worked in the van, but we were alone and I had powers beyond his understanding. Too bad that bitch had taken my book. Though… While Stone was too busy wiping witch cooties off his hand, I dropped my palm to the table onto one of his pens. He turned just as I slid it off. I stuffed my hands behind my back as he stared.

"Is it working?" he asked, his expression blank thanks to the shades.

Trying to not move while hiding the pen in my waistband, I said, "What do you care? Like to make sure your kindling's good and healthy before you burn them?"

He didn't laugh, neither manically nor to humor me, but sighed. "We do not employ such tactics any longer."

"Because most witches were hanged instead. What? I can read."

Stone extended a hand to the lone table with a single chair. "We do not hang witches either. Nor were most of those women and men witches, though I suspect you've already deduced that."

"Right, you're the real good guys, unlike those backwoods religious fundies whipped into a fervor because of bad wheat and boils on their junk."

Stone dropped his face as if to hide the smile rising. "We do ask our members to stow their religious fervor at the door. Please, sit." He said the second part with an edge, taking a step so I had to move back.

With the stolen pen pressing tight to my spine, I eased my way to the folding chair and sat down. Stone walked closer, looming over me. He draped a hand over the back of my seat.

*Oh shit! Did he see I stole the pen?* I stared, willing him to make a move. He hooked his hand tight to the metal back, his fingers nearly brushing against the cap of the pen. I clenched my toes, and he pushed me into the table like I was his date at a fancy restaurant.

"Wha—?" I stuttered.

Stone smiled and leaned so close he whispered against my cheek. "As for the state of my genitalia, they're quite pristine."

I ached to hurl him against the wall, but I kept my hands flat on the table waiting for him to leave. No spells, not until he looked away. He slowly returned his things to his pocket. *He'll notice, he'll put two and two together and—*

"Now, Ms. Leeland…" Stone cocked his head to the side. "Or would you prefer I call you Layla?"

"What do you think?" I hopped in the chair, scratched under my nose then reached behind my back as if I had to adjust something.

Stone chuckled. "Last name basis it is. Though yours is surprising given the weight to your book. I'd have expected a much longer lineage."

I clenched the pen and, as Stone turned to lift up a pad, I pulled it around. There was no way I could draw the ward fast enough on the table before he'd stop me, but what about under? I tugged myself closer, hiding both my hands below. The chair squealed in rage, drawing him to stare before I stopped and glared back.

"Miss Leeland, what is your date of birth?"

"I'm sorry, are you the DMV now? Is this a job interview? Gonna check my witch references next?"

"Humor me."

I nearly told him—that was the power of bureaucracy. Instead, I stared him down and said a solitary, "No."

Stone groaned and stepped back. He pressed more buttons on the cart I realized was wired up to something outside the room. "You had to make this difficult. Why are the talented ones always such a handful?"

*Talented? What is he on about?* I was barely scraping by. Every time I fell into conflict, I escaped by the skin of my teeth and the help of my guys. Ink all but scoffed at every spell I cast like the mean judge on a reality show. Thanks to my stupid dyslexia, I couldn't even read my damn spell book without…

"Daniel!"

I'd lost whatever senses I had. That goop had seeped into my brain and created a hallucination that my hot ghost boyfriend stood before me. He looked as he always did, in the same jean jacket with the tiger patch, his black hair falling from the pompadour. Slowly, Daniel glanced over his shoulder and purple lines strained from his deep brown eyes.

"Layla? Thank god!"

It was him! He'd found his way through the hunters' traps and wards. I reached for Daniel, needing to feel the chill of his form, but Stone turned.

"Excuse me?" he asked carefully, looking through the ghost to the weirdo who'd suddenly shouted someone's name.

"Bravo!" I called out. "Echo. Charlie." All that came to me were military codes. "Fox—"

"Trot. I get it, you're being cute," Stone said with a dismissal. "It would go better for you if you were less cute and more cooperative, but I'll work with what I have."

"Who's this asshole?" Daniel asked, jerking his thumb back to Stone who'd returned to the cart. The ghost stood half inside the table, caring nothing for their furniture. He couldn't do anything to hurt people, but just knowing he was here was enough to give me hope.

"How did you find me?" I asked Daniel, but it was Stone who responded.

"We've been tracking your movements for some time. Subtlety is not your strong suit, especially given your propensity for taking on creatures."

I tried to shut out Stone's bragging and stared at Daniel. "The locket. Calvin and the abomination came to me, said you were missing. I didn't believe them…so I came to find you myself. Are you injured? Did they do anything to you?"

"What was with the fucking spreader bar in the van? My ankles are killing me."

"A spreader bar?" Daniel snarled. The whole of his eyes churned with blackness as he rose up behind Stone.

Stone cracked open a small notebook with pages falling out and ran a finger over it. "Witches can be quite crafty. Would you believe some can cast spells with only their feet?"

"Sounds like what a pervert would say," I muttered, not believing him.

"I suspect my perversions would fill a thimble in comparison to the incubus you keep." Stone snapped his book shut and I used that sound to click open his pen. Working my fingers to the tip, I felt the nub, drawing a line over my skin, then placed it under the table.

*Please write.*

The raging ghost calmed and Daniel said, "He has a point."

"You're not helping," I whispered to my ghost, but it drew the attention of the one who had no idea he was there.

I finished the circle, the easiest part of this. *God, why didn't I practice these more in the dark?*

"You'd be surprised what my intentions are, Ms. Leeland."

"That so? You kidnap me on the street outside the witch's shop." I shook my head, raising my voice and bouncing my chin so my gaze traveled from Stone to Daniel and back. "Drag me into your pervert van with a bag over my head!"

"For your protection as much as mine," he said, causing me to snort.

"You're a terrible liar."

Daniel clung closer to me even as I finished the five dissecting lines of my ward. "Layla, the others tell me they tracked your scent to a culvert by the lake."

Tracked my scent? That had to be Cal. A strange urge to laugh and cry overcame me. My boyfriend cared enough to find me that he turned into a wolf. This was not the time to have a relationship breakdown.

"But they cannot get through a maze of traps. Where are you exactly?"

I stared Stone straight in the eye. "Where am I?"

Daniel gasped at the simplicity, but Stone had no idea my spy was here. He had no reason to lie. Instead,

Stone took in a deep breath and he raised a second book higher. "You know I cannot tell you."

"Why not? I'm already here. You can either kill me or tell me, because I'm going to find out."

Daniel yelped at my empty threat and he passed his hand against my cheek. I leaned against the cooling sensation, finding my face warmer than I expected. Why was I burning up?

With a click of his tongue, Stone stared over my head as if he were done with my conversation. But I sure wasn't.

"There was a ramp…had to be a boat ramp. Cement had small ridges, and a torn-out docking ring. How's Drake doing?"

"Do you have any idea the thinning line you are walking, witch?"

"There it is. No more niceties, no more pretending I'm one of the good ones. Just 'green skin witch.' Never takes more than a jab or two."

Rather than scowl or call me the real witch-ist, he raised the book and began to chant. Shit. Electricity zapped through the room and I recognized the rise in magic. "Daniel!" I called to my ghost, reaching a hand for him while I furiously scribbled the last of the ward. "We passed through a tunnel, dark. Took two lefts, then a right."

The wind increased dramatically, whipping around the room despite there being no source. Only Stone remained steadfast, not even a short hair on his head shifting. Daniel began to strain back, as if he were fighting against a hurricane.

"There's a fuse panel with a secret code! The numbers are four, three…"

Lightning shattered the air and Daniel vanished. I whipped around and leaped to my feet so fast the table buckled. The asshole calmly closed his book, which was when I grabbed him by the tie and snarled, "What did you do?"

He stared where Daniel had been, a ghost he shouldn't have been able to see. "I have cleansed the air of any unwanted specters." With a smirk, he drifted his gaze from the char mark on the ground to my chest. He reached for the locket holding a piece of Daniel. "It seems this was what needed to be purged."

When he wrapped his hand around it, I jerked back, falling into the chair. But he didn't let go of my locket even as I fought to keep from screaming. What had happened to Daniel? Was he *gone* gone? Just let him be banished to the library. Maybe I could bring him back from…extra death. I had to keep this piece of him, no matter what.

"Please," I whimpered, letting my fear slip through. "It was my mother's. It's all I have left."

There was no reason for the hunter to care. No doubt they'd make a pretty penny selling off the burned witch's property. He looked up from the heart-shaped locket with a handful of rubies that had to be worth something. I braced myself for the clasp to rip at the back of my neck, but Stone placed it back above my cleavage. He didn't say anything, but he stepped back to his cart of spells and worse.

Pressing a button, an intercom buzzed, and Stone said, "Please send in Ms. Monvoisin. This one is noncooperative."

He sounded defeated, as if I'd already failed some test of theirs. But I wasn't finished. I drew the last symbol for my spell, twin wavy lines, and stared him dead in the eye. "Mr. Stone," I said, directing him closer. "You have no idea how uncooperative I am." I slammed my hand against the ward.

Nothing happened. Fire didn't belch from the table, burning him in surprise so I could flee when the door opened. I slapped the ward again, certain I'd drawn it right. Nothing. Even with him staring at me, knowing it'd given the trap away, I dropped to the floor and stared up at the ward. It was pinched on the right but the lines were solid. *Why isn't it working?*

I screamed and slapped the table with both of my hands. More than the spell, something was wrong, something I'd been ignoring. Every other time I'd cast, hold my book, even when I'd stand in the rain, or kiss Ink, a warmth permeated through my body. I hadn't realized it was there until it wasn't.

"What did you do to me?" I sputtered, my palms collapsing to the ground.

Stone came around the table and took my hand. "We've gone off script, Ms. Leeland. I prefer to wait for the potion mistress to arrive. But it seems I don't have much choice." He helped guide me to the chair.

I stared at my palms, fragile and worthless. I'd thought I was terrible at magic, a witch of limited skill struggling to do simple spells. And now, I couldn't do anything.

"You have been stripped of your magic," Stone said calmly. I cast my stricken gaze up at him and his jaw flexed minutely.

"For how long?" If I didn't have my magic then…being with Ink would kill me, I couldn't save Daniel or Cal. My heart clenched in terror at losing everything with one slip of the blade.

Stone reached into his pocket and tossed a hunk of metal across the table. As its spinning came to a halt before me, I stared down at a silver badge with a pentagram in the middle and "Animal Control" written across it.

"Until you join us."

# Chapter Fourteen

*Ink*

Where was that formless fool? He'd been of a discontent and discombobulated nature when I'd fished him from his supernatural water closet, refusing to take heed of mine or the wolf's words. He was our only hope in finding Layla? If I had any truck with fate, I'd call her a harpy.

"Anything yet?" The wolf stumbled out of the backroom, a tunic around his arms. At my negative shake, he slipped it over his head, scattering the white-blond hair he kept infuriatingly short. I knew quite a few French aristocrats who'd have given him a countryside villa for his hair. Not that anyone cared for my opinion.

I clung tighter to the scrap of bone my bond had unearthed while the wolf stared forlornly at her slipper. He'd barely set it down since we found it in the alley. I half expected him to whimper and curl up with it by the fire. Rather sad how quickly humans could fall apart with the slightest provocation.

*Where are you, you gutless shell of whatever remnants of a mortal failed to be scraped to hell?* I shook the bone fragment, hoping that would encourage the man back.

"What if he can't find her?" Calvin inquired.

"What if he refuses to return? Perhaps he plans to whisk her away so he can keep her all to himself." I drummed my fingers on the table beside her in-house cactus.

"I don't think he's gonna do that," the wolf said.

"If you could rid her life of me and the ghost, would you?"

He closed his eyes in deep thought and breathed carefully. "No, because that's not what she wants."

"Layla!"

Tearing through the realms inside of realms, the ghost shattered into the living room, his hands outstretched as if he'd been trying to stop a runaway carriage. Or he'd been enjoying the ripe fruits of a woman's vine. I rounded upon him. "Enjoying yourself?"

Daniel, an obstinate bit of bone and little else, spun about as if his ass were on fire. "She's in danger!"

I glanced to the wolf who sighed. "Yeah. We know. We told you. Did you find her?"

"I…I talked to her. She's alive."

"Thank the moon!" The wolf collapsed in mourning for his mate, his hands clasped together as he whispered more to the heavenly bodies.

"What did she say? What is happening to her?" I ached to reach out and clasp my hands around his neck, but it would do little beyond freezing my arm. Still, I strained out my claws, wishing a demon could damage the dead.

"There's this guy, real asshole bureaucrat type in a suit. He's got her in...an interrogation room?"

"Was there any sight of kindling? Flints and twigs? Or a gallows being constructed?"

The ghost blinked at me as if the concept of hanging a person by the neck until they were dead had vanished from this world. Humans have always claimed to be above barbarism while disguising their bloodthirst under the name of justice and peace. It made the rare societies who embraced it refreshing, if not hard on the liver.

"Don't even start with that." Calvin leaped to his feet and pushed me aside. No, he kept his hand clasped to my shoulder, hanging on to me as he spoke to the ghost. "That doesn't matter as long as we can get to her. Where is she?"

Daniel crunched up his disturbingly perfect face, not even an errant mole distracted from his symmetry. With a slow sigh, he said, "I don't know."

I threw up my arms and was about to turn away, when the wolf dug his hand tighter. "What is the point of you?"

"Layla doesn't know. They kidnapped her from some...witch's shop. That's what she said."

The aura witch's emporium. The worst emotion in the pantheon smashed through me—not fear, not dread, not even grief but guilt. I'd abandoned her right outside that shop, left her to be tricked away by the foul hunters. I ripped up the realms, staring at the see-through chain barely clinging to my wrist. The far end was gone, faded to nothing.

"Will you stop doing that?" Calvin pleaded. "My stomach twists into a knot every time you do whatever that is."

When last I'd been plunged to hell, it had been at the tether of a binding chain. Now that I barely felt this one, I could not cease ripping apart the fabric of the realms, which increased the curiosity of creatures who did not belong. Stranger still, the magic seemed to be flooding instead of trickling through. What had happened to cause such a gush through the realms?

I clenched my hand tight, letting my claws cut through the human skin and pierce into the incubus fire below. I clung to the pain rather than face the betrayal I had inadvertently caused. "Where is she?"

"I told you…"

"Utilize the lingering synapses you have left to your disposal," I roared, shoving my fist through his chest. There was no heart to clench, no organs to rip free, but Daniel's eyes widened and he stared down at my wrist in shock. "Layla is not a fainting maiden. What did she say?"

"She mentioned a cement incline, a boating dock. And that there was a ring ripped off the wall?"

Calvin pulled on my biceps, trying to guide my hand out of the ghost. I gave in, finding no more use to the empty threat. With that done, he fished out his phone and scrolled through it. "There's a handful of close boat ramps, have to check them all out to find a missing ring."

"There's more. She said there was a fuse box, what looked like a fuse box, but it required a code to get in."

"And this code is…?" I prompted, growing weary with the ghost's stalling.

"Four, three…then." He fell still, his form fading in the harsh afternoon sun. It would be a lovely day to picnic in the grass, then lie with Layla among the daisies and daffodils. Instead, she had been taken, and I had to put aside the love for war.

"What's the rest of the code, Dan?" the wolf asked.

The ghost glared at the shortening of his name. A shiver came over him and I too began to panic. "I didn't get it all."

"Well, return to her to discover it," I prompted.

"I can't. That guy, that Stone. He did something, he banished me from her and I can't return!" The ghost's patient, almost melodic voice sharpened to a hard screech and I felt it in my marrow.

"That cannot be. A spell is required to purge a ghost."

"That's what he did. Held up a book, read it off. I've tried finding her, but I keep bouncing back to the library or…" He shook his head as if he'd walked across his own grave. "You never said the hunters used magic."

"They never did in my time. They'd spit at the ground and make crosses to their g-d at the sight of it. This is…" Hunters casting spells? There was only one explanation and it led back to where this had begun. "I must go."

"Yes, we need to find this ramp," the wolf said. He held out his phone with directions to the first, but I pushed it aside.

"I have my own errand to run."

Calvin frowned, but I took his hand. "You can find Layla better than I or the whisper." I pressed Daniel's bone fragment into his palm. "He might act as lookout or, barring that, you could toss his finger into the lake and we would not have to deal with him any longer."

"As if you've been any help. Where were you in all of this?" the ghost chided. "Aren't you supposed to be her bodyguard?"

Anger rippled up my lip. For once it was not directed at the ghost but inward. I was to be her bodyguard, a task I had agreed to as much to protect myself as her. I did not enjoy carrying the stink of failure. With a toss of my head, I walked to the door.

The wolf looked up from the bone and asked, "Where are you going?"

"To talk to a witch about the knife she put in Layla's back."

# Chapter Fifteen

*Layla*

It was a trick. They'd dampened my magic by putting me in a lead-lined room. Maybe it worked on magic like radiation. I couldn't be…

Normal.

"Fuck you." I flung the badge across the room, aiming for Stone's head. He dodged out of the way just as the door opened. A meaty fist that looked like a beef knuckle snatched the flying badge. The fingers clenched around it.

"Having a tough time, Detective?" a distractingly high voice asked, given the body it belonged to.

I couldn't see who it was until Stone turned away, though I laughed to myself from the asshole going bone white and his face falling. "Director Zimmerman," he groveled, no doubt before his boss.

Jesus, the guy in charge looked wider than that minotaur, and twice as ugly. If that was the leader, what did their muscle look like?

"I was just about to lay out the terms to Ms.…the witch," Stone said, sounding about to fall to his knees and beg for forgiveness.

The director turned over the badge. "He got you a new one. That's nice of him," he said, placing the cursed thing on the table.

I raised my thumb and finger up, about to flick it away again, when the man glared down at me. Every muscle trapped under his presentable suit bulged like over-yeasted bread. "I wouldn't do that if I were you."

Magic-less, alone, trapped in their underground lair—the common sense part of my brain swarmed over the rising anger and I laid my hands in my lap.

The director snickered. "Good girl," he whispered and turned away. I folded up my fist, about to slam it into the table, when Stone surged forward and caught it. The fucker in charge had to see it, the room was too small, but he didn't say anything. Just let his underling struggle to keep me from shoving that badge up his nose.

Stone guided my fist to the table, then patted the top as if it all had gone according to plan. I gave in to my urge to snarl at him. Rather than threaten or demean me, Stone stared at my wrists. "They look much better," he said.

I yanked my hand back and touched the wound only to find it was fully healed. Which he had caused—I couldn't forget that. I wouldn't.

"I heard that we had a lively one today. The head office is abuzz at finally adding a Leeland to the ranks."

"I'm not a fucking collectable."

The director chuckled patronizingly, like I was a dog barking at a stranger outside my fence. "Be careful with this one."

"She's already been depowered," Stone said so casually that I wanted to cry and smash his face in. I had never realized how much I needed my magic until all of it was gone.

Zimmerman stared longer at me, the jowls on his cheeks raising up in a not-smile. "Even still, Leelands are a dangerous lot. But I'm certain you have it all in hand. Oh, is that Valerie?"

The door opened once again, depositing not another asshole in a suit, but a grandma. Her white hair was pulled back in a knot, but a handful of textured curls had escaped. She wore harsh makeup, emphasizing a blush on her cheeks and dark, sparkling shadows across her eye lids. In a sea of black and white, she was a sprig of color. A fern and emerald dress with a check pattern swept to the floor, hiding her feet as she shuffled inward.

"Good evening, sir," the old woman said. She reached a wrinkled hand out to Director Zimmerman, who touched the tips.

"Poor dear, it's the afternoon," he said.

"Is it? Dearie me, time just slips on by."

Zimmerman swept around the old lady, his form nearly engulfing her as he turned Valerie to stare at me. "You see this, young one. This is what respect looks like. Best get used to it, or you'll have a short life in chains. I'll see you later, Stone. Big meeting at HQ. Won't be back for a few weeks. I expect you'll have all of this wrapped up by then."

That was my deadline. Either give in to their torture in a couple weeks or what...? Would they toss me into the cells beside the monsters, or with the monsters? I tracked Stone kowtowing to his boss who was shuffling away, and nearly missed the old lady hunkering over the cart. She pressed a button and an honest-to-god cauldron popped up.

"Is this the one giving you trouble?" she asked, her voice light and airy.

"Have a good trip, sir," Stone called, flustered. He slicked back his falling hair into the gelled goop at the top of his head and turned to the woman. "Yes. She's been proving uncooperative."

Valerie chuckled. "That's the young for you."

Unperturbed that he had kidnapped someone, the old lady took to uncorking bottles and dumping them into her cauldron. I wasn't about to go gently. "You're out of your fucking mind—"

"Language!" Stone sharply intoned, turning his head to the old lady. "Ms. Monvoisin, my eternal apologies."

I wanted to use every curse word I knew, but it'd just give them some imaginary upper hand. "If you think I'll join with the people who tried to kill…"

"We never intended to kill you, Layla. I swear."

"You're witch hunters. And I will fucking curse all I want."

Valerie sniffed as if she had much to say about it, but refrained. It was Stone who couldn't help himself. He slapped his hands down, trapping mine astride the badge. "We have evolved from random slaughtering of magical bearers. Now we work in tandem with them. Think what you can do with our resources and efforts at your beck and call. I know you've been trying to clear the streets of malfeasance. The kelpie."

How long had these assholes been following me? "I didn't need your help killing that thing."

"Perhaps not, but we would not have killed it in the first place."

"It was slaughtering girls, eating their organs. And you, what, wanted to capture it and donate it to SeaWorld? I saved them." It had ended with three dead college girls instead of god knew how many until they finally bothered to care. Why hadn't they leaped into action with the first death? Or even had some way to track a kelpie? I was already cleaning up their failures. I sure didn't need them telling me to fix more.

Stone scratched along his chin, drawing a white line against his golden skin. He toyed with the divot between his chin before asking softly, "What of the eggs?"

"What about them?" There had been a whole nest of kelpies, and when they'd hatched, more kids would have died.

"You destroyed the lot of them," he said.

"Yeah. I know." Ink had told me they'd be there and he'd been right. He could be infuriatingly right about a lot of stuff.

"Do you not think they deserved to be given a chance?" Stone asked without malice and my assurance stumbled.

No. They were going to eat people just like their father or mother or whatever it was I killed. It was going to eat me. I defended myself. "They drown people then eat their organs. Why do you think that should be given a chance?"

"Perhaps they could have agreed to consume the livers of cattle or pigs instead."

He was trying to guilt me into joining with them. He cared as much about kelpie eggs as he did the witches they enslaved. "And how many kelpies have you gotten to eat cows?"

Stone shrugged. "To my knowledge, none."

I laughed at his ploy shattering to pieces and leaned my hands behind my head. He was going to have try as lot harder to break me.

Stone slipped off his sunglasses and folded them up into his breast pocket. When he looked up, his eyes gleamed brighter than emeralds. "But we would try. What of you?"

"Detective. The brew is nearly ready," the old lady said. I'd nearly forgotten about her in our argument. "I only require her full name."

"Ah, not a problem."

I clenched my jaw, refusing to answer, when the bastard hauled up my purse. He tossed it onto the table, my spell book tumbling free. Instinctively, I snatched it up to keep safe, but there was no silent purring from the pages. I couldn't feel my book. Terrified, I opened the cover and found nothing inside. The spells had been taken from me along with my magic.

"She is Layla…" Stone held up my driver's license. I lashed forward to get him to stop but he kept reading. "Moesha Leeland."

The spoon clanged from the old woman's hands. Her shoulders clenched a moment before she smiled and leaned over the brew. I strained to hear her whispering, but I couldn't make it out. It didn't help when Stone put his hip on the table and asked, "Moesha?"

"What's your middle name? Rolling?" I reached for my license, as if that mattered anymore in this maze of monsters. He moved before I could take it back and stared at the awful picture.

Slowly, he looked from the old image of me when I'd turned twenty-one and was still hungover, to the me of twenty-five that was fuming. I tried a second time, snatching the card away. But Stone didn't move, and he said, "You take a good photo."

"Thanks?" What a weird thing to tell someone. *Hey you, you look good in two dimensions.*

"The potion is ready." The old woman…oh shit, she was a witch. They'd kidnapped her, probably yanked her off the street after bingo, ripped away her magic and threatened her until she'd agreed to do their bidding. All those spells the hunters were chucking about in Oklahoma, they had to have come from another witch. How many of us did they have chained up in their basements churning out wards and potions to fit their whims?

Valerie hobbled over and placed a mug filled to the brim with a clear liquid before me. She caught my hand and placed it against the freezing cold mug. "You drink that up," she said, patting my hand twice more. A tingling radiated up my arm that had to be magic. I tried to reach for it, but the power I'd been pulling in for over six months faded away like a winter wind.

I had expected Stone to toss the old woman aside, but he was at least decent enough to help her out and even thank her. No doubt this was the soft sell, trying to tell me that everything was just great. All their witch victims would get dental, casual Fridays and a shiny bucket in their cell. I glared at the reflection in the dark mug. Where were Ink and Cal? Did the incubus already sense I was no use to him…and had Cal stopped caring?

No. I couldn't even hazard a guess with Ink, but I knew Cal loved me. At least, he had before. I had thought my mother did too and we knew how that worked out.

"Drink it up," Stone said, his arms crossed.

I raised my exhausted head and stared him dead in the eye. "Or what?"

I heard the all-too-familiar cock of the gun before I felt it press against the side of my temple. "Or we get fresh witch brains for our pantry," Eve snarled. Where the shit had she come from?

Stone groaned in his throat, not as if he were upset, but that she'd gone off script. He was no help, and my boys were nowhere to be found. What choice did I have? I hooked my thumb through the handle and raised the mug. When it glanced against my lip, frost crawled across my mouth. I glanced to Eve, who didn't shift her gun, and started to tip the liquid back.

"Nice try." The bitch snatched onto my hair and yanked. My mouth popped open and I screamed in pain, but she shoved the butt of her gun under the mug. All the potion I'd tried to dribble down my shirt splashed straight down my throat and up my nose. Cold clawed in its wake and my hand fell, shattering the mug with a drop of potion left inside.

# Chapter Sixteen

*Ink*

"We're closed."

She tried to slam the door, but no witch was faster than me. I caught the edge and wrenched it forward, shattering the glass. "Strange," I said, catching the sign before it fell. I turned it around to face her. "Your hours proclaim you to be open until the cockerel retires to its perch."

"Well..." The witch glared at the sign as she took a step backward up the stairs. I followed, a smile straining my lips that we both knew wasn't radiating warmth. "I needed to take a break."

"Ah, I see. The kind that, perchance, a burner of witches would demand?"

She reached the floor of her shop and paused, crossing her arms under her floral and silk scarves. "What are you talking about, demon?"

"The mantle of stupidity. How strongly you mortals cling to it, as if we cannot smell the stench of falsehoods upon you." I landed a foot on the floor and my claws erupted from the ends of my shoes. They sprouted beyond anything even my bond had seen, true talons ready to gouge out the eyes of the betrayer.

"I don't like demons in my store," she said with her chin jutted out as far as possible.

"But you let a witch hunter in."

"What?" Her panic could be explained due to fear of the hunters. No doubt a mealy-brained ghost would dismiss it as such. But I remembered the man of glasses and black. As I stepped closer, my nostrils fluttered and I breathed her doom.

"Do you know what that scent is?" I asked, shaking my claws through the air.

"N-n-no?" Her cocky airs were slipping as I sloughed away the last of my human mask for the real monster within. My wings burst free, straining across the narrow shop. Every bottle and label they touched ignited and burnt to a crisp.

I caught her by the throat, tempted to plunge my claws into it and sever her voice box. But first I needed the truth, then I could silence her.

"Eucalyptus, a most potent smell that can dissuade the tracking powers of any werewolf. An oil you sold to the hunter that tracked my bond!"

She tried to laugh through my vise, but it came out a gurgle. The witch clamped her hands around my wrist, her powers bubbling over in a cloying stew of emotions. I shook them away, feeling nothing of their sting. "Tell me why I shouldn't kill you now for betraying her?"

“Her? Since when do demons give a shit about their meals?” The aura witch coughed and she cast tendrils of smoke from her lips. Snake heads strained from the thunderclouds, but I batted them away, knowing them to be false. If that was the only talent she had, no wonder she had given in to the hunters so easily.

“You know nothing about demons,” I intoned.

“Cut from the cloth of entropy, designed to destroy, crafted to kill. I know all about your kind. Play the pedantic game all you want, but you are the same as your forebears. You will as assuredly kill her as you will the world.”

“You don’t know me!” I screamed, unleashing the heat of the fires of sin from every crack in my skin. The witch yelped and tried to turn away, as if none of this were her doing.

“Where is she? Tell me where they took her and I may let you continue breathing. With or without eyes depends upon how quickly you answer.”

That was me being generous. No doubt this woman had turned Layla in for special favors or because she was vile down to the marrow. I ought to rip out her intestines and dangle them from tent poles across the town square as a warning, but my bond wouldn’t like that.

“You think I know?” the woman sputtered. She tried kicking her legs, but all that did was scatter one of her shoes to the floor. “They don’t tell me anything. All they do is show up, demand a potion, an ingredient, a spell, then they leave.”

“You put them on Layla’s scent.”

“Are you out of your fucking mind? I would never let them have a witch as powerful, as...as young as her.”

The truth at last fell from her lips. "You wanted my bond for yourself to grow your coven."

She laughed once as if the entire mess were hilarious. "Seems you're not the only jealous asshole around. They must have been watching her for a while."

So she had not given them Layla out of greed, hardly admirable in terms of human morality, but there was another matter. "You did not warn her of them either."

"What was I supposed to do when he was right there? I tried to get her away from them but she seemed to think she was fine with a wolf and demon. How are you getting on protecting her?"

Anger curdled through my guts. I raised the woman up, wanting to shriek fire against her face while also hurling her through her shop until a thousand potions broke over her flesh. What paused me was knowing I would have to explain it to my bond, and how deeply it would upset her.

The ghost and wolf were finding the entrance. I need only return to them, then we could rescue Layla. This was a needless errand. "I will save her myself," I said and opened my fist.

She tumbled like a sack of onions, her foot rolling under her and kicking the shoe away. I turned from her wretched self, tucking my wings back in and siphoning away the demon flesh. But the aura witch wasn't finished. "No, you won't. That place is covered in demon wards. You won't get two steps inside before you're pinned to the wall like a bug. Then all the little hunters will come and dissect you."

My lip curled and I tasted blood from how quickly my fangs punctured through my tongue. I felt nothing—a demon body was never designed for pain—

but I let the blood drip down my cheek as I faced her. "Then what do you propose?"

"I…I didn't suggest anything."

"You say the path is impenetrable, then provide no assistance? Tell me why I shouldn't gut you right now?" I drew my hand up, all five claws punctuating the air and my question. "You said yourself—my kind were only created to destroy."

All her magic was spent. I couldn't smell anything on her. No wonder she'd had her sights set on Layla. This woman would have treated her like a blood bank, siphoning it away like…like I did. But I needed it to live, not to entertain small children with purple butterflies. I advanced, my mind churning with revenge and skittering from the node of guilt growing in my heart.

"Wait!" The aura witch raised her hands high. "I may know something that would let you pass, but…" She trailed off, only enraging me more.

"But what?"

Her silent chuckle shook her shoulders. "You'll never do it."

"I'm an incubus. We'll *do* anything."

* * * *

*Layla*

The guy who had abducted me off the street and tossed me into a van tried to play good cop, while the woman who had nearly exploded my car then tossed me into a van chose bad. She laughed at me choking and coughing up the potion out of my nose while Detective Stone had that "very concerned" look. I swiped whatever it was on the back of my forearm, watching my skin turn silver where it touched. That wasn't unnerving at all.

"What was that? A poison? Did you turn me into your puppet?"

Eve snickered. "You'll see soon enough. Ask away." She at least had enough presence to take her finger off the trigger even as she waved her gun around. I laid my hands on the table, aching to snatch up a Sharpie and draw a shield ward.

But it wouldn't work.

God, I was helpless.

"What is your name?" Stone asked.

I glared at him. "You already know that."

"Your address?"

"123 Fuck You Avenue, just off Eat a Bag of Dicks Street."

It didn't matter what I said. Just like Conway, he had seen my ID. No doubt these damn hunters had ways to track people, or at least Google them. My only way out of here was doing the same as I had to Samuke and learning their real name. What were the chances he had been christened Detective Stone?

A little crinkle appeared at the top of Stone's nose that told me I was getting to him. I fixated on it, wanting to see it deepen with every frustration I could force on him. He tapped his little pad once more, then stared at me. "Who is your father?"

The question tossed me into a lurch. It'd been a long time since I'd thought of him. I clenched my hand tighter and rolled my lips up into a snarl. "Fuck off."

I felt the words on my lips, and my tongue, but what came out was, "I don't know."

The two detectives stared closer, growing more interested in me. My mouth fell open and more came without me thinking it. "My mother only told me he was a good man." Shit! I slapped a hand over my traitorous mouth, but even hooking my fingers under my jaw wouldn't stop it from opening. "And that I couldn't see him."

"Typical," Eve summed up. "Put him down as deceased."

I hadn't said he was dead. Though, the way she'd talked the few times I'd asked, how she'd grown quiet and turned her back to me, it had seemed the only answer. I'd never pushed because it almost seemed normal to not have one. What if she had lied about him too?

"The mother. Isabel Leeland," Stone said. How did he know her name? I hadn't said it. Did they try to recruit her too? Or had they succeeded? "Where is she?"

*Dead. She's dead. I can take you to her grave right now. Don't let the truth out. Dead dead dead!*

"I don't know," I repeated, my voice devoid of thought and emotion. I didn't care either. She chose to abandon me, so I'd do the same back to her.

Stone nodded and typed it down. "She's not in the system," he said aloud, which meant they hadn't caught her yet. A weird sense of elation filled me, then a crushing dread. That sounded like classified information, which one didn't say aloud unless they knew I was screwed no matter what.

"Move on." Eve jerked her gun, drawing it from my heart to my head. I jumped, dragging my nails down the table, which only caused her to smile. "I don't have all day for this."

"Is that really necessary?" he asked while skirting his finger across the screen.

She flicked her tongue against her teeth and leaned closer, nearly ramming the muzzle of her gun into my forehead. "Yes."

"You catch more flies with honey…" Stone passive-aggressively whispered under his breath before he focused back on me. "What type of witch are you?"

I started to laugh. Whatever truth serum they had used on me wouldn't answer that. I had no goddamn idea there were even types of witches. With a smirk, I dropped my chin into my hand and prepared to say a third round of *"I don't know."*

"I am a battle witch."

*I am?*

*What does that mean?*

All of his natural tan drained from Stone's face. Even Eve staggered away as if I'd gone Super Saiyan with my answer. How did I know I was a battle witch? I placed my palm to my spell book, and for a tiny second I felt a flutter against the cover. It knew, and it had told me without telling me.

For a second, Eve laughed. She reached up high, letting her gun twirl on her fingers like a mad woman as she stretched. "Of course you had to be one of those. Couldn't be some useless wellness, or aura or even potion." Her lazy stretch collapsed into a coiled snake, once again taking aim at me.

Stone finally moved out of his corner and he clasped a hand to her shoulder. I jerked out of the way, terrified he'd startle her into firing. Eve at least had enough sense to not blast me into meat. "We have our orders," he said, squeezing tighter.

I stared up the barrel of the gun into an eye of maddening vengeance. She didn't care about anything, not what these hunters wanted, nor what her orders were. I braced myself for the pain, when the gun tipped up. Eve laughed hard, then dashed to the cart. She hefted up a box surrounded by a chain.

"What are you doing?" Stone asked, but there was no stopping the woman.

She tossed back the lid and pulled out a bright blue liquid sealed in glass. The top narrowed to a tiny neck designed to be broken off, but one would have to be daring to drink from shattered glass. Laughing harder, Eve raised the vial to the light, then pointed her gun at me. "Now, before the truth potion wears off. Join us and you get your magic back." She shook the blue vial, which could either return what they stole, or kill me. "Don't and..." Eve glanced to her gun and she drew back the hammer.

I stared longingly at the vial, whatever tiny spark remaining inside of me pulling me to it. I had to drink it, to return my magic before...something bad happened. A darkness churned in my belly heavier than dread.

The truth potion held my tongue at its command. I couldn't bluff my way out of this. With a set to my jaw, I stared Eve dead in the eye and said, "Fuck you."

"Wrong answer."

A flash of light broke before me. It had to be the muzzle just before a bullet embedded itself into my brain. I waited for the pain, the blood, but I stared up at Stone, who held a...phaser? It looked plastic and futuristic, blue lights running up the middle of a toy gun. He reached over and plucked the gun from Eve's fingers. They didn't even bend as he ripped the Glock away, and I stared closer. She was breathing, her face slightly shifting in micro movements, but the rest of her was frozen.

"We do not go against our orders," Stone said, "especially in the name of personal vengeance." He fired at Eve once more and she pulled her trigger finger. But without a gun in the way, all it did was make her look foolish.

I met her eyes and mouthed 'pew pew.'

She snarled and wound up to smash the bottle. Stone ordered, "Do not make me freeze you again. Return it to the case. Now."

Eve shook her head and tightened her shoulder, prepared to defy him, but she smiled wider. "Fine." Stone kept his freeze-phaser trained on her as she placed the blue vial in the box and locked it up. "Your inane need to protect them won't matter in the end, Stone."

"I believe everyone deserves a fair shake," he said, slipping away his weapon, and—the dumbass—returned the gun to her.

She didn't aim it at me and blow a hole in my skull, but calmly checked to see if there was one in the chamber. "Wait until you watch one of them slaughter your entire crew. Then we'll see how solid your moral high ground is. She killed our own. By rights of the old code, we should have hanged her until she was dead."

"As I understand the situation, she was trying to flee and it was the nymphs you failed to anticipate who decimated your group."

Eve pulled a face at him, then she glanced to me. "Don't tell me you're a monster fucker, too."

Stone locked his jaw in and glared, a sure sign of guilt. He bundled his hands behind his back and said,

"The director gave explicit orders regarding her capture and treatment."

"Strange that he wants to get so involved with this one. Wonder why." She closed her gun's chamber and holstered it on her hip. "Doesn't matter anyway. No chance you're going to get this one to agree. And we all know what happens to witches without magic."

She tossed back her head and cackled, then drew her lanyard badge through a slit by the door. It beeped and opened, Eve glancing over her shoulder to glare at me.

*What happens to witches?* The question grew on my tongue, my panic nearly giving it voice, but as she snickered, the black hole in my stomach grew.

# Chapter Seventeen

*Ink*

A purple haze hovered across the floor as the aura witch turned round and round her wrought-iron pot placed upon a hot plate. I stared at the theatrics with an exhaustion quickly bubbling over into annoyance.

"You are aware I am not a brainless mortal who will feed you the contents of my purse for glittery sparkles and a spritz from a fog machine?"

She paused in her pointless machinations to stare at me. The only thing bubbling in her 'cauldron' was a chamomile tea. Instead of casting a spell, she'd palmed a small artifact from the collection behind. "It's up your sleeve," I said, pointing as she hefted the brooch out with only a slight tinge of guilt.

The witch smiled with her full teeth and she held the oval out. Instead of silver or pewter, it was made of the same elf-banishing iron as her cauldron. Dark and dull, the only decoration was a small raised circle in the middle. "With this, you can pass through the demonic wards unharmed," she said, her voice in the timbre of a fate weaver.

"Did you intend to give it a soak in your weak tea before passing it over?" I inquired, staring at the piece of old jewelry but not touching it. Magic of old sang through it, a magic someone of her ilk could never command. She knew I was aware, her fingers clenching tighter around the metal. Squiggles of radioactive green and yellow rose from her body, the aura witch unable to keep her emotions from getting the better of her.

She reached under her robe and drew a small dagger from a scabbard hidden below the belt. I tried to not snicker at the empty threat of her holding it near me. "This requires your blood," she said, as if I'd been concerned.

"That little prick won't even pierce my flesh." I extended my claw and placed it to my palm. Pushing in hard, I scraped down the skin, slicing through both human and demon layers until the nearly black liquid rose to the surface.

The witch cupped my hand and held it over the brooch. She squeezed harder than needed, watching to see if I'd react. "If you wish me to cry out in agony, you need to try much harder, or accept your desires to dominate me under your heel."

Her cheeks burned red at the truth given voice. I'd lived long enough to know humans rarely enjoyed having their secrets plucked free, often refusing to engage in them with the most willing of participants. It was an agonizingly confounding lesson for a young incubus.

I shook my hand, encouraging a full drop of incubus blood to plop right into the inlay. The brooch's dour exterior shifted to a crimson sheen. An image rose across its surface of an embossed creature of hooves and wings striding across the iron field. I held out my hand for the artifact, when she glanced to my wound that was yet gaping.

"Do not concern yourself with it. Tis a minor scratch." I clenched my palm shut to hide it away. The witch shook her head as if she had not shown a moment of humanity to the demon in her midst. "Now, if you please…"

She moved to extend the brooch, before pausing. "You do understand that by wearing this fixed to a cloak you will be human."

"Yes, yes, you read its quite dull terms and I signed the user agreement. If you please."

"Do you get what that means? Being human?"

I sighed at her antics. "I shall develop a sudden unholy obsession with cheese from a can? Do not worry. I've already known such pleasures. It's best when combined with a spritz of whipped cream."

"I can't tell if you're this stupid, or pretending to be."

My body churned at her stalling, and I wondered once more if she was not playing a part the hunters ordered. "Will you help me, or do I have to take that brooch from you myself?"

The witch lifted a fallen tarp from the ground, the ends stained by water and age. She draped it across my shoulders, the stench of mold filling my nose. "First, the cloak," she said. "Then…" With the end unfastened, she plunged the stick pin through one side of the tarp, nearly nicking my neck.

I smiled at the pointless jab and she stood before me, struggling to puncture the other side. "There is no second go with this. If you take it off, you will become a demon and all the wards will once again hold you in place. Do you understand?"

Her constant need to question had rasped off my last nerve. "Is it the question of your squishy mortality that you think I should weigh upon? I have known and *known* mortals for centuries upon centuries. Watched you muddle through life with your fragile bodies. A few hours in your skin will mean little to me."

"Is that so?" she asked and stuck the pin back into the brooch.

Weight fell upon me. A mass I didn't realize I was carrying crushed my shoulders. I stumbled away, trying to catch a mirror to spot an aufhocker or worse perched on my back. But as I stared, I saw only myself stripped of the glamour and sheen afforded to an incubus. In place of the pristine countenance, redness dotted the cheeks and pores enlarged down my nose. My eyes did not sparkle, the otherworldly fire dampened to a plain tan. Cracks had formed across my once supple lips, and there were small hairs upon my chin. She had turned me into an abomination!

Would the sight of me in this form turn Layla's stomach? Was that the aura witch's plan all along, to separate her from me?

"You already want to take it off, don't you?" she asked, taunting me.

She was in danger, and only I could save her from the monsters that'd hounded my steps through history and realms. A handful of acne wouldn't stop me from plucking her from their clutches before hell's doors opened wide. "I will not break the spell until Layla is in my arms." The words were for me, but the aura witch scoffed as if I was telling her.

"No matter what they do to you?"

"No matter what I do to them," I growled, finding my voice at least maintained its gravelly tone. *That should cause a few to piss themselves.* "Thank you for your admittedly forced…" I held out my hand to be the bigger gentleman, but started at the red blood dripping from the wound. My self-inflicted gash had not healed, and worse, as I held it out the air caused an inharmonic sting to radiate up my palm.

I clenched my hand closed, growing uneasy with the feeling I'd never before known.

The aura witch stared at me with such cockiness that I wanted to pluck her eyes out. But I was no longer the unbreakable demon. I was as fragile as her, as any human in the world.

It did not matter. I would walk through broken glass, crawl across the fiery gates of Tartarus, plunge into the frozen depths of Lucifer's heart to reach my bond. "I will save her," I said and took a step to the side.

The realms didn't fade, and I wasn't able to run without time's grip to the wolf's side. Right. Humans had to do all that walking. Bundling my cloak in my hand, I turned and clomped down the stairs. At the street, I whistled for a car to stop and plucked out Layla's phone.

"Wolf, I am coming. And the hunters will pay."

* * * *

*Layla*

"Is that all you people know?" I asked, quickly past caring and rounding back to a shrieking exasperation.

Stone looked up from his stupid pad to stare at me in confusion.

"First abduction, then death?"

"You do not have to…" He groaned and pinched his temples. As he did, the shellacked medium brown hair fell from its glue hell. Stone took a moment to fix it before he pulled over a chair and sat across from me.

Here came the good cop part.

"Our job here, my job, is the same as yours. We are on the same team."

"Last I checked, I didn't abduct women and stick them in mason jars," I said.

His face only fluctuated for a moment, as if he either didn't believe me or didn't agree with it. "Instead you openly attack and destroy on the streets where any human could see."

"What? You guys all about 'keeping the humans out of the paranormal world'?"

"Humans are as much a part of the 'paranormal' world as demons and angels. How do you not know this?"

Damn, that one cut deep. My cheeks burned at the simple question that revealed the depths of my ignorance. I'd been piecing together all of this mess I had been born into thanks to what my incubus and werewolf occasionally let slip. Cal seemed to be as unaware of the side of magic as I was, and Ink… Ink only revealed what benefited him.

A bubble caught at the base of my throat. I scrunched my nose, trying to fight back the truth wanting to escape. It wasn't just that my mother wasn't around to teach me. I couldn't let these assholes know she'd abandoned me. Who knew what they'd do if they found her? Probably the same shit they were doing to me. I coughed, the back of my tongue starting to tickle, then itch and finally burn.

Leaning forward, I spattered out a wet cough. I half expected to find blood like I was a pretty ingenue quaintly dying from consumption. Instead, a large globule of silver mercury sat on the table. I sat back and felt the same cold potion they'd forced down my throat cling to the side of my mouth.

"Here." Stone plucked the kerchief from his breast pocket and handed it to me. What kind of weirdo carried a handkerchief around? It looked like silk, with the initials RS embroidered on the corner. I stared at it but wasn't about to take anything from them.

"No thanks," I said, pulling my bag to me and digging inside. Under the mess of aspirin bottles I'd stopped needing, I spotted a dusty pack of tissues. As I pulled them out, my keys came with. They jangled loudly, drawing Stone's stare.

I met his eye while dabbing off the last of their truth potion. "You gonna take those too, while somehow acting like you're the good guys and not creepy-as-hell kidnappers?"

"We're not…" He groaned, his bottom lip thinning until it matched the top. "We're not the bad guys, nor are we the good. We're a line protecting humans from the realms bleeding through. Which is what you do."

"I've never kidnapped and poisoned anyone."

"This is not a kidnapping—it's a job offer."

"A job offer at the end of a knife!" It didn't matter what I said, nothing was getting through that thick bureaucratic skull. "You really think this is right? Capturing witches you find, telling them, 'Hey, either work for us, or we kill you'?"

"Would you prefer the alternative?" he asked, laying his hand flat on the table. The light caught a massive gold ring. Embedded into the top was a relief of a woman tied to a stake, metal flames rising to consume her. "You have no idea how dangerous you are to the world."

"Says the man wearing a ring with proof of how dangerous the world is to me. You really think this is the first time I've had people overreact just because of what I am?" I stared him dead in the eye, then jerked a finger to my face. "This ain't a tan."

"Neither's mine," he responded, as if that beat out my argument. "Your powers, your skills can be put to better use with our…"

"Force?"

"Guidance," he said.

"Your 'guidance' I can't say no to or I'll die. Work for free and never leave. Where have I heard that one before?"

Stone folded his hand up and banged the murder ring on the table. If it was supposed to scare me, it didn't work. He wrenched on his hair, tugging all the glued bits out until they fell to frame his face instead. With the wispy caramel-colored tendrils, he almost looked like some Latino elf late for prom. An orange light lit up beside the door followed by a buzzer. He stood up and muttered, "I do not have time for this."

Not caring what a hassle I must be putting on the poor detective's lunch schedule, I refilled my purse. I tugged my mass of keys across the table. Two to my apartment, my car fob, one to Cal's place, another to a locker at school. But it was the keychain that I drew my pinkie down. A black cartoon cat wore a purple witch's hat on her head, her green eyes staring impishly out from under. It was a gift from Cal, a little reminder that no matter how much the world hated witches, he wanted me.

*Damn it.*

I wanted him here with me. No, I didn't. God only knew what these monsters would do to a werewolf. But I didn't want to be alone either. For all my damn bravado, I needed him, and Ink and Daniel. I clenched to my keychain wishing I was holding them instead.

"Stone?" a scratchy voice came over the intercom.

"I'm in the middle of an interrogation," he said, sounding like he was about to crush some minion skulls.

"I know that, sir," the minion eeped, "but I thought you'd like to know we've spotted a werewolf outside the perimeter."

*Cal?*

"What should we do with it?"

Stone didn't speak to the intercom. He stared at me, trapped and fangless in a prison of their make. Adjusting his tie and slicking back his hair, he said, "Protocol. Tranq and collar him."

"No!"

* * * *

*Ink*

Horns blared as I rolled past, my mortality cloak catching in the wind. I gave a jolly wave when the pedals I'd had to utilize took on a life of their own. They, along with the wheel, spun madly as I tipped off the road and down a cement drop. One of the local lakes waited ahead, the waves slopping up in anticipation of snacking on my body. I hooked a hand on the bars and tugged on the little breaking mechanism, only for the chain behind my ankle to shatter.

"This is a problem," I said, my mechanical steed breaking into runaway pieces. With the watery grave looming, I took the only choice left and leaped into the air for my salvation. Alas, instead of a feathered bed or even the welcoming moss, I landed upon the cruel, knee-scraping cement.

That cursed feeling I was intimately coming to know lanced up my shin. Wetness seeped up my pants, but I shook it off and stood just as the wolf and ghost came running from around the bend. "Ink?" Calvin asked, then he stared at where my transportation struck the water and sank. "Why'd you use a bike?"

"Because none of the carriages would stop unless I plied them with gold."

"New question, what's with the…tarp?" He stared askance at my unfashionable wear, then stared closer at the brooch.

"Who cares?" the ghost answered for him. "The fuse box is up ahead. Come on!" He ducked his head back into the dark corridor, incapable of feeling the slop of water or the pressing dread.

The wolf waited for me to join him. He pointed to the wall. "Missing ring. Looks like it was just pulled. You think…?"

"That Layla gave them a fight they weren't expecting? Naturally. I only pray she's able to continue it."

"Well, you're here, so…" He held his hands out to me as if needing to touch my shoulder to make certain I had yet to be drawn to hell. I frowned at the link they'd weakened and stared at my hand. I could see nothing, nor feel the bonds. Had I, in my haste, severed them myself? Or were my new mortal eyes too feeble to see?

"Yes. I am here, and we should enter their lair with finesse. We do not want to endanger our… Did we ever decide on a term?"

"Babe?"

"I refuse to let that word slip from my lips, even in the event that I am tasked with holding an infant."

Side by side, we entered the mouth of our enemy's stronghold. I feared I was sliding down the gullet of a Leviathan, teeth about to collapse around me. The wolf looked startled as well, his eyes hooded as he tugged on a chain around his neck.

"Dearest one." The ghost popped in from the side, his face barely visible in the dark shadows. "That's what she is, after all."

"No one here is impressed by your penny poet wit, specter."

"What do you suggest? All of us call her"—he dropped his voice low and deadened all the emotion—"my bond?"

I scoffed. "Hardly. She is only bound to me, our souls forever locked as one by the chains formed of the other realms. The rest of you mean as much as a chimney sweep in comparison."

A low growl rippled from the wolf and he glared at me. "I'm sorry," I said, staring at him. Despite having the countenance and bone structure of a courtly knight, he had the manners of a privy digger. "Who was it that stomped off in a snit, leaving her vulnerable?"

"Don't even..." the wolf threatened, though he was far more bark than bite even in the worst of situations. Which was probably why Layla had been abducted.

"A...what do you call yourself? A boyfriend, that mate demarcation of wolves. Would one such as that not devote himself to her safety? To protecting her life no matter what? Yet you ran off, tail between your legs, to lick a wound you caused."

"Are you fucking serious?" he gasped, glaring at me, then the ghost.

To my surprise, and slight horror, Daniel shrugged. "He has a point. Though it pains me to say."

"Not as deeply as it does me to hear it. I'm rethinking my entire life."

"It was, what, a week where she didn't tell you? A week where she nearly died like thirty times. Where were you then? Why are you always not around?"

His blue eyes turned gray as ice storms as he glared past us, claws tensing for the kill. "Where was I...?" Calvin repeated, his voice adrift as if he too could not understand his failures. "Where were you?! You're 'bonded to her' as you keep bragging."

"It's not a brag if it's a simple fact."

"Well, Mr. If You Die, I Die, how did you let this happen?"

I started at his tone and the heat of his breath bursting from between fanged teeth. A strange sensation crawled over my scalp and my knees shivered at how close he'd drawn. If I didn't know any better, I'd say I was scared of him.

"Me...? She would not have been accessible to the hunters if you'd stayed by her side. And"—I glanced over my shoulder to stare at the ghost—"she would not have been in that store were it not for you!"

"My turn to wear the blame hat now? Goodie," the ghost said.

"My bond was only in that infernal snake's store to find a spell to give your wretched soul a meat sack to inhabit. Why she cares is beyond me. I'm more than enough to fulfill her needs."

To my surprise, it was the wolf who bayed like a hound with laughter. "Are you kidding me? Half the time she can't fucking stand you."

"I've only known her for two weeks, and she's mentioned wishing to abandon you in the woods twice," the ghost added.

"Tossed down a well."

"Fed to tiny sharks piece by piece."

The wolf and ghost chortled together at their shared hatred of me. I wanted to snatch their faces off for such insolence…but also cower in the corner from a feeling I'd never suffered before. *No. That will not do at all.* Summoning my strength of lived centuries, I stared Cal down. "Hate can ignite the passion twice as strongly as fondness. For every curse she lobs about me, she shrieks ten times more from my body."

That shattered the momentary truce between wolf and ghost. One could not even touch her, just play some strange masturbatory games. The other, while of decent skill, struggled to overcome his generous build, leaving him to let me take the final ride. I was the only one of the three of us free to sup upon every delight available with Layla.

"Now that that is settled, may we attempt to find our…mutual companion, before things get worse?"

The ghost nodded and he pointed to a small panel nestled beside what appeared to be a blank wall. I could barely see it with these worthless eyes. I took a step closer, when the wolf locked into my arm. "There's a hell of a lot more to it than just sex." He stared me down as if I was supposed to wither at his comment, but the perfect boyfriend award passing me by meant nothing.

"There is nothing to me but sex. If you will excuse me..." I pulled open the door on the fuse box and discovered a glowing panel inside. "I believe I will save Layla, and enjoy my just rewards first." With a wave of my finger, I plunged onto the first number.

Red lights descended from above. A siren blared through the tube, echoing down the cement walls until I could hear nothing. The wolf fell to his knees, screaming in pain while the ghost glared at me.

"What did you do?" he shouted.

I raised my hand up, ready to plead ignorance, when a dozen little red dots appeared from the now vanished blank wall. They all situated on my chest and I began to lift my arms, when another thirty joined them.

# Chapter Eighteen

*Layla*

"We have them pinned down," the cold, disembodied voice announced.

"Well…?" The bastard turned to look at me. I could do nothing but claw the table, wanting to choke the life out of him. "It seems we've reached the point in negotiation where—."

A pop burst from outside the room, like someone had tossed a firecracker into a pop can. Why would…? Stone turned white and he stood so fast his chair smashed against the door. "You idiots!" he shrieked.

*No.* Tears stung in my eyes and I clung to hope. Cal was resourceful, he might have Ink with him. They could escape, they—

A massive round exploded, a wave of bullets that'd tear through any meat or bone in its path. Under the pounding gunfire I heard it, the whimper of a wolf.

"I didn't give you an order to fire!" Stone screamed against the door. He pounded harder on it, trying to get their attention. "Is anyone listening?"

*He killed him. They all killed him.* A gulf opened inside of me and I started to shake. My head kept repeating the same thing—*he's dead.* They had killed him before I could say I was sorry. That I loved him.

I stared at the little kitty dangling off my keys. I could curl around the only thing I had of him and fall into despair until I was rotted away to dust. Or…

Coals of rage dumped into the gulf, the blackness igniting to a burning pit that nothing could quench. I threaded my keys between my fingers, forming a pair of makeshift brass knuckles, and stared down at Stone. He wasn't looking back, still banging away on the door.

I stood up slowly, the little kitty knocking against my wrist and my ward against evil tattoo.

"Hello? Can anyone hear me out there? Release the lock!" Stone pulled on the handle, then knocked once more.

I eased around the table, trying to keep myself composed, when he shouted, "What's the state of the dog?"

*Dog!* "You son of a…!" Shrieking, I lashed my only weapon forward. It should have punctured through his neck, but at the last second Stone dodged out of the way. My keys scraped against the plastic casing on the door.

He turned to face me and went for the gun on his hip, but in trying to get distance, he failed to account for his chair. "Fuck!" the asshole cursed, his stance crumbling though he didn't fall.

I had one chance to leap over and pin him, maybe take his gun before he could. I took a step, then caught my real salvation from the corner of my eye. Stone scrambled to his feet, his back hitting the wall. Just as he aimed, I dove not for him but the box holding my magic.

"Damn it!" He sneered, leaping after me.

I cupped the box tight to my stomach and swung wide with my keys. They slashed through his shirt, the edges sharp after hitting the door. Stone didn't even blink, but wrapped his hand around the box and tried to pull it free. With his other hand, he held his gun, but I was too close for him to do anything other than murder me.

Maybe if I'd had any sense, I'd have realized how easily he'd kill me. But all I knew was a bottomless rage to destroy every person who had hurt Cal. I didn't care how much blood I had to wade through to make it happen.

"You don't want to… Ah!"

I slashed him again, this time digging my keys into his biceps then straight down. Stone let go and stumbled back. He stared at the rip in his shirt and the red staining the once-white linen. Not so pretty now.

"Put the box down," he ordered, aiming his weapon at my head.

A demented laugh started in my throat. "You think that fucking scares me? I've had a gun at my head all day. You took everything from me!"

"That was a mistake…"

"I'm going to take it all from you."

It'd have been a good line if we weren't at a stalemate. I held my keys out like three tiny daggers, but I couldn't open the box. He had his gun trained on me, and, while he could shoot me, he'd lose his asset.

"Give me the box," Stone said.

"Give me the key."

"There is no key. It only activates with a proper fingerprint. You cannot get into it."

Fuck. "Then..." Not caring that he was about to shoot me, I raised the box over my head. "I'll smash it open!"

"No!" he shouted and dove to stop me.

The box flew through the air, on a collision course with the table. Stone was close behind, the gun clattering to the ground as he reached with both hands, but he wasn't going to stop me. There wasn't enough time.

Which was when a ten-foot-long tentacle shattered through the door, knocked the box to the back of the room, whipped around to rip off the ceiling lights then vanished out the way it had come. Only the flickering of the shattered fluorescents filled the void as I stared where the box had been. Stone froze too, his hands nearly pressed to my waist without the box in the way.

Slowly, I craned my neck. "What the shit was that?"

A klaxon blared above my head. "Warning. Detainees have escaped. All personnel report to forward stations."

The lunatics were running the asylum. This was my only chance to escape. *Get the box, find my boys...help him in any way I can. There's still time, there has to be time. Save the day, watch the place burn from a good distance.*

I nodded to myself, set on my path. With a lash of my foot, I kicked the stunned Stone away and turned...just as a spray of vomit-green goo burst through the hole in the door, straight at me.

* * * *

*Ink*

The radiating dots upon my chest multiplied once more. A low whine, like that of small engine revving, rose from the cavern. "Do not move," a voice droned from deep within.

"I say, hello? We are but three comely visitors who have come bearing treats," I called down the tube, before glancing to the wolf who was clawing the air apart. "We should have brought a basket of pastries. All will allow passage to the bread men."

Whatever robotic entity was at the end of these dots seemed unimpressed. "You are trespassing."

"Are we, though? I have yet to see a sign declaring…"

"Remove yourself from these premises or face the consequences."

This was going well. I turned from the wolf's chest where the spray pattern of dots shifted to perforate every organ inside. I had the same, hunters caring little for any innocent that wandered into their lair. They were the kind to use a halberd to slay a gnat, after all.

"Excuse me," I said, and took a step forward.

The lights increased in their vibrancy, but no bullets fired from their shadowed guns. I smiled wickedly and took another. "I would quite like to speak to your manager. You seem to have stolen something of mine I'd like returned."

"Do not move," the voice droned. I promptly ignored it and slipped further down the tunnel. When no ammunition perforated my body, I glanced behind to the two. "It is a farce. This is nothing more than a priest's mockery of smoke and mirrors to fool the feeble minded. Come along."

Calvin eyed up the revealed edge behind the vanished wall, the tube metal instead of cement and a low-lying fog slipping around our ankles. Then he took a step inside. I shook my shoulders, prepared to toss off my mortality cloak, when the tube lit up red. Dozens of wards reverberated on the walls, picking up on the introduction of the werewolf and ghost.

Growling, I watched the demon flypaper rise into view just ahead, high enough that no one save the ten-foot-tall could erase it. I'd have to play at human a bit longer. I dropped my shoulders, returning the tarp to smother my body.

"Are you sure about this?" the wolf asked. He'd turned to the side while staring ahead. The dots did not shift to make up for this change.

I laughed and extended a hand, watching them form across my palm like an errant case of measles. "They're nothing more than trickery."

The ghost strode ahead, the light vanishing into his skin and emerging out of the back. He stared deeper down the dry and foggy tube. I followed suit, struggling to peer through the darkness due to my lagging sight, when a drop of water caught the light. A black muzzle, no, a dozen more, were aimed at our chests.

"Oh dear." I launched back and hooked a hand to the werewolf with plans to collapse him. But the man was bigger than I anticipated, his weight sturdy and refusing to budge. In my human form, the best my willowier frame could manage was smashing him into the side.

"What are you—?" Calvin cried, his lips crushed by my cheekbone when the bullets flew free.

The bombast shattered my hearing into a bone-splintering quake and a piercing whine. I moved to cup my ears, as if that would stop the spray of death in the air. Before I could, the wolf swooped his hands around my head and plunged the both of us to our stomachs. A frozen chill erupted up around us, and I dared to look skyward. The bullets were impossible to see, but as they traveled, they left a momentary wake in the fog, hundreds of trails piercing the air to shatter a spleen or kidney.

That unnerving sensation rattled through me, my knees bouncing on the ground and my limbs hardening to ice. I couldn't catch the breath I needed and a fire burned in my chest. Just as a scream began to build, the werewolf clamped a hand over me and pulled me closer.

"Daniel? What do you see?" Calvin shouted to the ghost yet standing in the path without a care.

"A lot of little fires at the end of the hall," he reported.

"Helpful as always. Is there an exit we can reach? Preferably one with a door as we are not capable of transcending walls."

I expected the glare of the ghost, but it was the askance of the wolf that caught me. "Do that thing you do."

"Here? Now? In the middle of a firefight? You're kinkier than I give you credit for."

"Not that," Calvin growled. "Never that. Walk through walls, or turn a corner. Go out there and find Layla."

I glared at the ward taunting me. *Go ahead, toss off the only thing keeping me from being the hunters' latest demonic specimen. Take two steps into their lair and wind up on a dissection table, or worse, have to suffer their unending monologues about worshipping Satan.*

Another burst of gunfire shattered above us, sparks kicking off the walls. "And leave you alone? Layla would rip my heart out of my chest for such an action." It was a truth I was certain of.

The wolf accepted it, even as he pursed his lips. "Fine. But we need to get out of here before they figure out how to aim—"

"Guys...the guns just shifted," our stalwart scout reported.

"Sounds like our cue to find another entrance." I shoved at the ground, sickness leeching up my arms where I reached through the fog. But as I leaped to my feet, it faded. The wolf was slower, taking his time and looking up. I reached over to assist and wipe a spot off his collar, when a single, solitary gunshot pierced the air.

Panic crunched my heart, my eyes brimming with tears of pain as I slowly drew my gaze down. If there was so much as a scratch upon the wolf, Layla would banish me to hell in a second. His shoulders were staid, the sternum yet solid, and chest of an honest build. I could see no wound on him, no sign of blood or...

"Ink!" His staggeringly blue eyes opened wide and he pointed to me.

I glanced to my arm and there, between the tattered ends of my burned shirt, was the ripped flesh and blood of a mortal. "Ouch," fell from me. As the realization of injury rolled up my arm to my mind, pain struck through the whole of me.

"Ah!" I screamed, clamping a hand over the wound.

"Daniel?" the wolf shouted.

"I don't see anything else. There's..."

Calvin was trying to pry my seal away to look at the injury, but I pushed him off. No assurances that he was studying medicine would get me to remove my clamp. "Will you stop being so fussy? They could have poisoned their bullets, or cursed them, or…how did they hurt a demon?"

I dropped my grip, letting him peek at the tattered flesh, when the dull voice shifted. The once robotic male became a more urgent female. "Warning. Containment in processing has been breached."

"Containment?" I asked, glancing from the wolf who was busy with my wound, to the ghost providing no relief to anyone. "What does that…?"

A light flashed far within the tunnel revealing how deep it ran. Random bursts illuminated a shadow with a head the size of a lion and two long horns straining against the walls. "What would hunters keep in containers?" I calmly asked.

We had all turned to look when five giant tentacles burst through the fog to latch onto our throats.

* * * *

*Layla*

A single drop of the putrid green acid landed on my cheek and my skin curled in on itself in agony. I tried to take a step back from the arcing spray that would melt my body, but there was no escape. All I could do was raise my hand and…

Arms enveloped my waist, yanking me off my feet. The rush of acid blew right past me, the stench drenching my nose and momentarily smothering me. I struggled to breathe and looked up into the panting face of my captor and savior. He'd pushed me against the wall, his forearms acting like a cage against my hips. To escape, he'd nearly fallen on top of me, the lapels of his suit glancing against my breasts. If I breathed too deeply, I brushed my nipples against his chest, which was harder than his name.

He glanced down at me and I stared at his eyelashes. I'd never seen such thick ones on a man, making him appear almost innocent and genteel. Daniel won in the cheekbone department, but Stone was close on his heels. I held my breath, growing uncomfortably aware of how close he was…and how much my damn body enjoyed the tingle. It was Ink's fault.

"Your hair." Stone tugged on the end of my curls, revealing a charred end where the acid had landed and eaten through it. He frowned as if that slight marring was his failure.

"It'll grow back," I said.

For a moment, his harsh lips twisted into a patient smile, and he guided the burnt ends back to the rest. "I suppose so. Still a shame, though…" The smile faded and he whipped his gaze down, then took a step back.

The sound of a moose yelling inside of a trash can blasted from outside the room, and a creature stuck its nose inside. Like an elk but ten times bigger, it bore blue and white spots with antlers that shimmered silver. What stood out was the massive bulging goiter on its throat, which started to undulate.

"What is that thing?"

"Dangerous!" Stone shouted. He spun in place, taking me in his arms, and presented his back to the monster. A great blorp burst from the creature. In the reflection of the metal wall, I watched its jaws unhinge as it spat a baseball-sized loogie at Stone. He jerked forward, his hands clenching tighter to my stomach. But he didn't make a sound, only collapsed around me.

*Those are some damn nice forearms…*

*Yes, yes, notice after the monster's dead.* There! Sitting in the back corner was the box. I just had to get it. I was about to break free when Stone opened his hands and turned to face the creature. He dug into his pocket and raised up a silver pentagram. The monster bellowed, hooves flaring on the tile as it scrambled to get away.

"Go back to your pen, Lomie!" Stone ordered, fully focused on the creature. This was it.

I dove for my box, scrambling to avoid the acid burrowing through the floor. Reaching out, I tapped a finger against the locked surface. A bullet shattered the sheetrock inches from my head. Snarling, I spun around. Standing in the hole was the last person I wanted to see.

"Nice try, witch." Eve held her gun steady on me.

Stone had managed to tie a small rope of silver around the elk monster's neck. As he turned, I noticed his suit jacket had been eaten clean through, and shreds of the shirt as well, revealing burn marks on his back. He didn't even wince while guiding the creature like a petting zoo donkey to the door.

"Eve. Put down your weapon and take this."

"Not until the green skin gets away from the box."

Even buried in a coffin of metal, the magic cried to be returned, but I had enough sense to know not to move. "Why is it always about skin with you people?"

"I will collect it," Stone said. He glared at Eve, who held her gun with one hand and the leash with the other. With a sigh, he stepped past me and scooped up the box. "There. I have contained the problem. Both of them."

He nodded to the elk monster, which was cowering, its head bowed low as if the leash were burning it. Even though it had nearly burned my skin off, I could only feel pain for the creature. I rose slowly and picked up the only thing I could, my bag with my spell book. In this hell it meant nothing, but at least it was mine.

"If you would be so kind as to return it to its broken…"

A blood-curdling scream shattered the air. Not of another creature trapped in this prison. This was human and it bubbled over to silence in an instant. The detectives both gawped in shock before rushing to see what else was on a rampage. Eve ran out first, gun drawn. I tried to stay back, but Stone caught me by the arm.

I glared where he touched me, but he said, "For your safety."

"I'd be a lot safer with my magic."

"That's for my safety." Holding tight, he guided me out of the room and through the hole the tentacle had made. "Don't worry, no harm will come to you as long as you're…"

Madness awaited us. Not the last-day-before-Christmas kind of madness. This was Alice-deep-into-the-mushrooms madness. Lights of purple and green strobed from the ceiling while the rest of the room's fluorescents had failed. The fog rolled about like a rising tornado. Running through the mists and pulsing lights were shadows of things I couldn't even imagine.

"What is happening?" Stone shouted. Blood burst across the back wall, its owner screaming in pain before the sound of hooves stomping over bones broke the air. My stomach heaved at the image and a lightheadedness overtook me. I'd never been bothered by gore—hard to be a nurse with that. This was new and it sent me falling for the floor.

"Hang on!" Scooping me up in his arms, even while clutching the box, Stone rushed me past the rising chaos to put me safely behind a desk. The detectives were being tossed about like popsicle sticks, shattering on the walls and the impossibly gigantic heads in the fog.

"Stay here," he ordered to me before shouting out to the rest of them. "What is happening?"

"We've lost fucking containment!" Drake cried through the cotton up his nose. He had a giant water gun in his arms, but judging by the shrieking, I doubted it was water inside.

"On which level?" Stone asked. He deftly ran ahead, taking cover behind one of the overturned desks.

"All of them!" Drake responded.

"That's impossible."

"Tell them that!" he responded, raising his water pistol up and shooting it at the flames… walking? Yeah, they were walking through the floor, kicking ash into the air.

"Damn it!" With my box cupped under his arm, Stone slid over to the wall and yanked an extinguisher off one-handed. He aimed the white foam at the feet of the fire creature, blanketing his face. "Drake, what about the lockdown? Drake?"

We both turned to where he'd been only to find a shadow on the wall. Stone cried out and swung the empty extinguisher, knocking in the head of a rampaging scrounger. I couldn't stop flinching when its excess teeth scattered against me.

"We have to close the doors or they will destroy the people up above."

"Give me my magic!" I shouted to him.

"Don't you fucking dare," Eve called back. She too had set up shop in an alcove, taking shots at the creatures marching in with the fog. "A witch that hasn't been collared is just another threat at your back."

"I don't want to die either," I pleaded to Stone.

"The emergency button is in the director's office. We have to get back there."

I craned my head around and spotted the shattered glass labeled Director Zimmerman. "That's gonna be a problem," I said, directing them to the lashing tentacles ripping apart the drywall.

"Damn it, not now, Kevin!" Stone shouted.

"Listen," I called to the only cool head left. "These creatures, they're gonna kill people, right?"

"Yes. By the multitude if they get out of here."

"And I don't want that. You know I don't want that. So let me fucking help!"

I don't know why I was trying logic on the people who had kidnapped me, but it was all I had left. A moaning that did not sound human rolled from the director's office. They were pressing in closer, sending Stone scampering back a desk. Eve had to retreat as well, though she was on the other side of the room.

Oh, no. Worse than the moaning, chittering laughter broke from just behind the fallen desk. I clung white-knuckled to the frame and stared in terror.

"Stone!" I shouted. "Please!"

To my shock, he bent over the box and pulled the blue vial out. "Don't make me regret this," he shouted and lobbed it to me underhanded. I cupped my palms, my eyes growing wide as I watched it arc when the glass exploded.

"No!" A bullet ripped through, sending the potion that'd give me back my magic, that'd keep me from dying, soaking into the ashes. "You bitch!"

Eve stood proudly, her gun still held out as if she were posing. "An un-collared witch is a—"

A horn pierced through her chest, shattering her ribs. Eve gasped in shock, her dying eyes falling to find her heart on the end of the unicorn's horn. The creature cried out and bucked, tossing Eve's dead body until it struck the wall and crumpled. The blood-stained unicorn stared right at me, its eyes swirling with death.

"Ah fuck!" I raised up the only weapon I had left and swung my book, only for Stone to come barreling past. The unicorn swerved, its hooves scattering on the tile and causing the murder horse to collapse.

"How did…?" I asked, when he locked a hand to my arm and yanked me to my feet.

"No time."

"Don't they only stop for virgins?" I stuttered, my brain clinging to the ridiculous because my life and my magic were mixing with the blood of a unicorn.

Stone lashed a foot out, kicking away the last of the shattered glass door. I struggled to follow, trying to keep my bare foot off the floor by hopping. Which was when the chittering burst from above. Without a second thought, I swung wide, bashing in a tiny skull with my book. A body with a long, pointed skull struck the wall and slowly slid down.

"Good work," he said.

I tipped my head as if I needed his compliment when a horde rose from behind the desk. In a panic, I stomped my bare foot down right onto a shard of glass. "Fuck!" I swung with my only weapon even while trying to pull the glass out. The attacking creatures kept at it, their laughter buzzing like giant mosquitoes.

Stone wrenched a fancy chair away, rolling over the feet of two of the bastards, and he slapped a button under the desk. All the lights that had remained turned blood red and the floor shifted under me.

"Entering lockdown," a voice said dramatically.

"Come on!" He jerked his head to a small hole that had appeared on the side, then he kicked two of the advancing gnomes out of the way. I took a step, only for the glass in my foot to overwhelm me. My body crumpled just as arms scooped me up.

Holding me tight, Stone carried me to the small door. He dropped to a knee and placed me on it. I stared through the dark doorway and my stomach plummeted. "Hang on," he said, tipped his leg and tossed me down a black slide to god knew where.

# Chapter Nineteen

*Ink*

"That was quite the mess."

The wolf panted, his shirt ripped in strategic spots where the suckers had stuck to the cotton and pulled. I'd dare say the kraken seemed talented at knowing how to get a man nearly naked while still having plausible deniability. Calamari lay at our feet, the innards quickly drying out from the fog. I bent down to inspect a tentacle as thick as a man's thigh.

"Why didn't you demon up?" Calvin pressed. He drew his arm across his forehead, smearing the green blood of the kraken like a tribal mark. "You know, claws, wings, smug armor."

I smiled at him. "And take away your opportunity to shine? You had this well in fang. Or are you fishing for a treat?" I patted my pockets as if I were carrying a bone for the dog.

It only caused the wolf to frown, but he accepted my answer for the truth it was. He kicked into the ripped-open kraken's tentacle, rebounding its flesh off the walls. "Do they do this? Use squid monsters as attack dogs?"

I shrugged. It seemed unlike the hunters I'd known to give trespass to any creature not of this realm. Then again, the ones from my time would have been ripped in half upon confronting a kraken. This modern batch seemed to have embraced magic in an unsettling fashion. I stared at the ward, still out of reach, still glowing. None but a witch could make that, yet the ones who hunted them had. How?

"I rather doubt the hunters had intentions to send such a welcoming party after us."

"So how did they…?" he asked, before turning to me and chuckling. "Layla."

"Who else could it be?"

"They are gonna regret pissing her off." He scrubbed his face with his palms, working the kraken blood deep into his pores. While he continued to laugh, a sorrow warped his countenance that unsettled me deep in my marrow. "Your arm," the wolf said, jerking the wobbly tip of a tentacle at me. I stared at where he pointed, then raised an eyebrow. "It's still bleeding."

I clasped a hand to the wound and struggled to disguise the wriggle of pain from my touch. Stickiness clung to my palm which could only be the thinned demon ichor. How long did it take humans to repair their bodies? An hour? Three? Did they require an entire day to regrow severed limbs?

"Uh…guys," the ghost called, running toward us. I'd at least offered moral support in Calvin's war with the tentacles. The best Daniel had done was stand watch and point out when another appeared.

"Yes, welcome to the party, specter. You've done a terrific job of displaying your usefulness."

"Last I checked, I did all the fighting." Calvin hurled the last of the squid to the ground and turned to me.

"And I cheered you on. Fantastic claw work, by the way. Top marks."

"That's not the problem," the ghost said, running to us then through us. A chill sent the human goosebumps flailing up my body and I whipped around to glare at him.

"That is!" Daniel extended an ethereal finger in the direction of the water-spewing pipes. A shadow stepped into the spray—its head as wide as its shoulders, arms that could rival a Christmas ham and legs…surprisingly tapered at the foot.

A red light beamed from above, and another of those unnatural voices declared something about locks. I paid it no heed, the shadow stepping forward far more interesting. As it passed through the gushing water, its horns pierced apart the makeshift waterfall. Steam rose from its cleft nose and it struck a pose upon its hooves.

"Is that a fucking minotaur?" the wolf gasped.

"Good day!" I called, extending a hand. "How fares fair Minos?"

The minotaur stomped a hoof to the ground. I'd guess by the lack of udders and the hairy whip dangling betwixt the legs it was male, but I didn't like to presume. He, or she, snorted once more, and took off running with the horns in skewering range.

"Excuse me," I said, "you seem to be in a rush, but…"

"Get out of—" Calvin shoved me to the side, where we both struck the metal wall. The minotaur didn't even blink, running straight through Daniel, who—for a brief, blessed moment—had a cow's ass sticking out of him.

I began to point when a loud metallic clang shook the whole of the ground around us. I clung to the wolf for balance. The wall that'd vanished upon our entrance had slammed shut. A massive metal door that belonged in a bank vault had closed off our only exit.

It did not slow the minotaur, who plunged horns straight into the metal. Sparks shot off, but they didn't make a dent. Roaring, the minotaur swung their watermelon fists high and pounded on the door. *Bam bam bam!* Each hit caused the ground and my stomach to lurch.

"I say, excuse me." I switched to the old tongue and greeted the minotaur properly. "I don't believe that's going to work."

The minotaur bellowed like an ox in the mud, the cow tongue flailing in rage before it turned to me. "I'm finding another way out," it said in ancient Greek. "Follow me or don't." It loped on past, each crash of its hooves shaking the world around us.

"Do you have a preferred salutation?" I asked as the minotaur stepped back and charged headfirst at a wall. This time the bricks shattered, revealing a secret hallway.

The minotaur kicked the broken bricks aside with their hooves. "Elpida," she said, before leaping into the secret hallway and taking off.

"Well…" I extended a hand in her vanishing direction, the whole of the ancient sewer system rattling with every step.

"I don't like this," the ghost responded, and I failed to disguise my groan of exhaustion. He glared but a moment, putting all his ectoplasm into the flash of his eyes. "How do we even know Layla's down that way?"

"He makes a good point."

I sighed. "You shouldn't defend the dead. It'll fill your ears with grave wax."

Even while speaking, the wolf worked his pinkie in his ear canal. "Why don't you find her? We're in, you got to be able to zip zap next to her."

"Zip zap?"

"Or whatever it is you do. I don't ask for demon specifics." They both stared overlong, sensing all that was amiss.

I plucked up my wrist, expecting to feel the weight of the chain or the cold from the metal dangling into the ether. All I got was a rush of mildly warm air stinking of fetid plastic from the tarp. "Why don't you put your nose to the test?" I said, tapping my own. Even with a smile, I couldn't shake off the worry winding across my face. How did humans survive with such malleable expressions? It was exhausting.

"It..." the wolf said, when he tipped his head up and breathed deep. He held out a hand as if to silence the people who were not talking, then turned on his heel and walked to a grate in the wall. Crouched over, he breathed so deeply it was a wonder the grate didn't demand dinner.

"Layla?" Calvin whispered quietly before he locked onto the metal bars and tugged. "I can smell her, or at least jasmine and...um..." He mumbled the next part while straining to rip the bars free from the wall. "Ink, give me a hand."

"I…have a better idea. Elpida? Could you help us one more time? Our friend is in danger."

The others stared at me in shock, but the minotaur came roaring back. Calvin barely had time to roll out of the way before she kindly skewered the wall apart. The bars slammed down a second abandoned hallway where light peered in through crumbling bricks. "There you go," she said in her gruff voice. "I hope you find 'em." With that, she turned and vanished down the hall.

"Why are your jaws disengaged?" I asked to the two staring at me.

"Better question, why didn't you keep the minotaur?" Daniel fumed, as if entrapping a wild creature would somehow make him useful.

I leaned closer to whisper near his ethereal ear, "If you wish to chain her up to obey your whims, do it yourself."

While he imagined the stain his body would have left from Elpida's might, I strode forward into the hallway of the damned. The stone creaked around us as if it were about to crumble from the unnatural metal surrounding it. My hand rose to the ceiling, behaving of its own accord to try to hold the ceiling up. I shook it away and glared at my errant arm. Must be more of those human reactions. How could simple mortality play such a complicated symphony with my sinew?

"Wolf, can you still smell her sex?" I asked, struggling to see as the light faded to nothing more than weak candles.

"That's what you smell?" Daniel prodded and I chuckled at the awkward gasping from behind.

"Yes, Layla's around here. Like she flew past fast, or is near. I can't…" He pulled in a deep whiff before casting his haunting glare upon me. "Why don't you find her?"

"As I said, there are wards..."

"None in here."

"And your nose is a finely tuned instrument. I have faith in it leading us to our mutual companion. No, that is still an awful phrase. Bed mate? Any takers?"

The wolf ceased moving and the ghost stopped behind him. With exaggerated movements, Calvin crossed his arms before his chest telling me he had no intention of taking another step. I had no choice but to stop as well.

"You did it again. Being an ass, refusing to help—that I'm used to. But humility..." He shook his head as if I'd committed a cardinal sin, despite *being* a cardinal sin.

Latching onto my arm, the wolf stared me in the eye as he touched my bleeding wound. "What have you done?"

"What was necessary." I wrenched my arm back, feeling a pop in the shoulder. They could do that? The sting was only momentary, but it sent me twisting away from them and scowling. "There are demonic wards all over these walls, and ceilings and floors. If I took one step inside, I'd be as useful to you as Daniel."

"Hey!"

Calvin stood closer, his voice plummeting through his chest. "Then how are you in here?"

"I..." The bricks shook, not under or above us, but to the left. Curious, I stared closer, when a sharp force plunged through the crumbling wall. For a brief moment I saw a flash of green and purple scales and my heart dropped. "Basilisk!" I shouted as the snake creature reared up to attack the only flesh in the way, Calvin.

It must have been the human hormones winding through me. Oxytocin, adrenaline, serotonin, morphine—all those old words Layla studied when we lay in bed drove me to dive for the wolf. I knew there was no time to get both of us away, but shock still pierced through me when the basilisk sank its fang into my shoulder and bit.

"Ink!" The wolf slashed for the exposed throat of the giant snake and it had to release me.

*Satan's prickly ballsack!* Fire seared through my veins, wrenching the muscles of my shoulder and arm like a giant giving a deep tissue massage. I crumbled to my knee even though the danger yet remained, the pain too excruciating for me to toss it aside.

The wolf was the only one left as he faced down the dark hole where the snake hid. "Keep back," I gasped, my throat burning. "The venom is deadly!"

Oh. Yes. I was no longer a demon, ergo no longer immune to the simple venoms and poisons of the creatures of the realms. *Wonderful.*

Calvin snarled, fur sprouting across his arms. He did not bother removing the remains of his shirt nor pants, but spread his arms wide as they grew in girth. "I hate snakes!" he thundered as the basilisk sprang out to attack.

Its head stuck clean out of the hole, mouth opened wide and fangs ready to slice apart the mid-transformation wolf's chest. The venom would pump straight to his heart at that range. I tried to kick his legs out to get him to move, but the basilisk froze. Its jaw remained dislodged, the fangs dripping with venom and my blood, but the eyes rolled back. Inch by inch, the green and purple scales flattened to a dead gray stone. As it sealed up to the nose of the basilisk, the creature cried out once. The weight of the extended head became too much and it cracked in half, shattering at my feet.

"What in the…"

Gritting my teeth so hard my tongue bled, I inched up to my feet and slapped a hand over the wolf's mouth. Deep within the bowels of the parallel corridor I heard it—bok bok bok. After the clucking faded away, I whispered, "Cockatrice." I could not even make a bawdy pun to the man I held as my body writhed in pain and I fell to the ground.

"Your shoulder is bleeding blood. Red blood. You stupid demon, what did you do?"

He sounded near hysterics at my dying. What a strange concept. "As I was explaining, before being so rudely…ah! Interrupted. There was no way to get past the demon wards, so I reached the only logical conclusion."

"He's human," the ghost stuttered.

"They can do that?" the wolf shouted to the specter.

"Do not worry, it is only temporary. I can remove the spell and become my hale and whole self. But…" Why was it so difficult to move? I collapsed to the wall and luxuriated in the chill rising from the bricks. "If I do, I cannot put it back on. I will not take this off until Layla is safe. Or every hunter is a stain on the floor. Whichever comes first."

I expected a laugh, maybe a compliment for my ingenuity, but the wolf clasped his hands to his forehead as if he were the one in pain. "You… How did you—? How could you—?"

"I cannot answer a question you do not finish."

At that, he snickered. After a moment, Calvin breathed deep. "How long does it take basilisk venom to kill a human?"

"I've never injected a person and watched an hourglass to see…but I'd put it at anywhere from twelve hours to a day."

The wolf sighed and nodded as if he'd come to an arrangement on his own. "Okay. Here." He plucked a chain off his neck that held a small plastic purse with a seam down the middle. Into my hand, he placed the purse.

"Why are you gifting me a totem vagina?"

"That isn't…it's got Daniel's bone in it."

I stared from the wolf to the ghost who also looked livid. "I cannot say I approve of the crass metaphor. Far too on the nose."

He clasped a hand to my unbitten shoulder and faced the ghost. "Stay with him, guard him."

"What? No."

"I agree with the specter. I do not require a babysitter, particularly one whose greatest threat is slightly blowing an enemy's hair out of style."

Calvin picked up my arm, which felt heavy but otherwise numb. Strange. I hadn't noticed my hand fading to nothing. He slipped off his belt and knotted it around my shoulder. "I don't know if this is gonna work. It probably already got into your bloodstream. But it might slow it down." With all his might, he tightened the belt until my bones creaked.

Then he placed a comforting hand to my chest, ordered, "Watch my back," and stepped away.

"I never required permission before," I shouted as he disrobed. A pious demon would have turned his gaze. As I was a demon of sin, I ruminated upon the whole of him. Against the slew of muscles supporting his back were scars I knew to be from a whip.

The ghost dashed over to him and said in a fraudulent whisper. "You can't just leave me here. He's…he'll be fine. He always saves himself."

"Maybe," the wolf said. "I know he's infuriating and sometimes you want to throw him into a woodchipper, but it'd break her if anything happened to him. And I will not, I cannot watch her cry. Put up with it for her sake."

How noble. He was willing to sacrifice his pawn in the name of love. Truly, it was a tale worthy of the Bard himself. The ghost seemed resigned to his fate. He'd invested in the love story deeper than Calvin. With one last glance back, he shifted into his true form, fur and teeth and claws.

"I have a question before you go, oh noble beast. If your greatest fear is Layla's tears, then why won't you tell her about the werewolf politics hanging over your head?"

He turned back, light catching on the blue eyes of the wolf and his ears perked in curiosity.

"How the mother of your brother has approached you to be the new alpha in the woods."

Calvin flattened his ears and a snarl rippled his lips. I snickered at his threat even as my body failed me. Closing my eyes, I placed my head against the wall, the pain surging up my neck.

The ghost cheered the wolf on, wishing him luck. They were all fools, knotted in a twisted delusion that love would purify their hormonal lust. To think Layla would shed a tear at my departure…?

No one cried over a demon's loss.

# Chapter Twenty

*Layla*

The slide was mercifully short but ended with me ramming my bleeding foot into a cement floor. I yelped in pain and was moving to inspect it, when I remembered the hundred-and-sixty-pound man coming down behind me. I leaped up and hobbled to the side just as Stone emerged like James Bond on a playground. He even adjusted his tie while rising to his feet and looking to me.

"What the hell is going on?" I asked. My swooning abilities had died when he'd kidnapped me.

"We are in lockdown," Stone answered. He flipped open a box on the side of the wall, and the dim lights turned into bright halogens. I struggled against the sudden onslaught while blinking at the end-of-the-world bunker we had slid into.

Metal tables bolted to the floors were lined with boxes labelled with nondescript codes. Shelves filled the brick walls, all holding what looked like weapons sealed off behind frosted glass. Stone ignored the guns and probably bombs. Instead, he pried open one of the plastic boxes.

"I got that bit. It's more the how the hell do we get out of here without getting our heads bitten off that's my concern," I said. Out of habit, I waved around my spell book for emphasis, though Stone's gaze kept trailing it as if I were about to do real damage.

"Depends on if you have intentions to put your teeth to my head?"

He asked it so strait-laced I almost missed a small flare of humor at the end. "Depends. Do you have something other than Spam down here?"

Chuckling, he placed two familiar bottles on the table. "This is one of the secondary operating bases in the event of what just happened. The facility is in lockdown, which means no one can get in or out."

"So we die here," I summed up. My heart sank into the ever-growing pit in my stomach. I'd nearly had my magic in my hands before that unicorn kabob had gotten what she deserved. It wasn't just the monsters roaming the halls, or the hunter chained to my arm. Even if we got to the surface, my life was over until I found my magic.

Stone extended a hand to me as if we were about to break into a dance. He even bowed slightly, his left eyebrow crooked in invitation. Huh. I hadn't noticed the scar running across it until then. Even though I was uncertain, I took his hand and he swept an arm around my waist, then plucked me off my feet.

I reared back, ready to smack his face in with my book, when I landed on the table. "First order of business is repairing your foot. We're close enough to old sewers I don't want to risk you dying of a pilgrim's disease."

Before I could object, he squirted the white lotion into his hands, then picked up my foot and massaged in the soothing liquid. A tingle zapped from my wound, a discomforting but not painful feeling. As the anesthesia worked its magic, I wanted to slump down in bliss. But I caught the diligence with how he worked his fingers between my toes, spreading the healing ointment everywhere it could.

"Don't tell me you have a foot fetish," I groaned. If it were Cal or Daniel I'd be happy to indulge them, but having my captor methodically massage my feet was… It was wrong, right?

Yes.

Why was I even questioning it?

He swallowed and his rubbing paused. "I will keep it in check," Stone declared while rising. "How does it feel?"

Gingerly, I strained my foot for the floor, grimacing in anticipation of the pain. When none came, I put my full weight on it. "You know, I could have healed it myself much faster if I had my magic."

To my surprise, his gaze fell. "That is a problem. But I think I know of a solution. Once we contain this situation, I will find a way to return it to you."

"Or, you could tell me where more blue magic juice is, and I'll find it myself." All alone in the sewers with god knew what swimming around.

Stone seemed to find the idea as impossible as I did. He stared me up and down, then drew his hands back through his hair. "Even in these extreme circumstances, the matter has not…" His face twisted in pain, and he opened his mouth as if to cry out, but no sound came.

The poison acid had struck his back. How had I forgotten? "Take off your shirt," I said, plucking up the small bottle and squirting it all over my hands. They cooled like I'd reached into a freezer.

Stone blinked in surprise. "Excuse me?"

"You're hurt. We can't... Just turn around and take off your shirt. It's shredded anyway." Why was this proving so difficult? I kept anxiously rubbing my hands together, smearing the healing liquid more and more as Stone took his time.

The jacket was in pieces, making me wonder why he had kept it on. As that fell, I stared at the wounds below the tattered linen. Red like a cement scrape, the skin had not just blistered but calcified into tiny tan stones around the edges. That had to be agonizing.

Stone reached back to remove his shirt, and a deep grunt broke from him. "Hang on," I said and reached for his collar myself. His hands fell slack and his breathing became jagged as I carefully peeled his shirt away from the wound and down his back. All my attention was on the burns, my mind pinging with fear that they were third degree or worse. I couldn't see much muscle or bone, at least.

As I'd accidentally coated his shirt in the first round, I slathered my hands in more ointment, then pressed them to his back. Stone gasped like he'd gotten his head bitten and liked it. I shifted in place, feeling hot as I traced my palm back and forth just above his skin.

"You took a lot of damage back here. I don't know if this can heal it." With each pass, the redness faded a little bit more, but it was going to take a deeper touch to work away the hardened skin. As I massaged my fingertips into the edges of the wound, the calcified skin softened to silk.

"Seems downright stupid of you to take this much damage. Aren't you supposed to be highly trained in dealing with whatever did this?"

He chuckled, his back rumbling under my hand before he hissed. My pinkie had accidentally drifted too close to the open sore. "I'm afraid I reacted first, thought second."

To save me. Though I wouldn't have needed saving if he hadn't kidnapped me in the first place.

"Thank you," I whispered while squeezing the bottle's last into my palm. "For reacting."

Stone glanced over his shoulder, the light burning against his striking eyes. "It's my job."

"To find witches, pull them off the street, then kill or collar them. And I guess somewhere in there, you play nice so your new asset isn't destroyed in shipping? So what, even after you agreed to give me back my magic, we're right back to work for us or die?"

"That was a strategic calculation. We were bogged down. I feared I would not be able to protect you and we'd lose such a 'valuable asset.' I failed to take into account you could protect yourself even without your spells. My mission, my organization's mission, has not changed even with all of this mess."

What was I thinking, expecting sympathy from the devil? Scowling, I turned my head from what was supposed to be all of him, when a different wound caught my attention. Above the one I had put in his biceps with my keys was what almost looked like a white tattoo. It bore some of the same stylized lines of my wards but the curves were softer and I didn't recognize any of the letters. Stepping back, I found more, the white tattoo trailing across the back of his shoulders then circling around the other arm. It also trailed forward around his ribs.

Curiosity took hold and I reached to trace the line, when my finger dipped inward to skin torn then healed. That wasn't a tattoo, it was...

Stone ducked away from my touch, then he spun around. The entirety of his chest was cut apart by runic scars from his collarbones to his navel. He narrowed his eyes at my gaping shock, then closed them tight and breathed. "I'm afraid no amount of ointment will erase those."

While I struggled to piece together what I saw, he picked up his shirt and tried to put it on, only for the fabric to rip clean through. "I cannot catch a break today," he sighed, tossing the tatters away.

"Is that what hunters do to themselves?" I finally got out. "Oh fuck, is that what you're going to do to me?" They weren't just scars—they looked like a spell burned into the flesh like a cattle brand. I was not letting anyone come near me with a runic poker!

Stone didn't react to me struggling to get away. My hip smashed into the box in the process. "Don't worry. Animal Control is not so craven as to burn their employees."

"Then...how, what happened?"

His face collapsed into the brooding stare of a man with a tortured past. After dealing with Cal's cult history, Daniel coming to terms with his death and Ink's entire deal, I knew I wasn't going to get an answer. Not without having to pry it out of him.

He glanced a hand over the curve swooping down his left collar like a wave. "I woke in a forest clearing with these marks all over my body."

I wasn't expecting that.

Slowly, he traced the curved wave dipping down to his sternum where it formed a sharp V, then back to the other side. "I was only thirteen, my flesh flaming red from whatever they did to me, and the…I don't know what they were, chanting gibberish."

"Were they witches?" I asked, even while praying they weren't. Some preconceptions could be forgiven, but not that.

"No. Thin faces, with ears like bats and bathed in darkness and light. I've never seen their like again."

*Oh, thank god.*

Why did I care if he hated my kind or not?

"I don't remember much, only that were it not for Director Zimmerman finding me and 'detaining' them all, I would have been their sacrifice that moon." He finished by staring me straight in the eye, a plea in his gaze that I understood.

That was when he had signed up with the people who had hunted my grandmothers and burned them at stakes. Because something else had nearly killed him.

Stone shook his head, the cop slamming back into place to hide the vulnerable moment. "We should get moving before the creatures have time to form a plan of their own." He hustled around the place, gathering supplies and placing them on the table.

I watched his diligence with my head low, the silence growing deafening until I had to say, "I'm sorry."

Stone paused in his collecting to turn his chin over this shoulder, drawing me to look not only down the old scars but also at the one I'd added to his body.

"For making you tell me."

He chuckled. "It's hardly a secret. I quite love swimming and dooming myself to wearing a shirt in the pool for the rest of my life sounds dreadful."

It wasn't some deep confession he'd shared with me, just a thing to notice. Nothing more. So why'd he stare at his ripped shirt with a mournful sigh?

"Put these in your purse." He passed me two of the healing bottles in travel size as well as a six-pack of Gatorade.

"What's this for?" I struggled to cram the neon-blue drinks in my purse next to my book. It caused my keys to jangle and I slipped them in my pocket.

Stone turned from the wall where he was inputting a code. "You should drink one now. The electrolytes will help soothe the hole we…I put in you."

I twisted off the screw tap and stared at my Smurf reflection. The void inside pulsed back and I took a careful sip. "Ugh!" Warm Gatorade tasted like someone had dissolved a vitamin in melted popsicles. "I hate this stuff," I declared even while drinking more. With each swig, the doom in my gut shrunk a tiny bit more. Curious, I started to read the label to see if it made any mention of revitalizing missing magic.

"No!" Stone shouted, causing me to drop the empty bottle to the floor. He ran past, shoving his palm flat to every panel. The frosted window opened to reveal broken metal. "This can't be right. Every one, every weapon is destroyed."

"How?" I asked, spinning around to watch him. "Forget to maintain them?"

"These are all Hephaestus-blessed. Not the actual god, it's a…never mind. They should be serviceable for over a thousand years. But every one is sliced in half. Even the holy water." He picked up the same water gun

I'd seen Drake using, though this one's tubing was cut so the water had pooled in the cubby.

"Holy water? Like the stuff in churches?"

He scoffed. "This comes from a hidden spring in Iceland that's the only connection in this realm to the divine." Stone shook his head and tossed the pieces away. "I don't understand, unless… This wasn't a failure of our systems."

"Look, I don't much care about whatever politics your little kidnapping organization is playing. I'd just like to get out of here so I don't die from either murder gnomes or whatever happens when this void inside of me pops. Okay?"

Clacking his teeth in thought, Stone dug through every drawer until he emerged with a small derringer. He popped open the chamber and looked. "Daylight bullets, great. If we run into a gargoyle or wraith we're set, otherwise…"

I gripped onto his arm, wanting to get his attention. Instead, I got to feel his biceps in full and it was like holding onto a steel cantaloupe. *Focus, Layla. Death. Destruction. Donuts later.* "How do we get out of here?"

"My original intention had been to fully arm myself, then storm the castle, as it were. Now…" Stone wrung a hand under his chin and the scars on his chest shifted to a soft green. It had to be the weird emergency lights catching on them. Or my brain was melting from the lack of magic.

"There is a way out, but we will have to be careful. Quiet." He smiled at me. "At least you are well armed with book and key in hand."

God, it was so stupid, but I laughed at the idea of taking down a stable of very angry creatures from other realms with my heavy book. Or I could stab them in the eye with my keys. Yes. This was a brilliant plan.

"We should leave quickly, in the event whoever sabotaged this place returns." Stone slipped the tiny gun into his holster, then he filled another bag with supplies and hung that off his back. With a nod, he turned to me and slipped a hand around the back of my waist.

"Do you have to do that?" I asked.

"There are traps ahead I don't want you to trigger accidentally," he explained. I gulped at the idea, flexing my bare toes against the ground, when he turned and smiled at me. "And no, I don't."

# Chapter Twenty-One

*Ink*

"Will you cease that infernal practice?"

The soul spit finally paused in his incessant pacing, not that he could travel far due to his earthly tether clenched in my fist. I wished snapping the bone in half would rid me of him. All that would do was give the ghost two more places to haunt. With a great heave, I inched my back up the wall. Pain wrenched down the left side of my body, strangling my lungs within my chest. A single, solitary groan escaped, and I leaned my head against the cool brick. In the distance, all I could hear was a single, unbroken drip.

"Why did he leave me with you?" Daniel worried. I wondered if he had been such a fretting ferret when alive. It seemed more an inevitable time to chew upon one's nails, what with death being ever present. Yet he'd walked into a drug dealer's bullet. Perhaps it was being a spirit that had drained his bravery to only chastising and pleading.

"The wolf gave his reasons," I said, refusing to dwell upon his foolish beliefs.

Daniel snorted. "Which are bullshit…as you know." The ghost's ever-trailing eyes sharpened to near life as he stared down at me.

"After only two weeks of whispering in her ear, you have claim to Layla's mind and heart? Not at all a red flag for her."

"How she feels about you, whatever she thinks of you…it doesn't really matter in the end."

"I would argue she'd rate her feelings differently, but do go on. This is quite distracting from the venom seeping through my veins." I piled my hands in my lap, taking care to carelessly leave his bone dangling to the side.

Daniel glared, well aware that—if I dropped it—he'd be trapped in this archaic sewage system until he went mad and poofed out of existence. After tousling his hair back and forth in a manner more becoming of a common vagabond, he sneered at me. "Why are you here?"

"Oh dear, has the madness set in? Do you think yourself a Victorian lady who was murdered on her wedding night? All ghosts seem to fall back to that for some reason."

He snorted once, making me wonder if he'd been having visions of veils and poisoned hat pins. "I know about you. About that bond thing you claim to have."

"There is nothing to claim beyond the truth." I tried to raise my hand as if it weren't struck dumb from the poison. "What can you possibly understand of a matter beyond your ken?"

"You forget, I can read her spell book. I know more about magic than you ever will, demon."

Ah yes, his 'skill' to this coven of sorts. Calvin was the claws, Daniel the bookish librarian and I the witty repartee with a tongue of gold. It left him leaning over her shoulder often, and even perusing her spell book when she was asleep in the wolf's arms. A fact he'd never felt the need to tell her. It left us on a strange seesaw footing.

"And…? If you have discovered a vital spell or ward that would protect our companion, why have you not shared it with her?" I prompted, growing hotter under my collar. Or perhaps it was the poison sweats drenching my back. How did humans not explode ten minutes out of the womb?

Daniel had enough sense to look chagrined, whether he felt it was debatable. The only reason I suffered him was due to his connection with this Mr. White. Butting into the affairs of such a man once was coincidence, twice was folly, but so many times and even I could not shake off a lingering concern. Whatever Daniel knew in life that had ordered his execution, he wasn't giving up to us in death. Which meant he took my accepting his needling as weakness instead of strength.

"Whatever you've found in your hour or two of reading the ancient recipes of witches has little bearing on me or my decisions."

"Really?" he scoffed.

"I am not a demon, nor am I entirely of this realm. It's…how do they say? Complicated. Witches conduct magic to their whims. I have little to do with it in any form."

My hopes that he'd be silenced were cut short as he turned his full fervor on me and asked, "Then how did you cast the spell to bind yourself to her?"

A single drop of water struck the pool, the sound echoing down the long hallway as we—incubus and ghost—stared eye to eye.

"What? No smart-ass excuse? No half-lie dressed up like the truth? Not even surprised I figured it out?"

Wait. There was more within the drop. Each striking plop cast a note, a high G, sailing through the air. I closed my eyes, listening for the fall of the drop and the slow, nearly hidden song within the water itself.

"Ink?"

My lids opened over sandpaper eyes and I struggled to focus on the ghost. His body grew hazy, as if a gust of clouds had dropped from the heavens to hide him away. I reached out to bat them away, but it only sent Daniel scampering back.

"What are you doing?"

The heaviness that'd kept me pinned to the ground flew from my fingertips. With a great push, I rose to my legs. Calvin's belt pinched tighter, the slack end slapping against my back as I gazed down the corridor where he'd vanished, then to the right. I turned to speak to the ghost, only to discover I'd been humming under my breath the entire time.

How strange.

"Someone is calling," I said, raising my heavy arm in the direction of the song.

"I don't hear anything." Daniel shook his head like a wasp-stung bull.

With a great jolt, I pushed my foot forward. My body did not collapse, so I tried another and another. The pain that had sundered me to pieces abated until I felt nothing, my feet little more than bones and meat to move me ever on.

"Demon?" the ghost kept screeching from behind. My head was too weary to turn back to him, so I kept forward.

The song. It grew around me, the rhythm syncopating up my veins and pausing the venom from pulsing inside. I took in a breath that filled the aching mortal lungs and felt a shackle fall from me. A voice sprouted within the water, growing ever stronger as it beckoned me.

"You dropped my bone. Demon. Demon!"

The raven cawing from the grave faded to nothing as I stumbled for the balm beckoning me onward.

* * * *

*Layla*

I was being led around by a shirtless man covered in creepy scars. Exactly the kind of thing mothers warned their daughters away from, or mine would have if she hadn't... *So not the time to be thinking that.* I kept one hand inside my purse, caressing the spine of my spell book in the hope I'd finally feel it respond. In my other, I carried my last weapon, my house keys, threaded through my fingers. At least Stone walked ahead, taking point and scouting out every turn as we walked down culverts half-filled with stinking water.

And I was not asking what I was walking barefoot into.

Stone flattened to the curved wall as best he could while he darted his gaze down a right turn. I stood behind, trying to not stick out too far when a shadow passed. His hand flew out to smack my chest and he pushed me back until my spine hit brick. Stone crumpled next to me, his eyes closed while I risked staring.

As whatever it was passed, circles of blue light followed and tiny silver fish leaped from the pools.

"I think…"

Those annoyingly attractive green eyes cut me off as Stone glared a warning to keep quiet. I locked my jaws but could see whatever it was had passed. After a time, he leaned further out while pressing his hand to me. "I believe it's moved out of range," Stone said.

"A-hem." I coughed almost silently.

He darted his gaze back to me a moment, then did a full double-take to find he'd smashed his arm right into my boobs. Stone's eyes went wide, nearly glowing even in the dim sewers and he clenched his open hand at air.

"You gonna…?"

"Sorry." He pulled away, flailing his errant arm like it had fallen asleep. "It should be clear ahead. Come on, before the wisps return." Without a thought, he reached behind as if to take my hand, but it was full of keys. Before he could grope me again, I cupped his shoulder.

"How about I keep ahold of you instead?" I asked, trying to keep this kidnapping from getting too embarrassing. I'd failed to take into account how hard his scarred shoulder would be. Even Cal didn't have that much muscle.

Like a determined kindergarten teacher who had accidentally led their class into a tiger pit, Stone guided us down the pipes. "We should be coming up on a switching station. There we can regroup and pray it hasn't been taken over…or damaged."

I nodded, hoping the movement would transfer to my arm. We passed out of the halos of the working caged lights into near darkness. What had been nothing more than slimy water felt like the testing fingers of tentacle monsters with every step. I clung tighter to both Stone and my keys, ready to attack at a moment's notice.

"I'm sorry for…it was an accident. I'm used to working with River in such matters and he isn't quite so, um, blessed in the chest range. This is making it worse."

I laughed at the scary man in black bumbling through an apology. It would be cute if he weren't trying to enslave and or murder me. "River," I said, remembering his silent partner. "Stone. Eve, and there was an Adam. Guessing none of those are your real names."

"Names have power," he said, like reciting from an employee handbook.

"So what, that's it? You sign on the dotted line and you're Stone forever?"

"I know better than to give a witch my real name."

I groaned at him putting up the defenses for nothing. "But you have to have something other than just Stone. Or do your friends all call you Detective? Happy Birthday, Detective!"

"Why do you care? Hoping to improve our working relationship?"

I scoffed hard at the very idea. I didn't care in the slightest. I was just trying to get him talking. Could arms feel smug? If so, Stone's was rock hard with smugness. A soft green light rose ahead. At first, I tried to peer past his shoulder, but the Nameless Stone blocked me off.

"Keep your gaze to the ground. I fear the gorgon is out."

I dropped my head as he kept inching deeper into danger, but I couldn't stop myself from saying, "Don't they only turn men into you? I should be fine."

"Your concern for my safety is touching," he said in a sly remark as we emerged into a wider berth for the various pipes. At least three stone tunnels trailed off to the left and another four to the right, but it was the glowing green orb that drew my eyes…which I then pivoted to the ceiling. The shadows undulated as if the light were being blocked by a pile of writhing snakes.

That damn hand clamped to my arm again, pulling me to the side like a doll on a rope. My foot plunged into the freezing cold water and I yelped, which was when the monster caught us. Its voice rose through the brick under my feet, echoing in ripples off the walls. I tried to crush my ear to my shoulder even while staying armed, but it didn't stop the pounding.

"My lady, I…" Stone began, trying to shout over the not-sound pulverizing us. "Wait a minute…Kevin!"

"The gorgon's name is Kevin?"

I risked facing a lifetime holding a bird bath by looking up to find a wriggling pile of tentacles batting a child's ball back and forth. With each slap of the suckers, it lit green, providing the unnerving atmosphere.

"He's sort of our pet. Mascot. I don't know." Stone stomped for the tentacles that were the width of a human leg and strained through the grates from a darkness beyond. He snatched the ball from them and the tentacles all flailed wildly at that.

One reached out to slap Stone across the face, but he caught it and held on. "Kevin! What are you doing out of your cage?"

"Shit!" The pulses struck like cranking up the bass on whale sounds. My stomach lurched as I rocked back and forth from the sound waves.

"Mm-hm, I see. Well, I'm going to need you to return to your room."

The pounding slowed to a more gentle ripple and I was able to stand when the tentacles swiped for the ball.

"I'll be keeping this until you can prove you're a good kraken."

They all slammed against the wall, breaking the bricks with each slap. I lurched on my unsteady footing, struggling to keep upright as the kraken kept up its tantrum.

"Just give it the damn ball!"

"How else will it learn if I give in to its fits?" Stone asked.

*Shit!* Two tentacles somehow popped out from behind me. They too slammed against the wall, this time taking out an exposed pipe. Water gushed from above. I locked my mouth shut and tried to not think about where it came from. Running, I snatched the ball out of Stone's hands and hurled it at the tentacles. For a brief second, I feared the monster's wailing would only knock the ball back, but it stuck to the suckers.

Like flipping off a switch, the tantrum ended. The creature cooed as it tossed the ball back and forth between its tentacles and all of them—including the new ones—slunk away.

"Why did you do that?" Stone turned on me like I had just given a toddler a cake before naptime.

"Because that's an ancient sea creature that doesn't deserve to be treated like your errant puppy! And who the shit names a kraken Kevin?"

He crossed his arms and gave that whole disappointed-professor vibe. Though, the fact he was shirtless and covered in runic scars ruined the effect. "We took a vote. What concern can you have of Kevin's treatment? Do you not rampantly slaughter any monsters that cross your path?"

"No, I fucking don't!" I shouted, stomping my foot into the ankle-high water. "I only kill when they're trying to kill me. Even then I try to ask nicely if they'll stop."

"Oh yes? What of the kelpie then? Seems he didn't have much choice."

"He was going to eat my liver!"

"And the werewolf alpha? What intentions did he have upon your organs?"

Given half a chance Lucien probably would have put my heart on a pike, but only after he'd finished with his sons. "You think I killed him?"

Stone tipped his head. "He is dead and a witch was on scene. How else should I read it? Or are you saying someone else killed him?"

"I did…" If I didn't get out of here, or fix the hole inside, they might come for Cal. I couldn't tell them the truth, and I didn't want to. "Fine. But he was going to hurt someone…special to me."

I tried to be careful, but Stone tossed the soggy hair off his cheek and he said, "Yes, the werewolf cub. Strange for him to be so beholden to a witch, but I suppose that makes sense."

I couldn't escape the damn snicker at him. "And you think you're so much better, on your high horse, throwing people into unmarked vans like some…oh shit, you are a secret police force. I'm so dead…" All of this infuriating fighting was for nothing. Even if I lost him, even if I got out of here, what then? They had me, they knew my name, where I lived. And something told me they'd never stop.

"I fear we both are," Stone said.

I risked peering over my shoulder to find he'd walked to the pipe gushing water from the kraken tantrum. As I did, I noticed the water level had risen to my thigh. "What the hell?" I sloshed through the chilly water to him. "How is this building up? There's grates everywhere."

"They're all closed off in the event of a lockdown. Nothing in or out."

"So we killed ourselves. No, you killed us because you pissed off a giant calamari."

Stone hustled to the left, wading as fast as he could through the thigh-high water. I wasn't doing much better. It pooled to my stomach, freezing me from the waist down. Ink would hate that. Or he might take it as a challenge.

My heart skipped at the thought of him, all of them, out there. I wanted to hold his stupidly handsome face and kiss him until he was out of breath. Then pull Cal to me until our foreheads bonked so I could run his browbone over mine like a massager. Hopefully they were all far away from this madness.

"Leeland!" The reminder of my timely demise shouted for my attention. He'd hunched over so he was submerged up to his shoulder, but he strained one arm out for me.

I lurched closer, my stomach growing colder than the rest of my underwater body. The hole was getting bigger. Stone plunged his face into the water. I reached over to try to save him, when he whipped his head out. His wet hair slapped against my cheek and he paused with his lips nearly on mine.

For a beat, we stared, with the water rising to our dooms. I couldn't move and he was underwater. All I could do was take in the unfairly elegant swoop of his jaw and his lush eyelashes.

A deep pain from beyond this realm pulsed from my stomach. I lurched back and shouted, "What do you want?"

"On the other side of this room, there's a valve like this. You have to turn it."

"Why don't you?" All of this—the kraken, the unicorn, the kidnapping—was his fault and I was tired of dancing to his whims.

"Because this damn thing keeps closing on its own. I can't let go or else…"

*You're being an idiot. Play along, then…* I'd figure it out once I had my magic. Same as always. Sure would be nice to have a plan just once.

"Fine!" I said, half paddling away to the right.

*Next guy needs to be the planning type. Not Cal's rugged lone wolf, not Daniel's deep research dive, not Ink's…chaotic spontaneity.*

*And the fact that Stone man seems to have an idea for every turn you take?*

*Shut up, brain.*

I made my way to the other side, the water to my shoulders. It wouldn't be long now. "I'm here!" I shouted, then stared down into the murky depths to find two valves. "There's a red and a yellow one here. Which do I turn?"

"The yellow!" Stone shouted so fast, I stared back at him. He spat out the water already washing against him. "If you turn the red, it'll drown the entire facility."

I touched the yellow, but stared at the red. *Turn it, finish not just Stone but all the hunters and the monsters running amok.* What alternative was there? I wasn't getting out of this alive no matter how hard I fought. Even if I did, this hole would eat me alive, or a gorgon named George would. If I drowned the hunters, other witches would be safe.

I shifted and gripped the red valve, when a shadow passed over my head. No. It had to be my imagination. Why would a gray wolf…? "Cal?" I barely called for him, my voice a whisper of uncertainty. But when the shadow of gray fur passed again, I shouted his name.

"Cal!"

The rushing wolf paused and it turned a single blue eye down at me. *Oh god!*

"The valve, Leeland!" Stone shouted from the far end. Could he see the werewolf above us? Seemed he had bigger problems. I released the red one and gripped the yellow.

"Damn thing's stuck!" I called back, gritting my teeth and giving it my all. It turned ten degrees, then froze. I cursed incoherently under my breath, my fingers falling numb from the cold water I'd plunged them into.

"Layla?"

Cal's soft cry invigorated me and I cranked with all my might. "Come on, come on!" The valve shuddered and it slipped fully around. Yes! I spun it the rest of the way, only for the dial to come spinning off. That couldn't be good.

As I stood up, showing the broken dial to Stone, a second pipe burst from the other side of the room. "Damn it!" He dove under, then resurfaced. "I'm going to try one more thing."

I nodded as if all my focus weren't drawn to the naked man standing on the iron bars above my head. Wading through the freezing water up to my neck, I fought off the chattering in my teeth to call to him. "Cal, what are you doing here?"

*You have to get out.*

"Finding you. So…" He reached down through the bars, his fingers slipping past. I tried to jump up to them, but I couldn't get more than an inch out of the water.

"Trying something else," Stone reported before he once again dove back under. At the rate the room was filling, it wouldn't be long.

"Who's in there with you?" Cal asked, but I shook it away, my eyes stinging.

"Doesn't matter. I'm sorry. For…for reading your memory, for stealing it. I didn't mean to. I don't care about the red wolf or any of that mess. It doesn't matter."

He went quiet a moment before calling out, "We can talk about that later. For now, use your magic to burn these and I'll pull you out." Cal strained as far as he could, his voice full of hope.

And there I went, crushing it like a butterfly. "I can't," I gasped just as the water rushed into my mouth. I tipped my head back and spat out the metallic taste.

"Daniel's…I can go get him. He can read you the spell—"

"They took my magic!" I screamed, each word forming the noose around my neck. Cal's face dipped from confusion to worry then back.

"What do you mean…?"

"I don't know how, but I can't…I can't do anything. I can't even read my spell book. Cal, listen to me." My body finally became buoyant, the water pushing me higher toward the ceiling. To him. I reached out, the tips of my fingers brushing over his, but with each gallon of water they grew closer.

"You've got to get out of here," I said. "This place…it's about to blow with god knows what."

He yanked his hand back and my heart plummeted with it—my last lifeline ripped away. But Cal bent over the bars and pulled with all his strength. The veins on his neck and arms bulged in agony, but the grate didn't budge.

With a great scream, Cal slammed his fist into the iron, doing nothing but hurting his hand. Only the sound of rushing water and Stone's flailing filled the air as I stared at his bent-over body. Slowly, he shook his blond hair back and forth and he swiped at his nose.

"Stay calm," he said, his voice steady though I could see the red in his crystal-blue eyes. "Ink is…I can go get him. Assuming he'll be any help." Cal shifted a moment as if he was going to make good on chasing after the incubus. But before he could turn his head, he rushed back and bellyflopped onto the brick above.

Straining with his fingers, he managed to wiggle his hand through and I caught it. The warmth overwhelmed me, causing a single whimper to slip past. I wasn't going to get to hold it again, or feel his gentle touch.

"I can still find him. He can save you," Cal pleaded with me to let him go. I pulled his hand to my cheek and nuzzled against it. There wasn't any time. He knew that as well as I.

"Cal…"

"Don't do this. Please. I need you to get out of this. We need to fight about how I can't stop running away from shit. I need you to be mad, then understanding, as you always are. Layla!"

The water almost had me pushed to the ceiling. I tugged on his hand, pulling myself closer until our faces nearly touched save the bars in between. Cal's lips twitched and tears ran down his cheeks.

"I need you," he gasped.

With the last of my strength, I launched out of the water. Past the grate, I was able to get a grip on his hair and pull him to me. "I love you," I whispered, kissing him with the cold iron of my cage between our lips.

The water shifted, and I slipped from his touch. Cal reached for me, but he missed. What was happening? While holding his hand, I glanced back to find a sluice gate slowly rising from below. Water gushed out of it, draining the rising levels. A miracle!

*No, wait…!*

"Cal!" The current ripped at me, pulling me down with the pressure. I tried to leap up, to catch the grate, but my fingers slipped right on past. It sent me whipping back, with only Cal's tight grip to keep me from flushing away.

The water tore at me, bashing my purse into my spine and legs, but I held on. I had to…

From deep in the void, a pulse of loss erupted through my body and my fingers went slack. In a heartbeat, they slipped from Cal's. "Layla!" he shouted as I plunged under into a labyrinthian horror.

# Chapter Twenty-Two

*Ink*

A pleasant spring wind ripened with pomegranate blossoms blew petals across my path. They tumbled from an open doorway made not of industrial iron and brick but white marble. Light from a hundred braziers danced in the threshold as the gentle plucking of a lute strummed through the air.

The hundreds upon hundreds of years, the miles I'd etched into my feet, the taste of millions of lips fell away, and I emerged into a Grecian bathhouse as fresh as the day I was formed. Springwater more potent than the rivers of Lethe dribbled from the mouths of Eros, Aphrodite and the Fates. It pooled in a sunken bath filled with people lounging and caring naught for their state of nakedness.

I breathed in the unbidden desires of men fresh from their toils in the nail-breaking mines of the amphitheater and library. Some cast their eyes to the buxom ladies pouring fresh water from vases, but even more turned in curiosity to the demon slipping into their midst. I raised my head high, my shoulders steadied for a hunt I'd been hungering for.

"My dear Eros." Fingers caressed the back of my neck, drawing me to turn to the only blonde woman in the Greek bath. "You must walk before you can run." Lust perched on a chair with more regality than would any queen on her throne. She tented her delicate fingertips and my legs wobbled as if to pull me into a bow. Before I tumbled, I lashed a hand out and held onto a statue that felt strangely cold for the summer day.

"Lust?" I sputtered, my cheeks burning at her level gaze. "I thought, was it not you who put me to this task?"

She leaned closer and dabbed a cloth across my brow. "Oh, poor Eros. Your body is growing weak with hunger." With a single fingertip to my forehead, she pushed me to my knees. As they struck, pain jarred up my spine and a flash of dark gray and unforgiving metal ripped apart the golden marble baths. What…?

I looked again. Whatever delusion that was vanished. All the people in the baths raised their cups of wine to me. I nodded in gratitude. Their desires for my cock and ass flitted through my mind like one of Orpheus' tunes. It would take nothing to catch one by the arm, take him or her behind the curtains and eat my fill.

I reached for one of the waving hands, but paused before touching it. My gaze skipped past the brunette to an inlaid mosaic below the naked asses and scrotums. It was a classic of Medusa, her mouth wrenched apart in her death throes, snakes of hair writhing. Yet the eyes felt more realistic than anything

I'd seen in Alexandria. A soft yet tenacious brown, they pleaded up at me to do…what, I could not guess.

Nor did I care to. This was a feast and I the guest of honor. Anything unpleasant was best to be ignored. My attentions homed in on the incubus who'd found me limping from that mousy man's chambers. I could have succumbed to rot and confusion were it not for her intervention and her training.

She smiled brightly at my cocksure grin. "You seem to be in finer sorts, Eros."

"Why wouldn't I be when the wine flows freely and inhibitions even freer?" I tried to put a foot under me to rise when Lust clasped my shoulder.

"Remain at my feet, where you belong."

"Humorous as always, Lust. But I don't think a predator should stay…" I moved to stand again, but she pressed harder.

"No!" Her voice boomed like Lord Zeus thundering apart the skies. Darkness erupted from her face and all light leeched from the cracks.

In a heartbeat, it vanished. Lust drew her finger down my cheek and bent over, almost placing her lips to mine. "The baths await you," she said in her belladonna voice. "Go on and join them." Lust smiled at the others who raised their cups just as before.

Exactly as before. Not a one was caught mid-drink or too enthralled with the curvy thighs or buoyant breasts of another. A pain crawled up my throat that I'd never known. Was this that late stage of hunger she'd warned me about? Or was more at play?

Lust tried to push me to the pool, but I tossed her grip aside. "I think I'd prefer to remain dry, if it's all the same," I said.

Something was rotten in that pool. I could smell it now, the heady scent of blossoms barely able to cover a rot festering up from below. Tendrils seethed in the water, green and vibrant as dawn's rays. They rose up to ensnare the people who were unaware of what was coming.

"Don't be this way, Eros. You're supposed to be charming." Lust crossed her arms and pouted.

"I believe I can be whatever I wish. Is that not the point of my very existence?"

Free of her strength, I was able to stand but only with the help of the statue of Circe beside me. Who would put that in a bath? This version had hair of great volume and curl with a round face of engrossing features. She carried a book in one hand and a marker in the other.

*What is a marker?*

With a grand huff, Lust tossed her golden braid off her shoulder. "You are to be what I tell you to be, Eros. Lest there be no point to you at all." She gestured to my groin to drive home it was a threat. They came often from her. She did not want a partner to hunt with, nor a fellow sin of desire to trade barbs and stories with. I was her protégé, her toy on invisible strings only sent out into the world at her whims. I'd grown weary of her puppetry and abandoned her centuries prior.

"This does not exist." The world presented before me cracked, the marble dirtied then buried under decades of decay. All the jugs shattered, the wine splattering to the floor, then staining to blood dashed across the ancient mosaics. It never took humans long to ruin an empire. Maybe they got a good four hundred years in, maybe it was simply one generation, but everything fell in time. Everything except for the sins of their making.

"Ah!" My chest constricted and I fell. I tried to catch myself, but my hand went numb and it nudged the vase off its pedestal. As it shattered, the pieces reverberated across the floor and rose up as if floating in air. There was more below even this illusion.

"What are you?" I asked. "A witch like her?" I nodded to Circe, who'd shifted. With one hand, she clung to a heart around her neck, her lips parted as if about to speak.

"Don't be foolish, Eros. I am as I have always been." She collapsed to her knees, the peplos of old replaced with a wool and velvet dress. As she drew her hand across my brow, a chill trailed her touch. "I am your Lust."

A low laugh rumbled in my aching chest, one that only further enflamed the angry organ at the center. "I do not know what you are, siren, sorceress, elven queen. But I do know you are not her. If there is one thing Lust cannot do, it's share."

Anger bubbled in her eyes. She wrapped her fingers tight around the back of my skull and pulled me closer. I realized her intentions at the last second and turned away, causing her kiss to fall unwanted. I belonged to another.

*I do?*

Pain boiled my brains as I chased that thought's origins. I belonged to no one—none would be foolish enough to chain themselves to an incubus either in marriage or love.

"Ink…"

A sound whispered on the wind. No, a word. I looked past the raging illusion to the puckered lips of the Circe statue. They did not move but it called for ink. What use would a statue have for papyrus or inks?

Yet there was a familiarity. When it struck my ears, the tight lock around my heart lessened and I felt lighter. My Circe was freeing me.

No, not Circe. Another name, sweeter and fiercer. From a different land, another time.

*Layla.*

"Where is Layla?" I snapped my gaze to the creature, its face shrouded in shadow. Dead vines choked the baths, clogging all the windows save a shaft of light that fell on me.

At the name, the creature shuddered. "Why isn't this working?"

"Delightful attempt at an illusion, whatever you are. But I'm not in the mood to play your games. Tell me where Layla is and I will let you live."

With a great heave, I stood up to my full height. The one I had thought to be Lust shrank. The figure grew wider around the bottom as the rest slumped into a petite sack. "Don't come any closer. I'm warning you."

"Yes, yes. First the warnings, then the pathetic attempts at trickery. Why not go for a dove up your sleeve or a dinar behind the ear? It'd go just as well for you." With a steady step, I advanced on the woman. Her once melodious voice crackled with consternation, fear and age. It was an old creature I dealt with, though doubtful it was an elf.

Without pause, it hopped up a stair and the world washed away beside me. From the edge of my vision, I could finally see through the layers of lies. It was not a gleaming fresh bathhouse at the height of Macedonian Greece. Nor a dilapidated one after the fall of Rome where brigands and vermin nested. No, I stood in the sewers under land forgotten by half the world because I was trying to find my bond.

"Where is Layla?" I shouted, and the mosaic shattered in half. One side was the gorgon, terrifying and terrible. But on the other, the coiled snakes became ebony with hints of honey blond hair, the green complexion a softer tan, and the lips mouthed my name—Ink.

Ugh! The last of my control spiraled out of my legs and I plummeted to the ground. Lucky for me, I struck the limp body of a human pitched over in sleep, but smiling and softly giggling. I moved to slide my hand out to look up at the creature fleeing. As I did, fire wrenched through my muscles, burning a path up the entirety of my arm and striking my brain. There was no power on earth that could keep me from releasing a scream of pain.

The fleeing monster paused. "You're dying." The older voice sounded interested and slightly entertained.

"Truly? I suppose that would explain the throbbing in my veins. Thank you for your diagnosis." With the tips of my toes and fingers, I tried to crawl along what had been the pool's floor. The humans in my illusion were real, though instead of resting in a bath, they were all slumped over in various states of joy or terror. That creature had been busy and no doubt intended to get to consuming delicious gray matter.

"You could see through my illusion, yet you're dying of a venom bite?"

"Basilisks are rather capricious serpents." Endless agony I might be in, but I had no fear of death. My name would never appear on any of the Reaper's lists. Though the deadening of my limbs that slowed progress to a crawl was beginning to grate.

The woman, that I could be certain of, hopped up a series of stairs until she stood outlined in what I'd taken to be a doorway to the atrium. No doubt some other cruel arena for creatures awaited beyond. Her silhouette shifted, the illusion fighting to take hold at a distance, but if I closed one eye I could see the squatter woman of quite some age.

"You'll be dead in under an hour," she pronounced, and still I kept crawling. All that earned me was a derisive snort and she turned to leave. Before vanishing out the door, she cocked her giving hip to say, "Don't worry about Layla. I've got her."

*Damn you, cretin!* The brain eater sauntered away, about to attack my bond. Never. No harm would befall her as long as I drew…painfully sharp breath. I tried to crawl another step, but my elbows turned to slush and my chin struck the ground. I stared at the doorway where the woman had been, my heart bounding about in my chest as though it was fighting a duel to the death.

I had to get to Layla. If she died, I'd…be taken to hell. That was why I fought through every jab and strike to save her. Gritting my teeth, I willed my hand up to my throat and knocked my fingers against the clasp. I was no good to my bond prostrate on the ground. With a numb forefinger, I reached to undo the clasp, when I looked up to find a damn demon ward above where the woman had vanished.

Its haunting red glow taunted me, daring me to break the seal so I'd rid myself of the pain of mortality only to be trapped in this hunter's den. Darkness encroached upon my vision. If I did not decide soon… *Why is it becoming so difficult to think?*

An obnoxious ring, like that of a drunken town crier, echoed in my ears. I tried to shake it away. Layla needed me to protect her. It was my job.

It was what I had promised her.

Somehow, my hand hit the floor without my wrist giving out. Maybe the venom was subsiding. A bit of luck for the first time today. I reached for another and every joint in my body exploded. My chin slammed against a broken stone, my teeth scissoring into my tongue. Warm blood drenched the back of my throat, overflowing the narrowing windpipe as I struggled to breathe.

"Lay..."

I could not die. I was an incubus, desire made flesh. Nothing could kill me, not even...

Even as the world darkened, all my senses fading to blackness, I felt a touch on my cheek, as soft as a pomegranate blossom. Her whisper, hot breath against my ear, was the last voice I'd ever hear. "Ink..."

# Chapter Twenty-Three

*Layla*

All I knew was cold battering my body, like a feather sucked down the drain. The darkness thickened, dragging away the last source of light. A familiar ache burned in my lungs, but after the kelpie, I had better sense than to override the panic. A lungful of water wouldn't help anyone. The darkness shuddered before me, a door raising like the one that began this. Submerged, I watched my watery tomb tumble like a waterfall ahead of me.

Oh shit! I tried to paddle against the rapids, but there was no chance. Gravity took hold and I plunged over.

Pain sliced up my leg and I cried out, casting the last of my air into bubbles. Wait. Bubbles went up. Ignoring the ache in my calf, I paddled after my breath, kicking with no skill. In the darkness, I couldn't see the line between air and water, only felt the sharp parting as I burst free and gasped in oxygen.

Small, recessed candles flickered in alcoves lining the walls. They barely lit the room, but at least I could see I was in a chamber with brick platforms crisscrossing the whole area. I paddled for the closest one, needing to get out of this damn water. As I swung my arm, I realized in all of that, I'd managed to keep my purse at my side.

"No doubt your doing," I whispered to my book.

A wispy chattering answered me. Did that mean my magic was returning? I whispered the healing spell even while swimming, hoping it'd at least mop up the blood I was spilling in my wake. Nothing happened.

*So much for that.*

I reached the platform and heaved my purse onto it first. My bleeding leg kept waving back and forth in the water, no doubt infecting the wound with every exotic disease possible. "If I have to amputate it, maybe I could be a pirate witch. Arr, hands up, matey, before I curse ye for a thousand years. Oh god, I've lost it."

Placing both my hands onto the brick, I willed the last of my strength into my arms and tried to rise out of the water. Then, from the corner of my eye, I caught a small green glow. It pierced through the brackish water like a laser and I turned to stare.

Stone lay at the bottom, his back pressed against the wall as if he had hit it.

Pure madness drove me under. I kicked fast, trying to get him. What was I going to do if he was already dead? Die in some watery grave, either from starvation or whatever happened to magic-less witches? As I drew closer, the strange light faded until I couldn't understand its source. None of that mattered. I reached a tentative hand out to his cheek, terrified I was about to touch a dead body. Warmth ran up my fingers. There was still time!

I dropped my feet to the ground and locked my arms around his chest. With a great heave, I pulled him off the bottom and up into a float. His arms hung loose like a knock-off Jesus, but he was moving. *I'll get you to safety, you goddamn idiot. Just don't die.*

Putting all I had into it, I kicked wildly while guiding both of us to the surface. But as I went, the chittering stopped being so wispy and grew rather menacing. *Worry about whatever fresh hell that is later. For now…*

Stone's face pierced the surface, but he didn't pull in a breath. That was bad—that should be subconscious. *Shit!* I swam up as fast as I could beside him, when a sharp wire slit my arm. I reared back to find my blood blooming through the dark water. Then the chittering got louder.

"What the fuck now?" I shouted, breaching the surface and getting a hand around him. Overburdened, I could barely move, while near-misses of whatever had struck me whipped back and forth in the water. Panic tried to take hold and my strokes grew erratic. I slapped at the water like I was trying to take down an elephant-sized swarm of gnats.

Stone's head bonked into the platform and I nearly cried in relief. "Sorry about that," I said to the unconscious man and worked my way out of the pond. Bending over, I hooked my arms under his. I should have kept going and not looked up. The entire surface of the water shivered like it was made of razorblades.

"Forget the new death trap," I shouted at myself. Clinging tight to Stone, I pulled him as fast as I could. "Why are you so fucking heavy?" His shoulders, then back rose out of the water, but those cursed legs dangled freely. The razors struck, bouncing off his ankles until more blood wicked into the water.

Then the roar began. The surface of the water dropped, nearly dragging Stone from me. It didn't drain so much as get sucked into the razor-toothed sea monster rising from below. With two hundred rows of spinning blades of death, the blender from hell was coming for Stone's legs.

Nope!

Planting my foot on the edge, I put all my weight into it and—with the last of my strength—hurled Stone up. The whirring Kitchen Ninja rammed straight for us. "Come on, come on!" Tears in my eyes, I tugged harder, a loud splash shattering the air as we both tumbled backward.

He nearly wound up on top of me, but I pushed him to the side and grabbed my spell book. It didn't need to go toe to toe with the rampaging ice crusher as it dove below the surface just before striking the brick wall.

"Yeah, you better run!" I taunted—waving my book around—before tumbling back, all my energy drained in an instant.

A strange laugh of survival bubbled up in me and I turned to share it when I caught his still face. Fuck!

I threw my leg across his waist and bent down. No breath. I pinched his nose and leaned over, prepared to clamp my lips over his and breathe for him.

Stone's chest heaved and he coughed up sewer water across my shirt. I let go of his nose so he could turn to spit out the last somewhere not on me, but I was too exhausted to move. Only the slop of waves from whatever was boiling the water and Stone wringing out his lungs filled the air. I waited in the near darkness for anything to go right for once.

"You…" His voice sounded like it'd been dumped on a charcoal pit and turned to ash. And he looked like a rat drowned in a toilet, not that I was in a much better state. After coughing twice more, Stone sat back on his elbow and stared up at me. "You saved my life."

"I don't want to die down here with whatever the hell those razor things are."

He winced and looked past me to the water that was slowly calming back down. "Ah, blood razors. Nasty if they sense…you can probably guess."

My damn leg must have set them off. I looked at it, my jeans a wreck not only from where the debris had punctured them, but also from a handful of cuts that nearly hit skin thanks to the blood razors. Barefoot, in shredded jeans and a sopping wet shirt covered in hunter spit. I was going to ritually burn this outfit when I got home.

If I got home.

"What do we do now?" I whispered, fearing the answer would be wait to die.

Stone's eyes glowed even greener in this gloom, which he kept aimed behind me before slowly moving them up. "I am wondering if you had any intentions to move?"

"What?" God, I hadn't realized I was still straddling him. With a wince, I tried to scramble off of him. In doing so, I planted a hand on the ground beside his head and ducked down. My wet hair fell around us like a privacy curtain and he sat up, causing his nose to bump against my cheek. I paused in my mad scramble to stare at him, and we both breathed in time.

Stone raised his hand to pierce through my soaking wet curls and cup my cheek. I lowered my backside and felt something long and hard press against it. Shit!

I tumbled to my side, yanking away his hand and…other lower male extremities that were hopefully in the throes of rigor mortis.

*That only works if he's dead.*

*He was nearly dead. It's still possible.*

*Because you saved him, your kidnapper. Why?*

Stone took stock of his injuries, barely frowning at the cuts the blood razors had done to his legs. He glanced a hand over his stomach, damn near daring me to stare. I wasn't so easily tricked and avoided his svelte abdominals for my waterlogged purse. A sticky mass of wet Kleenex formed a film all over the inner lining, which I dug out and threw to the side. Was there anything worse than the squishy feel of soggy tissues?

"What do we have left?" Stone asked.

"You mean what do I have?" I came back with. He slowly raised an eyebrow as if he'd worked hard to perfect that sardonic stare. "My book." I held it out for him. "And what looks like a half-opened packet of crackers that are mush now. Anything in your menagerie that's terrified of soggy peanut butter?"

"'Fraid not. I see you've lost your three-pronged sword as well."

"Shit!" In all the commotion, I hadn't even realized my keys were...somewhere down there with the razor-sharp blood-hungry monsters. I wasn't getting those back.

While mentally toiling over the mess I'd face trying to get duplicates of my lost keys, I stared over the brink as if I might spot them. The cruelest cut was losing Cal's keychain. Stone stared with me, his ragged breathing slowing as he seemed to get over his near-drowning quickly.

A mouth of razors snapped out of the water and sent me jerking back. Sturdy hands pressed against my arms, holding me safe, and I turned to glare at the reason we were trapped down here.

"Raul," he whispered so softly that the glug of the submerging creature nearly covered over it.

"What?"

A single tendril of his soaked hair dangled in front of his eyes. "My name. It is Raul, not Detective."

My tongue stilled and I had to fight to keep from telling him mine again. Absently, he pushed his hair back and I'd swear the once chin-length locks now nearly brushed to his shoulders. That didn't make any sense. How hard had I hit my head?

Stone…or Raul pointed to my leg and held his hands out. With a groan, I twisted around to let him have a look. He reached for the wound and I winced in anticipation, but he was gentle, carefully peeling back the tattered jeans that were already scabbing into the cut.

"Any chance you've got a secret stash of vodka down here?" I asked.

"Sorry, though a shot of whiskey would be a delight right now." Stone tenderly massaged my calf, working away a knot I'd barely noticed, while taking care to avoid the slow-bleeding wound. "I'm sorry I'm without any healing draughts."

I shifted off my hip and it caused my jeans' tattered edge to fall right back into my wound. A searing pain shot up my leg and I gasped, clawing it down.

To my surprise, Stone winced. "Perhaps it would be in your best interest to remove those."

"I can still beat your head in with my spell book."

"And no doubt dump my corpse in with the blood razors to clean up the evidence. Doesn't change the pain they're causing you."

I shook my head, feeling the weight of my soaked hair dragging it back as I did. Even through the pain, I wrenched my leg out of his range. Heat burned on my cheeks at how empty his hands looked.

Stone looked about to argue, no doubt with some point he considered valid, when he raised his hands in surrender. "As you wish."

Silence, save the plink of water striking pipes and the whirr of ravenous razors, fell around us. I didn't want to ask what happened next. I was exhausted with not knowing. It was he who broke first by softly chuckling. At my look, he explained, "I was only thinking, after you saved my life, we're even."

*What the hell is he talking about?*

"Eve…may the earth take her bones, was not lying. Your attack upon our fellow detectives is considered a death sentence. I spoke against it."

He said it magnanimously, as if I should fall at his feet and kiss him. My spine bristled. "You think that makes this square?"

"I put my reputation on the line. It's a lucky thing Drake's ego's so large he wouldn't report your injury, or else…I'm uncertain what the director would have done. But it would have been unpleasant."

"Oh yes, how dare I take a swing at the men who kidnapped me off the street and hurled me into a van!"

Stone whispered Spanish curses under his breath as he wrung a hand over the back of his neck. "This again?"

"I'm sorry if I don't just 'get over' being kidnapped. Did you thank the weird cultists who cut you up?"

Oh shit. I knew it was stupid the moment it left my mouth, but I couldn't stop. His cocky while also patronizing attitude made me see red. In that state, every button was the nuclear option.

He clucked his tongue hard against the roof of his mouth, his cheeks pulling inward until he looked like a skull. "Ah yes, these…" Drawing a finger across the curved lines above his ribs, Stone chuckled. "Every morning in the mirror I find the proof that you, witches, demons, creatures from other realms are a threat."

"I didn't fucking do that! I've never cut up anyone."

"But you killed..."

"Someone trying to kill me! Yes, even your goddamn detectives. If they didn't start it, I wouldn't have raised a fist."

He cocked his head to the side. "How do I know that?"

"Because I just told you, you..." I managed to force out every cruel curse word in one go while leaping to my feet.

Stone followed quickly, though he took the time to dust off his wet pants as if anyone down here gave a shit. "And I am to take your word on that? To put trust in a woman gifted powers that could slay hundreds with a snap of her finger?"

"Why do you get to decide? Who made you judge, jury and executioner?" I clenched my stomach, the hole pulsing faster. Or maybe it was my heart beating more rapidly in fear and rage.

Stone chuckled at my question, only enraging me more. I didn't realize I'd stomped across the cold ground to face him until I felt his warm breath across my cheek. God help me, but it smelled like a meadow. A meadow of hypocritical asshole.

"Can you fault us for wanting to save our people from magical threats?"

"That's what I do!" I reached out to smack him in the shoulder, my anger needing an outlet. He snagged my wrist before I could even make contact. Before I could blink, Stone pressed me back against the brick wall. Water dribbled through the mortar, rivulets running the length of my spine. I didn't squirm or whimper, but glared at the bastard who had dared to shove me.

Stone took a step closer until his hips nearly knocked against mine. His eyes flared in the same anger stewing inside of me, his voice rising in flames. "How can any of us poor, powerless mortals know whether you're a gun that'd take out the monster or turn on us?"

"I'm not a fucking gun!" Screw this guy. I caught the back of his neck and I dug my nails in, prepared to wrench him off me. He bent his head low and I kissed him. No, I tried to bite him, with my lips. Stone gave back twice as hard, heat snapping off his mouth as he nipped and sucked on mine.

I pulled on the hair at the nape of his neck, scraping the skin below as I crushed him tighter to me. Stone reached back and caught my wrist, yanking me off him. His once staid lips trembled and burned red from the force of his kiss. I kept glaring at him, a snarl raising up my swollen lip.

Lightning quick, he slammed both my hands against the wall beside my head. A low growl rumbled from deep in his scarred chest. The sound sent a shiver racing from my heart down to my thighs and I fought to keep my teeth from clacking. He drew his smooth cheek against mine until reaching my ear.

"No gun does what you can."

I broke free of his hold on me. It startled him so, he nearly reared back, but I fisted his hair and held him against me. In charge, I faced him. "You can't own me." Hauling him closer, I declared, "You'll never control me," and I kissed him. Stone's mouth parted, and I went in. He tasted of an ancient glen in the middle of a forest. With his hot tongue, he tried to tussle mine into submission, but I wasn't going down without a fight.

We twisted around in a circle while pawing at each other's clothing. I fought against his belt while he fumbled with my shirt. When my back once again struck brick, I gasped against his open mouth. His teeth snagged on my chin and he groaned.

Stone nuzzled against my neck while I scraped my nails down his back. Instead of wincing at every scar's divot, I dug in, causing him to buck against me. He rose taller than me, pressing his hips and the thick cock behind his pants against my belly. The strength in his stance nearly caused me to wilt as he toyed with the hem of my shirt, softly raising then lowering it.

He pushed aside my sodden hair and breathed against my ear even as he thrust his cock against me. "I don't want to control you."

"Fuck you!" I shoved him away, grabbed my shirt and yanked it clean off.

Stone's cocksure posture cracked. He could only pant in single puffs while staring at my chest. "Aw shit, there's freckles," he moaned, beaming at my cleavage.

He bent for my breasts, sucking on the top with his teeth as he caught under my ass and lifted me off my feet. "Fuck!" I clung to the back of his head, my thighs spreading wide with each jerk of his hips. My jeans' fly rubbed in just the right spot, causing me to moan and thrust back.

All the while, Stone bit down on the exposed top of my tit. Every pinch of his teeth filled me with rage that went straight to my inner core. I slammed my leg around his waist and kicked with all my might. It got his attention. He looked up, his eyes feral.

I reached under to snag his belt and hauled him right against me. "Are you done playing?" With the leather end, I pulled his hips so he ground against my hot, soaked pussy.

"I assure you," he said, unbuckling his belt and lowering his pants. Not far enough for my liking—it only exposed the indent of his hips and a tamed patch of hair right above the trapped dick. Stone clung one-handed to his pants, then wadded my hair in the other. He tugged my head back until the pressure tingled down my spine. "I never play."

He bent down to kiss me when I took his cock in my hands. All that powerful force crashed once I wrapped my palm around him. His forehead smacked into mine and I started to pump up the shaft with a vein thick as an ancient oak.

The low growl deepened until I could only feel his chest vibrating against mine. He ripped at my bra, tearing the hooks clean off until it slid down my arm that was working his cock. When Stone clasped his palms around my naked breasts, I drew my thumb straight up to his crown.

"No turtleneck?" I asked in surprise. I'd gotten used to Cal's double-wide foreskin.

*Cal? Wait, what am I…?*

Stone pinched both my nipples and the overwhelming pleasure knocked my head back into the wall. "Even splayed against this wall, you're still a threat."

"Fuck!"

He raised his knee and drove it between my legs while stimulating my tits. Not just the nipples—no, he went for every curve and swoop of the breast, diving down to take another bite and send me reeling.

"If I'm such a threat, why aren't you dead?"

Stone snickered in my ear as he toyed with the button on my jeans. "Admit it. Admit you're a killer. All from beyond the divide are." My pants fell clean off despite being soaked and shrunk. I looked down in confusion, when he slapped both his palms to my bare-naked ass and pried the cheeks apart.

With each rub, he swept his thumbs just outside my lower lips, taunting me. The twin fires of rage and lust burst. I clamped my nails into the single ounce of fat on his hips and, while tugging him closer, said, "You're the one who's killing me, hunter."

Before he could answer, I pulled him inside of me. He spread my legs wider, moaning at the tight fit. The crown was so thick I felt dizzy, each tiny thrust of his hips jarring through me. But the pain became an inferno of pleasure, soaking my vagina around him as it sucked him deeper and deeper in.

Stone slammed a hand beside my head and he bent close to kiss me. I lashed out and bit his lip hard enough to hear him squeal. His cock hardened to his name. "You're going to pay for that," he threatened, taking my breast and squeezing.

"How? You gonna kill me more?"

He thrust faster, digging my spine into the brickwork. With each pump of his cock, road rash scraped down my skin, and I wanted more. Stone shifted, taking my legs in his hands and pulling me off the wall. I rested on only my shoulders and my clit fell straight onto his pubic bone.

I cried out at the sharp sting of pleasure. Every ache, every curt word, every cross look only made my body boil more for his touch. My turn. I pushed back, grinding against him until my clit burned white hot. Stone groaned, his arms lagging at the weight, but I didn't care if he cramped every muscle in his body.

It was what he deserved.

"I never wanted to kill you," he whispered in a plain, almost tender voice wiped clean of the rampaging filth between us.

For a moment, I stopped grinding on him and looked up. Something was there past his shoulder, a large head with a long… Stone bent down to me and whispered in my ear, "I wanted to fuck you."

He bucked hard and fingered my clit while kissing me. His ass flexed harder, my heels barely able to make a dent as I wound up tighter to fight against the tide. "I hate you!" I gasped, giving in to the orgasm pulling me into its inescapable abyss.

Stone pulled back my sweaty hair and he whispered, "I know," just as he came. He didn't pull out as we slipped to the filthy ground, Stone's bare ass taking the brunt, then my knees. Cold raced up but it didn't touch my skin. *That's…*

He blinked up at me, his eyes uncertain and his hands demurely placed across his chest. Slowly, he brushed the tips of his fingers across my breast, playing with the freckles as I tried to catch my sense. *What in the hell just happened?*

"You're enchanting," he breathed.

I wanted to roll my eyes at his pun, but no, I didn't. I couldn't give a shit what stupid thing he said to me because none of this was right. I wasn't the kind of person to hate-fuck someone that'd tried to kill me just because he looked good in a suit. Someone who treated me like a dangerous weapon to be tagged and kept on a shelf. Cold bit my brain, seizing it up to remind me who really mattered. *Daniel, Cal, Ink…*

I slammed my hand forward the second my vision flickered. Instead of the empty air I'd been shown, I clamped down onto the soft and easily crushable larynx of a panicking creature. It shrieked as I turned and stared dead-eye at the siren.

# Chapter Twenty-Four

*Ink*

"He's here!"

*Please, if I must be yanked back to this mortal coil, let it be a bevy of comely lads and lasses inviting me to their orgy.* With the last of my energy, I pried open my sticky eyelid and stared face to face with the damn ghost.

"So much for a dying man's last wish," I muttered to myself.

"And he's still alive," Daniel harrumphed. If he'd wished my demise, he only needed to wait a minute more.

"Leave me be and I'll get right on fixing that." I couldn't say how long I'd been out—five minutes, two days. Only that returning to this land of burning joints and dead limbs was too much to bear.

"Take your time," the ghost said beyond me, trying to be funny. Failing, but at least he gave it an effort compared to his usual moaning.

For all I knew, he had thrown his lot in with the hunters. Perhaps he'd been a plant by them all along to sniff out Layla for their attack. I struggled to flip over when the long strides of a naked werewolf dashed into the room.

He stared around a moment, needing time to adjust his eyes to the gloom while I was free to openly gawk at his physique. I didn't know why I'd avoided the furry beasts prior. They looked like they could handle a demon's full thrust and give back just as good.

His blue gaze finally dropped to me and I gave a half-hearted wave. Calvin dashed to my side, tenderly lifting me up like one of his infirm patients. The purse containing the ghost's bone dangled from his wrist. "What in the hell were you thinking?" he chided me.

"Delightful. I get to be bathed in shame before the end. Would any of you drooling denizens mind offing me now?" I called to the rest of the ensorcelled who had yet to move.

The ghost shuddered after staring at their inebriated faces, while the wolf uncorked a bottle in his hand. He squeezed a large serving into the palm while berating me, "You weren't supposed to move."

"I did not have much choice in the matter. As you can hopefully piece together with your meager mind, there is sorcery afoot."

"That can affect you?" he asked before splattering his hand against my open wound. I lashed out, nails slicing into his shoulder, then clamping down at the pain roiling down my once dead arm.

"What are you…?" The pain lessened even with his touch remaining, and a cooling sensation chased down my arm, wiping away the fire.

"Better?" he asked, revealing a surprising bedside manner.

My jaw twisted as the pain raced up my neck, but I was able to gently nod. The clenching in my heart had lessened, wiping away the imminent fear of death.

"I don't know if this will completely cure you, but I found one and noticed a drop wiped away a pimple I had. Hoped it'd do the same for a basilisk bite."

"Oh blessed Hades and Anubis!" I cried out, in near orgasmic bliss as the agony of the last hour downgraded to a minor pain.

The ghost scowled at my proclamation, but Calvin chuckled. It was hardly his first experience with my exuberant reactions up close. He pulled his hand off me, and pain burst from the air striking my wound. I slapped his palm back and pressed it tighter.

"That is far more enjoyable than the lack of your…" My words failed me as I had to face the reality that he was helping me. "It pains to admit this, but your touch is quite welcome. Nowhere near as erotically talented as mine, mind you."

"There's the Ink we all know and put up with," the wolf said, but he did not draw his hand back in disgust. The ghost provided that, along with a toss of his head.

It must have been the exhaustion, the brush with death and the abyss before me, but I could not stop myself from saying, "I can understand why Layla reaches for it often."

To my surprise, the wolf winced. He turned from me, though kept his hand in place even as the healing ointment faded. I looked to the ghost to find him also staring in concern. *What had I missed while passed out in a puddle of my own drool?*

"Wolf…?" I began, before softening my tone. "Calvin, what has happened. Layla…?"

"I found her. I mean, I saw her. She was behind these bars and I couldn't rip them out."

I patted his bare shoulder in that familiar show of male camaraderie. "No doubt this place was built with the angry werewolf in mind. But, her magic. Surely she could have—"

"That's just it. They did something to her! They stole it."

Every brick in the Colosseum dropped in my gut. "What do you mean?"

"I don't know. She just, she told me she lost her magic, and that she was sorry, and…" He mouthed the word 'love' but little else.

A witch without her magic was like a dragon without its heart. Or nearly anything without a heart, come to think of it. In time, the realm itself would devour her until she ceased to exist.

I launched to my feet, only for the world to warp and nearly send me toppling back. The wolf was still of a calm enough mind to catch me. But that could only be due to his failing to understand the dire situation his mate, our Layla, was in.

"Where did you last see her? How many hunters are there? What is the terrain like?"

"Whoa, take a…take a minute. You can't even stand."

Anger was a tool for the sin of wrath. I'd never found much use for it in my existence, but a rage lanced through me like crimson lightning. It wasn't enough for them to steal her away—they were trying to poison her forever. Not as long as I drew breath.

I clamped onto the wolf's bare shoulder and hissed in his face, "Cease your endless dodging and tell me where she is."

"The corridor, room, whatever she was in, it…it flooded."

"What?" the ghost gasped.

"I tried to hold on to her hand, but—"

"How the hell could you let her go? She was right there with you!" Daniel berated the already crumbling Calvin. The wolf turned to him to explain, offering up excuses that felt limp even if there were no action he could have taken to alter the end.

Pain clenched around my heart, though I did not suffer in my arms or lungs. An underground dungeon flooded, her magic taken, hunters and devil knew what else stalking the corridors… *My bond.* I looked to my wrist, wishing to see the shackle, but I stared at the abrasion that punctured the skin.

"If I yet walk this earth, then Layla lives."

The two arguing men paused and looked to me. I pushed off from Calvin and took my own weight in my proverbial hands. It was touch and go for a moment, but I managed in the end and raised my head higher. "We must find her, and soon."

"Where? This place is huge and built like a labyrinth."

"It did come with a minotaur," Daniel unhelpfully added.

The wolf shook his shaggy head. "We need to take the time to plan and let you heal."

"Time is the one luxury we cannot afford. To take a witch's magic is…it's a death sentence."

I'd seen it but once, thought it impossible without the interference of a celestial when one of their realm guardians overstepped her bounds. "There is a hole inside of Layla slowly devouring her, bone, blood and brain. It devours the magic forever leeching from the other realms. Without the magic, it consumes what is available. If we cannot find her, if we cannot repair the damage they've done…I'm uncertain if it's even possible."

I hefted my wrist, feeling the weight of the bonds more like the noose. I'd escaped so many attempts in my demonic days, but this one held the weight of an end I could scarcely comprehend. I had to break this connection as quickly as possible, or worse than hell could await me.

"No." The wolf threw his shoulders back, his stance and voice firm in its conviction. "We will save her. We'll fix whatever moon-damn thing they did to her, and she will be safe. You hear me?"

He'd moved beyond the valley of sorrow into the lava fields of revenge. My human body erupted in goosebumps from the strength of his command. Shame that I could not share in his fervid certainty, as much as I wanted to.

Calvin glared at the ghost, who jerked his hands around, his gestures becoming more animated with the passing of time. "Of course I want to save her. But how the hell do we go about doing it?"

"The enchantress of before." I stood taller and peered past the drooling leches to the doorway where I'd believed Lust stood. It could not be her, but someone prying into my mind and using that as a cloak. "There was a woman, or it could have been a man in the guise of a woman. She's the one who lured me here, lured all of them."

"To sacrifice them?" Calvin's eyes bugged at the thought, as if we hadn't seen worse already.

"No," the ghost spoke up. "Look. There's protection wards around them. Whoever she was, she wanted to keep them safe from everything else out there."

"That door." I pushed myself forward. Each step was a thousand knives gouging the bottom of my foot, but I could not stop. The pain pierced to my knees as I stumbled up the stairs, Calvin and the ghost fumbling behind. "This is how she exited, and I suspect she may have plans with Layla."

"You think this enchantress of yours can find her?" Daniel scoffed. Ever the dour dead man, that one.

"I don't know, but you are incapable of offering a better suggestion." We were two useless lots, the mortal man near death, and the dead man thirty years late. Together, we turned to look to the only competent one left.

Calvin peered through the doorway, his jaw twitching. Was he contemplating the path untraveled? Or worse, was he weighing the sting to his conscience should we turn back and abandon her?

"Here." He picked up my arm and drew it across his strapping shoulders. "You're barely moving already, and we have to do this fast." Together, we slipped across the threshold. I held my breath and stared at the purple wards dashed all along the ceiling. Not a one lit up at my presence, the cloak still working.

Neither did anything attack the wolf at my side. It seemed to matter little with the ghost—a gnat would do more damage. We abandoned the metal cistern for an industrial corridor. Grates of black steel pressed in from all four sides, infecting me with a sense of claustrophobia.

"Anyone else feel like we're walking into the abandoned ship on the edge of space?" Calvin asked.

"If you see any giant eggs, don't stick your face in them."

I turned to the ghost in disgust. "Why in the outer realm's name would anyone do that?"

The ghost snorted, while Calvin calmly explained, "It's from a—"

A great tremble rattled every grate below our feet. They shook one by one in a wave toward us, then behind. Calvin clenched tighter to my arm. "That can't be good."

Another struck, harder than before, buckling the grates and causing us to slip and slide. I crashed against the wall, then took the weight of a grown werewolf. "I believe you cracked one of my ribs," I groaned, every breath punctured by a sharp pain.

"Ink…" the wolf howled for me when a black tentacle pierced from below.

"Fuck! It's the alien!" Daniel less than helpfully screamed.

The tentacle lashed for Calvin, who punched it right in the suckers, then he darted back. I clung to a pipe above my head as the unstable ground continued to buck.

"Behind you!" The ghost now offered assistance. Without blinking, Calvin lashed his foot back. As he did, he transformed it, the claws slicing a gash through the rubbery skin of the flanking tentacle.

Whatever it was shrieked in teeth-shattering rage and all the tentacles withdrew at once. Green ichor stained Calvin's cheek and naked thigh. He kept his stance wide and arms akimbo waiting for another attack.

"We should continue in case it regroups," I said, inching my way along, courtesy of the pipes.

Finally, the wolf stood taller and wiped off his cheek. "We should be good. Sounds like I..."

The grates crumpled, a tentacle wider than Daniel puncturing through them and smashing into Calvin. It batted him back from whence we came. I turned even as my bones cried in agony. Whatever magical healing he'd used on me was already wearing off.

"Wolf. Calvin!"

"Get out of here!" he shouted to me, hacking wildly at the trio of tentacles punching up from below and to the side. "Ink! Find Layla, save her before it's too late."

"What about...?" I called.

He smiled at me, his teeth sharpening to fangs. "I've got this." Calvin put on the fur of his wolf. Armored and armed, he launched off his haunches and plunged his teeth deep into the monster's flesh. Daniel shouted directions, guiding him even as the tentacle warped through his ephemeral body.

If not for the cloak, I could have dispatched the kraken in a moment. I fumbled for the brooch, my finger nearly on the clasp. No. If I gave in now, and there were wards ahead, Layla was as good as dead.

Biting my tongue, I clung to the pipes above, my feet barely touching the vanishing ground. Even with the pain throbbing through the very marrow of my bones, I inched closer to freedom, to her.

"I'm coming, Layla. When I find you, it's your turn."

# Chapter Twenty-Five

*Layla*

"Please don't kill me," the siren whimpered, and reached out with its spindly arms. I looked down to swat one away and spotted the wolf howling at the moon image straining across my breasts. Shirts, bra, jeans—I wasn't naked. Did that mean…?

I started to peer over my shoulder, when the siren touched me. "Not so fast," I threatened, jerking the thin neck back. Her head bobbed like a balloon, but she dropped her hands.

"All of that…" I finally peered at the scene of crime. Stone too was dressed and crumpled up on his knees. Even at a distance though, I could see a full mountain in his pants. "You did that?" *To him? To me?* I wanted to collapse her trachea for that violation alone, but a breath of relief cooled my anger. *At least I didn't…*

"You weren't supposed to break out of it," the siren whimpered, as if that'd protect her.

"Too bad for you he's not my type." *Yeah, who'd go for a cold, confident man with a dark past? Only weirdoes that are certainly not me.*

"I'm sorry. Please don't kill me. It's all I know to do. I saw the hunter and panicked!"

My mouth still tasted his tongue and my skin tingled from his touch. I tried to shake it away, telling myself it was all a dream. A nightmare, more like. *Who'd want to sleep with…? Stop looking back at the shirtless man on his knees. Focus.*

How long had she been messing with my mind? "The blood razors?" I started to peer over the side, when a gnash of teeth rose up to bite my reflection.

"Those are real." The siren's cool skin started to prickle under my fingers, raising her tiny scales until it felt like I was holding a pinecone. She swallowed hard and focused her giant pink eyes at me. "I've been trapped down here, trying to keep everything from finding me. Then you dropped in and…"

"Why?"

"It's what we do. We aren't fighters. We illusion people into their greatest desires, then flee while they're distracted."

"Not that. Why did you make me think I was…why did you pick that vision?"

"I didn't," the siren full-on squeaked. "You do. At least, one of you does. Ensnaring two people is trickier without involving them in the same illusion."

"Him. It was his," I insisted to the world. All that wanting to own me shit…yeah, not hot in the slightest.

"Th-th-that must be why you broke free. I'm so sorry. Please don't kill me."

Standing next to the tiny creature, it was easy to see why it feared death at every step. The willowy limbs and pipe-cleaner-thin body made it look like the siren would snap in half from a light breeze. A deep grunt broke from behind me, and I shivered as I realized just where Stone had gotten in the vision. Or maybe he went for a second round.

*Why am I even wondering?*

The siren blinked her giant pink eyes, then swerved them up to me as she forced an inhuman smile. I sighed and opened my hand. "I'm not going to kill you, not while we're both trapped down here, at least."

"Thank you, thank you, thank you… I know I'm outside of containment, but all the doors disengaged and I didn't know what to do."

"Stop explaining it to me. I'm not a hunter. I'm like you, another specimen they rounded up for their collection." I fell to my ass and curled my knees to my chest. As I did, I caught the wound on my leg, sending up a flare of pain that did not lead to anything pleasurable. This couldn't be a siren illusion… probably.

"You are?" The siren remained standing. Maybe they couldn't sit. "But…but you're like them. Human."

"I'm a…was a witch." Out of the vision, I could feel the void growing until it pressed against my lungs. My breaths shallowed as I struggled in the forgotten air in the cistern.

"A witch? Eeek!" She collapsed behind her hands and muttered something in Greek. "Are you going to drain my liver for one of your potions?"

"I'm not that kind of witch. I keep any vivisections to my day job."

We were two lost souls plucked from our homes and tossed into this hellhole thanks to Stone and everyone like him. The fool crumpled over to his side and curled up like he was spooning an invisible person. Who was me. God, this was never going to stop being weird.

"If you're a witch, why aren't you working with him? Seems like you kind of hate him, and also don't."

"I hate him, okay? Him and all the rest of his witch-burning friends. That enough of an answer? Only an idiot would help their enemy."

The siren held her hands up and the human gesture felt even more alien on the strange body. I goggled at her movement and noticed a metal necklace at the base of her neck. "What's with the collar?" I asked.

When she touched the piece, it lit up a pulsing blue that began counting down to zero. "It greatly limits my illusions."

"That was your skill on low?" I gasped. It'd felt so real, I could remember the tug of his cock on my palm. Not that I enjoyed it or anything.

The siren tipped her bulbous head in fake humility. "Without it, I could control the minds of everyone in the bureau."

"Is that so?" Every mind that knew who I was, where I lived, how to find me.

"Collared, I require near contact in order to confuse any would-be threats. It's why I have to sit here very quietly while you make strange grunting noises."

I full-body winced at the reminder she'd sat there listening and watching us like some magical perv. She seemed to know humans well enough to catch my reaction and she raised her hands. Before another round of pleading for her life could begin, I asked, "Could you wipe someone's memory? Or is it only 'here's your greatest wish come true'?"

"Oh, memory alteration is child's play. The human brain is surprisingly squishy and malleable," she said offhand before her eyes opened wide. "I don't eat human brains!"

"Uh huh..." That sounded like what someone who ate brains would say, but I had bigger fish to fry. "What about every hunter in this building? Could you wipe their memories?"

The siren bobbed her head. "Provided it's a simple memory, and not too deeply buried."

"Can you make them forget about me?"

"I...maybe. But not with this on." She tugged at the collar, before dropping it. "I'd have to get close to everyone and they'd kill me on the spot."

"The only hunter here is fast asleep. Take it off."

The siren shivered, her dull tan scales momentarily shifting to a vibrant green before fading back. "No. I can't. I touch it too long, see..." She picked up the collar and the flashing resumed. "It'll shock me. Dead. They showed us on a pig."

"What the fuck is wrong with them? Here, let me try." I reached out with a finger. The siren scrunched her face up and leaned away. When I touched, no light pulsed, but there was another problem. "I can't find a clasp. How did they get it on?"

The siren went white as a sheet. "I don't want to say."

"If I just had some tools...or my magic."

"Their alchemic kitchen is down that hall."

I whipped my head around to follow her point. "What hall..." Where once had been an inescapable wall, there was now a doorway helpfully labeled with a sign pointing in the direction of said kitchen and a unisex bathroom. I turned to glare at the siren and she smiled painfully.

"Instinct?"

"Here's the deal..." I bent over to the side of the platform and reached under the water. It didn't take long for the blood razors to start keening in excitement. Before they could turn my hand into a stump, I pulled out a sharp tooth wedged inside the brick. That'd do.

The siren clasped both her hands over her mouth as I held it out. "This is for a ward to break off your collar. Stop crying."

"You want to free me? Why?"

"So you can help me. I need you to erase Layla Leeland from every human mind in this place. Can you do that?" I tugged her collar up and peered close. With the tiniest of cuts, I formed a destruction ward that'd pop that thing clean in half.

"I...yes. No problem."

"Here's the trick. This ward won't do anything until I get my magic back, which I will hopefully find in their kitchen cauldron. Maybe a box of 'witch's magic' cups in the fridge. I don't know."

The siren yelped again as I drew in the middle pentagram. There was always a pentagram in these things. "You want me to go with you? To move? I can't... If I shift from this spot, he'll wake up."

"That isn't necessary. I can ignite it remotely and find my magic on my own. Do we have a deal?"

Even if I escaped with my life, they wouldn't stop. Not if I didn't cease to exist in their minds. "Siren? What's your name?"

"Like I'd tell a witch." She snorted.

*Jesus Christ.*

The siren narrowed her eyes at me. She already had the ward, but without agreeing to help me, she was on her own in this blood-razor-infested hole. "You'd make a deal with me without question? What if I do not do as you asked? I will be free to flee into the night."

"You do that, you don't erase their memories so they capture me again, and they won't just send me after you. There will be an enraged demon dogging your every step across this globe until the end of time."

"A…a demon?"

"He's very attached to me and really hates hunters. So what's it gonna be?"

She extended her tiny hand that was barely bigger than my thumb. I carefully cupped my palm around it for a soft shake. "I will remove you from their minds once you break my bondage."

I gathered up my bag, making certain the spell book was still inside. Armed with only the tiny tooth of a murder creature, I stopped before the exit and looked back. Raul lay curled up on his side, one hand out as if caressing a soft belly that wasn't there. He looked almost…sweet in that vulnerable position.

"What about him?" I asked.

"I believe he will sleep for many hours. You humans seem to exhaust so readily post coitus."

I nodded at the explanation even as my cheeks burned hot. He wanted to fuck me, not the other way around. The siren had even said so.

Another pulse erupted from my void, this time splintering against my ribs. I dug my nails into my bag and limped for the door. Before I left, I stared at the creature I was leaving alone with Stone. "You aren't like, some bloodthirsty siren that's murdered thousands, right…?"

I expected a giggle, a reassurance that she would never. But a cold, hollow voice spoke. "What does it matter? You require my services and the bargain has been made."

I opened my mouth to argue, only for another pain to wrack my chest. If I didn't get my magic soon, I wouldn't be alive to fuss about the murderous siren I had let loose.

* * * *

I hadn't been expecting this.

Instead of a rusted cauldron over an open flame, glass fridges lined the wall. Plastic bottles filled the shelves, each bearing a label that looked like a generic medicine. Waist-high counters with slate-gray tops took up the middle of the room, and standing at the sink with a book open was the last women I thought I'd find.

"You!"

She wrenched her hands out of the water, which stopped flowing, and looked up. Sure enough, it was the old woman who'd brewed up the truth serum they'd force fed me. Not that I expected to find a lot of seventy-year-olds running around down here. *What did Stone call her?*

"How did you get down here?" I asked, taking a step closer. As I did, my bag swept over the counter, causing my book to tumble out. She looked to it as I stared to hers. The pages appeared blank save a multitude of colored stains on the wrinkled paper.

"I imagine the same way you did." The old woman's once soft and guarded voice lost all pretense. She spoke more like the wise old guardian just before the shit hit the fan for the hero.

I started to laugh at the idea of her tumbling through the pipes to escape drowning. "For your sake…ah!" The void struck my heart. It was only a single missed beat, but it felt like a giant clamped his hand on both of my lungs, then squeezed my arms. Tears rose in my eyes as I fought against the pain and I looked up into genuine horror.

"What did those fools do to you?"

"Same thing they did to you." I struggled to speak. She was a witch too, which meant they'd also taken her magic and threatened her with death until she agreed to poison her fellow witches. "Fuck!" Another pulse struck and I crumbled for the cement floor.

At the last second, gentle, wrinkled hands caught me. The old woman barely came up to my shoulder, but she had the strength of a lion and used it to guide me to a stool. "I thought you'd have found your magic by now."

"Tried, but one of the hunters destroyed the bottle."

She pursed her thin lips, her wrinkles piling up until she looked like an enraged pug. "They do not think, only act out of malice."

"I'd hoped to find a replacement down here, anything to stop me from…" I choked up at the word even though it was as plain as the blood weeping from the gash in my leg.

"They keep those under lock and key," she said softly and all the tears I'd fought against, the hell I waded into and out of, slammed into me at once. "Hey, hey." The old woman wrapped me up in a hug and patted my head. "You're not going to die. Not as long as I'm here."

"You mean…?"

She snickered and her eyes gleamed. "I'll need a few minutes to brew it up, then you should be back to a fully-fledged witch."

"Thank you!" I cried, reaching for her hands even as she dashed away for the ingredients. She moved around the room like a jet-powered Roomba, bouncing from cabinet to fridge and back to the central stove. "I'm Layla," I called to the old woman as she hefted a cast-iron Dutch oven onto the counter, then lit the gas burner.

"I remember, dearie."

"I...I'm sorry but I didn't catch your name when they were..."

"Torturing you. Understandable given the circumstances. They call me Ms. Monvoisin, but please, you may call me Valerie." She dumped a handful of herbs I couldn't place, then a silver liquid into the pot.

"You're the first person to just give me their name down here."

"They think they can protect themselves with a handful of tricks, charms and wards. The rituals of minor vigilance keep them from noticing the gathering storm."

I strained my toes out, trying to will the pain out by sheer force. As it passed, my brain put together what she said. "Meaning...?"

She snickered. "The grid did not fall. It was pushed."

"You...you broke free." Holy shit! The old, assumed-frail woman tipped her head, revealing a hairpin with a skeleton hand holding a bottle.

"I'd hoped that the fools would have taken after the creatures and left you alone in the room. I searched for you, but...it seemed the hunters did not wish to give you up so easily."

"Tell me about it." I massaged my wrists, feeling the pinch of their cuffs even though no sign remained. It was more in my mind than anything. "We…who are you? I haven't met many witches. How did they get you? Why did you finally break free?"

Valerie chuckled. "You are a fount of questions. To your first, I am a potion witch. It gave me quite some renown even among the untainted sort."

"They must have taken you like they did me. Forced you to toil in this underground dungeon for…years?"

"Nearly thirty, I'd hazard a guess."

"Fuck!" That could have been my future. My spells, my magic, my life lost to their whims. Would I have even seen the sun again? My shock twisted into another round of pain and my body began to shake off the stool. Valerie held a hand to my back to keep me in place, but nothing could stop the agony.

My bag! I fumbled open the flap and latched onto the last Gatorade bottle. With a calming breath, I started to break the seal on the cap, only for another round to begin.

"You're succumbing so quickly." Valerie took the bottle from my fingers.

*She works for the enemy. She could still be playing to their tune. How can you trust her?*

Quickly, she hurled the cap off and guided the liquid to my lips. Some of it splashed out, but as the berry blue dripped down my throat, my shaking stilled. I took over holding it, letting her return to her brewing. Valerie pulled out an old egg timer and cranked it.

I only had to hang on for five minutes, then I'd finally be free.

"Most witches give in by the time the void escapes their stomachs. There must be a lion's strength inside of you."

My cheeks blushed at the idea and I took another careful sip before placing the bottle down. "How long did you hold out before…?"

"It had climbed to my throat and was about to obliterate my brain. There is nothing to come back to after that."

"Holy shit." I pawed at my head, terrified of feeling a pulse of nothing where my skull should be. "I fought with everything I could, just like you did."

"We are quite similar indeed," Valerie said with a slow smile. "And it is no wonder the bureau hunted you down so. A weak witch, she can sustain the void for days, even weeks. But a powerful one succumbs in hours."

I sure as shit didn't feel powerful. I was weaker than when a werewolf had sliced open my thigh and I had nearly died in a roller rink. All I wanted was to get out of here, to fall into Cal's arms, to feel Daniel's cool touch, to hold Ink's cheek and tell that damn fool not to leave me.

But he wanted out, to seduce and drain millions of new people. I was only holding him back. Even knowing that, knowing he wasn't capable of loving me back… *Oh no. No! I have not fallen in love with the incubus. Your stupid heart. Cal, fuck yes. He's unfairly perfect. Even Daniel without a body has that whole courtly love thing going on.*

*Ink?*

*Yes.*

*He can't love me back. It's only going to end in heartbreak. I know, and I don't care.*

"...cease your infernal screeching, you harridan!"

My beaten heart heard the voice before my ears did. It sent my body tumbling to my feet, ignoring the pain raging through me. I stepped to the door just as it blew open and my demon hero stepped through.

"Ink..."

"My bond." He greeted me like it was a Tuesday. I stumbled for him, Ink reaching a hand out to me, when my stalwart incubus fell.

*Why is he dirty?* I'd never seen him with a hair out of place. His skin was broken and... "You're bleeding!" I cried, swooping to his side. He'd crumbled to a knee and carefully lifted a shaking hand. I helped guide it to my cheek and he smiled with such serenity it was like gazing into the eyes of an angel instead of a demon.

"Do not concern yourself so, my bond. It's nothing more than a scratch now that I've found you." The damn fool couldn't stop smiling, his trembling thumb tugging on my cheeks and causing my tear river to redirect.

"What are you talking about? You don't bleed, you heal. Why isn't it healing?"

"Ah, a simple trick I can finally release myself from. I must say, this mortal life is not to my tastes." He struggled to reach for a strange brooch around his neck. I looked to it and swore the eyes on the embossed face looked back. "How was your day? Exciting?"

He couldn't stop acting like everything was normal. I ruffled through his hair, the once feathery locks weighed down by oil. "Ink...please tell me you're okay."

"Yes, in but a twitch of a lamb's tail." He pulled on the brooch, but nothing happened.

I tried to count his cuts, but they were numerous, and his eyes...instead of the fiery amber fields, a terrifying yellow leeched across the sclera as if his liver was shutting down. "Okay. This is all very funny, whatever the joke is, but..."

He gritted his teeth and tugged harder. "This cloak should be falling away. It's masking my nature, making me mortal." Ink gulped and his hand fell away. "Layla, I fear I've been bamboozled." Before I could ask what he meant, his eyes rolled back and he slumped over.

"Ink? No! You can't... Valerie, can you do anything?" I cried out, trying to take his pulse, check his breathing, and remove the brooch. But the pins were sealed shut, no mechanism there to undo. What was this thing?

"Hm, I'd guess he was poisoned by a venom. Whatever it is, it's run its course. I'm sorry."

"No. No, no, no. He's not human. He's an incubus. Ink!"

"A demon. Child, get away from that thing." The old lady bustled over and dropped a hand to me, but I slapped it away.

"You have to help him. How do I get this cloak off?"

"That's a witch's charm on his throat."

I grabbed the first thing I could find, a tiny knife, and stabbed at the brooch. Nothing happened. No, I wasn't letting him die. I stabbed twice over, only causing sparks to fly.

"Why won't this fucking thing break!" I wrapped my fingers around the flimsy cloak, the plastic and fabric already tearing. It wouldn't budge, not even the knife could cut through it.

"My dear..." The old witch patronized my feeble attempts at saving him.

If I had my magic… I looked to the timer, but another five minutes remained. He'd be dead by then. How did I convince her to…

"We're bonded!"

"What?"

"Him, he's bound to me. If he dies, then I do too!" I raised up my arm despite there being no shackle or chain. Valerie squinted and my wrist grew heavy. Suddenly, the bindings of my demon glittered from my wrist to his dangling hand.

"Damn." She stepped back and waved her hands. "I'm going to purge every spell in this area."

Yes, that had to work.

What about the siren?

"How far?"

"A hundred feet? I never fully measured the radius. There is no other choice." She parted her hands between her fingers and, from them sparked a line of purple. I watched the tendrils grow longer and fatter, each one fracturing into another three until the entire room sparkled. Valerie threw her head back and the purple sparkles exploded.

The first wave knocked into the brooch. The second tore at the cloak. When the final hit, the clasp came undone and it fell to the floor.

Except Ink wasn't getting up. Oh god, he looked even worse. His skin sunk against his bones. Cracked lips barely moved over his exposed gums, and his eyes…they faded to a red gray. "Ink! What's wrong?"

"He's been drained. He'll require nourishment before—"

He needed desire. My desire. I took his poor, wizened chin in my hand.

"No, wait!"

*I want you, you damn idiot. I need you. I'll always need you.*

His lips moved, and with barely a whisper he said, "Lay—" I captured them in a kiss before he could finish my name.

# Chapter Twenty-Six

*Ink*

*"When you take your prey into your arms, you devour them not with tooth and fang but lips and fingers."*

Lust's words floated through my mind. Her first teachings had been her only.

*"Do not pause, do not let them breathe. They desire you, and you in turn desire what they can give – nourishment."*

I'd never felt so weak before, not even in my first days of life. Heat pressed to my quivering lips, then a taste more delectable than the nectar of the gods dripped across my tongue. I filled my arms with her body, her curves softening more as I drank my fill the only way a Sin could.

*They are food, an endless supply aching to fill your bed. Not a one matters, only the whole.*

Yes! My energy soared as I sucked upon her lip. She moaned as I knew she would, her mind pinging with desires for me to caress her breasts and buttocks. Still weak, all I could do was take her cheek and plunge my fingers into the hollow behind her jaw.

Her lips parted with a gasp, and I delved ever deeper. Not just with my tongue but with my unending hunger. A stolen kiss barely filled it. I needed more.

*When they've given all they can, find the next one and never look back, Eros.*

A song carved from the air, water and earth from when the Celestials formed the realms danced in my blood. I felt her slipping away—whatever she once was, whatever she could have been. That was the coda to our dance, one I'd pursued a thousand times before. Always alone at the end, never giving them another thought, never pausing to wonder if…

"Ink?"

My name, but not. It overpowered the rising trill in my bones, the hunger demanding its fill. I blinked, and the darkness of chaos faded to a supple cheek, a caring but concerned eye, and the hard-kissed lips of my bond. "Layla," I whispered to her.

She floated in my hands, not her physical form but her energy. I'd snatched it from so many, like snipping the end of a thread once the tapestry was finished.

*Take it. Do as we were created to, as they made us for. Consume her.*

The ringing grew desperate, the strength in my body demanding I take what I was owed. I was the hunter, she the prey.

I broke the kiss.

As I'd learned, as I'd done hundreds of times after the thousands. The life in my hands returned to where it belonged and Layla, my bond, breathed again.

*What are you doing?*

*I'm no hunter, Lust. I can eat without death, and I can look back again.*

The feeble trappings of the mortal cloak burned to ash. My wings spread free, blanketing against the walls as I leaped to my feet. I opened my eyes and felt the unquenchable fires of desire burning inside. I was back.

"Demon!" the unexplained woman in the room shrieked.

I moved to adjust my cuff, the fabric already repairing itself, when a swoon fell over my bond. Without pause, I ensnared her safely in my arms, my wings folding around the both of us. As I bent close to her, the tip of my nose glanced against her cheek. She'd paled to an unsettling shade. Her eyes fell shut and her hands crumpled to her breast.

"Put her down!" the witch threatened, but my attentions were where they belonged.

"Layla…?" I whispered. Like a petal on the breeze, her eyelids lifted and so too did her smile.

"Ink?" she croaked in her adorably froggy way. When she placed her hand to my cheek, I turned to place a kiss.

"Child, are you all right?" the elder lady called. "The demon did not drain your life?"

"What do you take me for, some kind of human?" With my regained demonic grace, I eased Layla up to her feet and held her steady. She wobbled, but other than needing a long sleep, would suffer no consequences from my kiss.

"Why were you in that cloak? Where are the others? I'm so glad you're here." Layla's spitfire response could only draw a chuckle from me.

In genteel mode, I raised her fingers to my lips and kissed them. "They are close behind and should be finishing with the tentacles soon. I wore it to find you. And I am grateful to be here as well."

She smiled ever brighter and swept her arms around the back of my neck. I moved to kiss her, when she gasped in agony instead of delight. The rosy reunion punctured into ashes and I raced to keep her in my arms even as Layla crumbled.

"My bond. Are you still without magic?"

"You heard?" She gulped. "Don't worry, that problem should fix itself in…" Layla swiveled her head back to the counter and the bubbling cauldron. A dial ticked slowly for the center which must be the end of her exile from the realms. Good.

"That is against Animal Control Policy!"

"Ah shit."

Limping, with all the bravado of a man who found his courage at the bottom of a bottle, appeared a man of fair features and greenwood eyes. He held a small firearm, the exploding end pointed at my midsection.

"No one move! Monvoisin? You're all under containment for this insubordination." At least he did not waggle his toy around, causing it to go off at the most inopportune time. That was the only plus I could give him.

"Excuse me, my bond." I placed Layla in the care of the older woman who was no doubt facing a long list of treasonous charges.

"I said not to move!" the hunter ordered.

At that moment, a ding broke from the metronome behind me. I flew forward, taking no chances with a hunter's weapon. It could be stained with unicorn blood, a satyr's tears or old-fashioned feces. With a fast swipe, I knocked it away, the ferocity causing it to crumple on impact. The hunter's fair-folk eyes went wide, his mind no doubt realizing the misstep he took, as I clasped a hand to his throat and hauled him up.

"Your power is nothing, mortal. Your threats are impotent. Know how little you mattered as I crush the soul from your body."

"Ink, stop!"

It wasn't the man at my mercy who cried for salvation, but my bond. She dropped the ladle she'd drunk from into the pot, splashing a drop of blue down her cheek. Without bothering to wipe it away, she dashed to my side and held my arm.

"Put him down. Please." Her eyes begged me to obey even after all we'd suffered this day at their machinations.

"This is your pet demon?" the fool squelched out from between my fingers.

"Not the time, Stone!" Layla snarled at him.

I focused on my bond, unable to find sense. So distracted, I missed the glint of silver until the damnable hunter pierced a blade into my wrist. My grip collapsed and he fell to his feet. The pain was nowhere near the same as when I'd been human, but I could not fight back, the whole of my arm falling numb.

"This is insanity from the both of you. Do you have any idea what you've done to your career, Monvoisin?"

The old woman stared over his head as if she'd already removed herself from the conversation. I wrapped my palm around the blade yet wedged in my wrist, but fire burst on my fingers. Damn it!

"And, Layla…whatever you've done, the director could very well order your destruction."

He reached for her hand. I tried to bat his grip away, but when he touched her, Stone's eyes rolled back. Her lips barely moved but Stone fell to his knees, then he crumpled onto his side. Had she killed him with one touch?

I was mightily impressed, until a small string of snores burst from the agent of chaos. Layla clenched her hands into fists and she smiled at her work. "I guess my magic is working. Here." She ripped the dagger from my wrist and tossed it aside. Then, with a gentle touch, she smoothed her witch's healing magic across the wound. It aided in my natural demonic skill, quickly sealing away whatever damage the hunter's infernal weapon wrought.

"Thank you, my bond. Now allow me to finish this." I raised my foot, prepared to turn his brains to tartar.

"Don't!" She did not just hold my arm, but swept protectively in front, putting herself between me and the hunter. What in the world was she playing at?

"It might seem disquieting to let the demon do your dirty work, but..." the old woman spoke up for me, while I only had more burning questions. For what reason would a woman shield her captor? And why did the hunter smell of self-gratification?

"Listen to me, I already have a plan in motion and if he dies...it'll mess it all up."

"If you think a hunter will vouch to protect a witch..." I began, but Layla shook her head.

"Not that. I've got a siren."

A siren of Greece? "You move in august company. Or are they more of a July creature? April perhaps."

The old woman smiled wisely. "You're going to purge their memory."

"I'm sorry, she said she could only do it for me. But if we ask, maybe..."

"Do not concern yourself with me, dear. I have my ways out."

Layla nodded sharply and cupped her hands together. "Right. Well…time to try this." I could see nothing, only my bond clenching her fingers then her eyes tight before she gasped and opened them. "Ah shit, I forgot about their system. The computers—"

"You've been logged as being administered the neutralizer. Without anyone remembering you, the system will default to assuming your demise and you will be registered as dead to them."

So that was to be it. No great battle where I severed the head of her captor? Nor would we ride through the halls on the backs of winged horses, obliterating all in this dungeon of lawlessness and chaos? I glanced to the man happily snoring away, uncertain if he or anyone else already had Layla ripped from their memories.

She was busy thanking the older woman profusely. "If it weren't for you, I'd…"

"I know, dear. You're welcome, of course." The two hugged in a distant and uncertain way.

"You should come with us. Ink can get you to the surface."

I tipped my head at her certainty. "While my skills of travel are legendary, would she not paint upon us the bullseye you tried to remove?"

"Oh…" Layla withered at the thought. While it pained me to crush this fledging friendship of covens, it would hurt more to put her in harm's way.

"Don't worry, child. I've been here since before this place was built. I doubt even Detective Stone knows the tunnels I do. But you should get out with him."

"I have so much I want to ask you. About witches, about magic, about…"

The old woman sighed sadly and patted Layla's cheek with all the love of a grandmother. "You poor thing, your mother has left you in the dark. I wish I could be the one to unfog it for you, but your demon is correct. If I visit you, they will resume hunting you. I must go."

Layla flinched but nodded in acceptance. She turned to me, her eyes wet with tears, when her mouth dropped open. "Wait! There's this spell I need. I've been trying to hunt it down but I can't find a trace of it."

The old woman stopped filling her bag with war spoils from the fridge. "Yes?"

"How do I bring someone back from the dead? Not like raise their corpse, it's really decomposed."

"Without the soul…"

"I have that. I mean, not in a jar. He's a ghost. But he's around and he deserves…I need him to help me."

"Help? A ghost? In what way?" The old woman chuckled at the idea.

"I ask her that every day. It seems he might know some trick to defeating a Mr. White."

The old woman's face didn't shift. She did not blink, nor close her mouth. She very actively didn't react, which meant she knew more about this White than she wanted to say. "I'm afraid I don't know of any such spell, but if…"

A great roar burst beyond. I swung to face it, putting my body before Layla's. She cupped my shoulder and raised her hand, fire spurting from the palm. We smiled together at the stance, prepared to face whatever monstrous, venom-spitting snake-headed creature came barreling for us.

A shadow loomed in the doorway, footsteps trampling on the metal floor. I prepared my claws and she lifted her hands when a blond head thrust into the room and a voice shouted, "Layla?"

"Cal!" Full-on waterworks burst free. She shook away her fire even while running to him. The rampaging beast shed the last of his wolf as he swept her up into his arms and spun her in a circle. Layla clung to him, her heart bursting with a desire that stuck in mine. She dropped her forehead to his and the two stared eye to eye.

"Go ahead, I'd say your wolf earned a kiss or…"

Before I could finish, they shared a passionate one. I bent over to pick up the body of the still living hunter. Layla's spell must have been even more powerful than usual. He didn't make a sound as I hoisted him over my shoulder.

"I was so scared." Calvin made his usual proclamation after she was out of danger.

It was Layla who threw us for a loop as she gulped and admitted, "So was I."

I looked back and caught his eye just as the ghost appeared.

"Daniel!" Layla reached for him and let the specter possess her for their strange half hug. As she wrenched her arms around both and whispered her devotion to them, I popped away to deposit the sleeping man in the cistern with the rest of the slumbering hunters.

With little grace, I dropped him like a sack of potatoes, his head striking the ground. He frowned at that, but could not fight against her magic. "Hear me in your dreams, hunter. If you dare to come for her again, I will pierce your back, rip your lungs out and lay them like wings."

Groans began around me, the others beginning to stir. Before they could notice the demon, I dodged the ward and returned to my bond's side. There were more happy tears on cheeks, both hers and the wolf's. Even the ghost looked like he was tear-stained without being capable of crying.

"I see the witch has vanished," I declared, breaking up their happy moment.

"Who?" Calvin inquired, extending his long neck around the room before he landed back on Layla.

"I'll explain it later. For now…please take me home."

I reached out, taking her into my arms. With her warm body pressed to my chest, I felt lighter than air. I kissed her cheek and whispered, "I'm here to answer your every desire."

With that, we popped out of the underworld and back into the sun.

# Chapter Twenty-Seven

*Layla*

I woke feeling like Dorothy fresh out of Oz. Instead of the would-be Tin Man, Scarecrow and Lion, I focused my gummy eyes on a pile of cardboard boxes. Then I heard the voices of three men arguing from beyond the door. *Get up and deal with that mess or stay here and sleep?*

I didn't have much choice. My blanket had slipped off and my toes were freezing.

When I placed a foot to the floor, numbness swelled up from the point of contact. But it wasn't as bad as last night. Yawning, I stuffed my wayward breasts back into the cute camisole top that could never keep them contained and made my way toward the site of the commotion.

"Give me a hand!"

A gentle clapping broke free.

"Very funny, now maybe help with all of this."

"I am helping. I daresay I helped more than you managed in a lifetime."

"Then why is he carrying all the boxes?"

"It's called emotional support. I can understand why it's beyond someone dressed like he fell into a load of fieldworker's denim and forgot how to lay down a stitch."

"You wouldn't get it. This is vintage."

"The same is said of old spinsters' porcelain cat collections, though even they are kept in better condition."

I walked into my living room to find my three men vaguely bickering. Ink and Daniel were ranting near each other but not close enough for it to be a threat. Daniel raised a finger in his direction when he turned and spotted me. "Layla!"

Cal's head appeared from behind a stack of boxes in his arms. "Babe!"

"How are you feeling?" Daniel asked, floating beside me.

Cal dropped the boxes and he took my hand in his. "You were out cold for so long, I was getting worried."

With a swagger, Ink cocked his hip and said, "I wasn't."

I smiled at the three men in my life before I finally took in my apartment. The couch was missing, as was my TV stand. The walls were bare and all the odds and ends from my kitchen were piled up inside the open boxes on the floor.

"What are you doing? I thought we were gonna wait before doing all this packing. At least for the weekend."

Cal tossed his head. "I know you erased their memories, but who knows what those hunters still have on you? Better safe than sorry."

"What about my lease?"

"Don't worry, I handled it." He smiled wide at me, his arms crossed so tight his biceps bulged. "I sent Ink to talk to him."

"Took me three minutes," he said with a bow. "You are in the free and clear, once we have removed your valuables from this place. In the meantime, I suggest relocating you to better quarters."

They all looked at me as if I should be grateful. I was. After everything that damn place had put me through, I couldn't think. Cal stepping in and taking charge was a relief, and yet... "Can I have a few minutes here? Before I have to say goodbye."

"Of course," Daniel answered. He dipped his fingers into mine and clenched my hand as if I was holding his. I gazed into his eyes that held such hope it almost caught my breath. "Demon!"

"What ho, useless spec?"

"Let's pack up her bedroom and give our...beloved." He smiled warmly at me, as did the others. While I appreciated the sentiment, I could tell I had missed something. "Time to bid farewell to her apartment."

"Very well." To my shock, Ink hefted a box and he trucked down the hallway. "What help do you intend to add to this? Going to blow on her curtains?"

"I'll make sure you don't miss anything," Daniel said, striding confidently beside him.

Ink chuckled. "Don't worry, whisper. I, of all people, will not forget her dildos."

"That wasn't—"

Whatever new argument they picked up was dulled to a wordless groan when Ink closed my door. I took in a breath and looked up to find Cal lingering beside me.

"I was wondering if I could talk to you. But I can go if you want."

"No." I caught his hand before he smooshed back his hair and clung to it. "Please. I…want to talk to you too."

Now that we both said we wanted to talk, neither of us knew what to say. We both stared at the other, then looked to the side. The sound of an incubus dumping my most valuable possessions into a plastic bin only amplified how little we weren't talking.

"Thank you," I said. Cal frowned in confusion. "For letting me stay at your place until… My getting kidnapped didn't fix anything. And that everything, between us, is a mess."

He'd offered because there was no other alternative. I'd told myself that when Cal said I'd be moving in with him while they'd all undressed me for bed. Hoping for everything between us to be back to normal seemed too far a leap.

"I don't want it to be." Cal drew his tongue across his teeth and he clenched a hand beside his head. "I don't want to be the way I am. I know it's fucked up. I'm fucked up."

"You're not," I began, when he turned so sharply I caught my breath. "No more than could be expected given the circumstances. It's my fault. You told me what you wanted and I didn't do it. I…panicked."

"I wouldn't listen. I kept it from you because I am fucking terrified that all of my werewolf pack bullshit is just gonna—" His waving hands collapsed around my shoulders and he pulled me to him. With his lips to my forehead, he whispered, "I'm sorry for putting all that on you. I didn't realize how much I was hiding out of fear that…"

"That I'd get hurt?"

He laughed without mirth and leaned back. Staring at the ceiling, Cal said, "That you'd hate me for it."

"Cal..." I cupped my hand to the back of his head and directed him to look at me.

It took him a moment to open his eyes. A deep sigh escaped. "I just kept thinking if I'd been there, they wouldn't have gotten you. I should have been there. But what did I do? I ran away, tried to pile more sandbags on my past, on the...the cult shit. I don't want to run away anymore."

"You don't have to. I'm here, and...I can't know what it was like growing up under all of that. But I'm not afraid of it. Or you."

"Layla." He collapsed me into his embrace, his head bent over mine, his arms safe and welcoming. "I wanted to be perfect for you."

"That's not possible. All we can do is try." I swept my hand up his back, Cal's wide chest shaking as he fought off the sobs that'd tormented him.

"Talk to each other." I finally got him to look up as I threaded my fingers in his hair. He smiled tentatively, as if testing it out, when I pulled him close. "And fuck every chance we can."

I kissed him just as he broke into a wide grin. Cal swept his hands under my ass and he lifted me off the ground. I yelped in surprise, nipping his lip. He licked where I bit down. "That I can handle," he purred against my neck before kissing me harder than before.

"The demon has broken everything in your room."

Trying to not sigh, I leaned away from Cal as Daniel strode before Ink, who carried a box that jangled more than it should.

"It's hardly broken." He glanced down into the box. "An application of epoxy should solve the problem nicely. Wolf?"

Cal frowned but accepted the box. "The truck's nearly full. I think just one more load and we should be good."

"Then you best get to it." Ink shooed him like he was an obstinate cat.

For a moment, Cal backed off, but he placed the box in the crook of his arm and swept me up with the other. I giggled in surprise and he kissed me once more. I clung to his cheek as he whispered, "I'll see you, every inch of you, at home." Boldly, he swept his eyes down my body and flashed me a Cheshire grin.

Cal left me breathless and panting for more. As he turned for the door, Ink stepped forward to drop a coin purse in his hand. "Take the ghost with. He can prove quite useful at being useless."

"Tch. Says the demon that cannot understand the simple mechanics of bubble wrap."

"If it's not meant to be slammed into the wall via my fist, why does it make such a satisfying sound when I do?"

Cal glanced from me to the demon as I fiddled with the locket around my neck. "Come on, Dan. You don't want to stay here."

"Why?" he asked, before looking back and frowning. "Oh. Well, if you require me, my meadow flower, you only need call."

As Cal walked out the door with Daniel in tow, the ghost asked, "Please tell me you have a library where I can study Layla's spell book in peace?"

"Well, there's a dining room I never use. I guess it could be a good place to haunt. Maybe get you a few candelabras to float about..."

They vanished to the truck, leaving me standing before the demon who had risked his life to save mine. Who had said he didn't want to be with me any longer. Much like with Cal, it was time to face the music. I took a breath, but Ink spoke first.

* * * *

*Ink*

In all my travails across the continents and oceans, I'd never found much need for collecting objects. A few changes of clothing, should the engagement require it, were all that I carried. Any other gift bestowed upon me by smitten prey was left once the deed was done. I had no idea how mortals could stand carting about so much stuff. Perhaps that was how they dealt with having so little life, ignoring the drop of the sand by dusting their little knickknacks for the ten-thousandth time.

Calvin and the ghost swept out the door. At least he was able to withstand the specter's blather. If I spent one more minute in his company, I'd suffer a headache—which was impossible for incubi. I glanced back to my bond to find her staring expectantly at me. Ah, yes.

"Here." I extracted her phone from my pocket and passed it over. "I kept it warm for you, I suppose."

She snickered to herself. "I damn near forgot about this poor thing. Oh...that is a lot of messages from Dana." Layla groaned at the exuberance of her friend. I knew she intended to concoct whatever story was necessary to appease her worries.

"I shall leave you to it," I said, when she shook her head and placed her phone on the kitchen passthrough.

"I'll talk to her later. And Fariah. And my professors. Please don't let me have missed any quizzes due to magical kidnapping." She scrunched her cheeks up as if trying to wipe away the internal scars of the last day.

I reached for her, and she smiled at my touch. Her desires churned in such a turbulent wake I could not discern which would make her melt. I settled for the old standby of gently massaging her neck. Her head lolled as she gazed to the middle of her living room.

"To think, that's where it all started. You in that tiny red G-string. Whatever happened to it?"

"I returned it to its owner. I may be a sex demon, but I am no thief."

"And your usual outfit?" She drew a hand down my standard crimson shirt and black pants.

"A gift."

"Someone just gave you all of that on the streets?"

"Is that strange? It's how I acquire all my clothing. Accepting coin for my services feels rather one-sided given how much they nourish me."

She pursed her lips, but I knew my bond well enough to discern she was not judging my lagging business acumen. There were more turbulent matters on her mind. At least she seemed to have patched the tatters with the wolf. That would make this new arrangement more livable.

"I keep thinking about that night, Halloween night. You standing there, declaring you were bound to me. I didn't ask what that meant. I don't think I wanted to know how or why."

*Ah.* "You've determined the reality of the situation."

"Not entirely. But if I hadn't snatched you out of hell and bound you to me..."

I smiled almost serenely at my tongue loosening with the truth. 'Twas the curse of demons that we were incapable of lying, but with that came a skill in never telling the truth either.

"It is as you've discerned. I was the one to bind myself to you. As for my escape out of hell..." I sighed at the rare, exposed glimpse into a heart I should not have. "I had no cause in that, nor did another. A hole appeared and I took advantage. No one summoned me, no one freed me."

I was not the valiant, realm-striding sin I wanted to appear. Only a minor demon-adjacent entity who had seized an opportunity when presented.

"You did." Layla brushed a hand to my cheek, drawing my gaze to hers. "You freed yourself, which...is not an easy thing to do."

I smiled at her candor. "Coming from an expert, I thank you for that."

Her warm grin sharpened and a sour note swept across her features. She cast her eyes down and her voice softened. "You helped me, a lot. Not just with magic, but keeping my ass alive."

"It is a fine and firm ass worthy of such diligent guarding."

"And...as much as I don't want to say goodbye, you've more than earned your freedom."

Oh. I'd forgotten my request prior to the hunters' attack. By the harsh light of day, I'd felt so certain in my steps. I'd thought the hunters gone or so diminished they would not threaten me. This last ordeal proved otherwise. But far more stuck in my throat and slipped down to the aching chasm between my lungs.

I didn't want to leave her.

"Daniel helped me find the spell to break the bonds. I think. There's like ten different options, so I wrote a few out." She raised up sheafs of paper covered in the ghost's interpretation of the spell in her book.

Before her lips could part a single syllable, I caught her hand and lowered them. "My bond…" I smiled at the phrase, the reminder of what she was to me, what I was to her. Not in servitude, as how I'd learned and suffered under this spell. She was something else, something I could scarcely understand.

She had risked her life for mine without question, even knowing what I was. No one, not even Lust, had ever done such a thing. That connection, as fragile as it could be, was a difficult thing to abandon.

"I would like to amend my earlier statement regarding our dissolvement."

My tongue stilled and a thousand thoughts ran rampant. What if she refused? What if she'd already decided upon a future with her as queen to the werewolf's future throne? A future where I didn't belong?

As Layla stared, an unholy flush came under my skin. It felt as when the basilisk poison had flooded my system, my heart squeezing. I could only stare at her a moment, like gazing at the sun, before the pain returned. Was this what it felt like to care? Lucifer's sake, how could anyone stand this?

"You want to stay with me?" she asked, her lips parted and eyes bright with hope.

I took her cheek and held her tight. *Yes, until the moon falls to the seas, I wish to remain by your side and in your heart.*

*What is that thought?* I frowned at the sentimentality that could have only come from the mortal cloak. Some remnant must yet be floating in my veins. No incubus, no demon would waste his unlimited time on such frivolity. We did not love, for we were never meant to love.

"Given what we now know about the hunters, it seems dangerous for you to join a coven. Any one of them could be working with the enemy."

"Oh." As her hopeful smile faded and she dipped her head, the lingering pain struck one last time. "That makes a lot of sense."

"I do try from time to time." I could not give her what she wanted. It was not in my nature to be the beloved the others found so easily. Instead, I tenderly brushed back her hair, hoping the small touch would help.

"What now?"

"I believe…" I swept her up into my arms and pinned her back against the wall as I had that first night in her apartment. She smiled wickedly at me and my being surged with her desires.

Catching her wrists, I extended them high above her head and pressed my full advantage against her hips. Layla sighed so deeply, I felt it. "You deserve one last ravishing between these walls."

# Chapter Twenty-Eight

*Layla*

Ink clenched my wrists more tightly, a low rumble rising from him that sounded like a dragon guarding its gold. It sent a shiver straight down my spine that left me panting. He drew his nose up my cheek until he reached my ear. I waited for a sinful request, but instead of antagonizing me, he used that wily tongue to lick around my earlobe and pull it between his teeth.

I groaned, arching my back. My incubus cupped my belly and tugged the tissue-thin fabric barely hiding my skin. With an almost chaste coyness, Ink let his forearm haplessly caress under my breasts. He tipped up my chin with his nose, then caught my lips in a hard kiss.

On instinct, I squirmed, raising my leg. Ink caught it before I could do any accidental damage. He kneaded into my inner thigh, lifting my leg to wrap around his waist while I precariously balanced on the other.

His deep rumble of laughter echoed against my cheek. "This is how I like you."

"In a flamingo pose?"

"Strained to the near breaking point." He thrust his hips, grinding his cock against my soaking panties.

*Fuck, it feels so good.* I wanted him to strip me naked and slam me against the wall. Ink reached for my waist, about to remove either my panties or shirt, when a pair of green eyes flashed in my mind.

*No, that wasn't real! I didn't…ask for that. I didn't want it.*

Ink paused, instantly reading my reticence. I leaned forward, hanging off the grip he had on my wrists, to kiss him. He pressed back, flattening my spine to the brick… Plaster, that was a plaster wall in my cheap apartment.

"Actually." I turned away from his kiss, a disquieting seed planting in my stomach. It was the wall sex that had made me keep thinking of Raul. Stone. "I'm not a hundred percent. Do you think we could…?"

"Do much better?" He opened his tight grip on my wrists, but did not release them. Instead, he guided my palms so they clenched behind his neck. With a smile, Ink hefted me up until he held me. My ass bounced against the crown of his cock as he whispered in my ear, "Always, my bond."

I reached up to kiss him, expecting to be whisked away to my stripped bed. Ink took a step back, and a chill caught me. In surprise, I opened my eyes and found we were standing in Cal's house next to the staircase. Boxes filled the hallway, cramming us in.

"What are we…?"

"Shh. Trust the maestro. He knows how to wave his baton for an unending crescendo." Ink bent over, placing me on the worn carpet of the staircase. It was far from comfortable, but I didn't care. My incubus was busy lifting away my shirt.

"How come I never have to take yours off?" I asked. He was careful to place my sleep shirt on the banister before he fell to his knees astride me. Like swirling paint in water, Ink dipped his two fingers across the top of my chest.

"I thought it easier for the sake of the festivities. Do you wish to?"

He caressed over the fullness of my breasts, letting his palm brush against my awakening nipples. I sighed and reached for his shirt. Despite being an agent of sex chaos, Ink always kept his shirt tucked in. That was changing. I tugged like mad on the crimson tails, letting them fall around his waist. How his tightly controlled body looked at ease flipped a switch inside me I didn't know I had.

"You enjoy this side of me." It wasn't a question. It was never a question with him. Ink released my breasts and he coyly undid the second button on his shirt, then the third. All the while, he stared at me as if this were the hottest thing he'd ever done. His shirt fell open, revealing his taut shoulders, then his glistening pecs, and…

I reached out tentatively, nearly cupping but holding back from a tattoo on his left pec. It was faint, as if it'd faded over the years, but I'd never seen it before. A loop of chain shaped like a heart had appeared directly over where his heart would be.

"Is that new?" I asked, daring to let my fingers fall on the old but fresh ink.

He glanced down without concern. "I suppose so. You're welcome." As he spoke, his chest lifted and the steady beat of his heart pulsed a louder symphony in my panties.

I wrenched off his shirt, catching on the wrists, but Ink didn't even wince. The force set off his dragon rumble and his cock grew inside his pants. That needed fixing. I caught him by the belt, tugging him closer, when a chill blew through my hair.

"Layla," Daniel whispered in my ear. I shivered, certain I'd imagined it, when Ink's touch paused and he looked behind me.

"You're here. How?"

He licked his lip while staring down my naked chest. "Their wicked curse must have worn off."

"The ghost can haunt you again. Huzzah."

Ink's complaint was the only thing to pull Daniel from losing himself down my cleavage. "Should I leave you two alone?"

To my shock, Ink said, "No." Even Daniel stared in surprise. Ink tousled my hair back from my ear and he whispered, "We three bonded together to save her. I say she deserves we three in celebration of our victory."

"Ink…? Ah." He took my right breast in his hand while he sucked on my ear. Daniel drifted lower until he sat on the stair above me and reached into my hand. Using my palm, he massaged my left breast with a hungry ferocity while Ink was a gentle tumble of fingers. My incubus tenderly swept his palm around the side and under, before he'd lightly caress my nipple. Daniel tugged on my nip, causing me to squeak more with each one. I could barely get a grip before one of them drove me mad.

Both pressed my breasts together until Ink's hand knocked into my own. The pair stared at each other, fingers knotted in my cleavage. I grabbed Ink's hair and pulled him to my lips for a kiss. His stern growl slipped to a sensuous pout while Daniel ran his hand across the whole of my chest.

"Take both her hands," Ink said, pushing away. I had barely released his hair before Daniel slipped in. He crossed my arms like a slumbering mummy, my forearms propping up my breasts, while he pinched my nipples and whispered in my ear.

"Every cry from your lips makes me come a thousand times."

"It's a good thing ectoplasm isn't real, or we'd never get the carpets clean," Ink said.

"Where are you going?" I called out to my wayward incubus. He didn't just slide away for Daniel but got off the stairs entirely.

"Merely attending to the door, my bond." Ink gave a deep bow and pulled open the front door just as a box and my wolfish boyfriend entered.

Cal greeted Ink with mild surprise, when he turned and found me nearly naked, my legs spread, panties drenched, and hands rubbing my breasts. The box fell to the ground and I jumped at a growl rolling in his throat.

"Full moon," Ink said just as Cal leaped forward like a man possessed. He wrapped his arms tight around me, hefting me off the stairs. It ripped Daniel free, leaving me completely at my werewolf's mercy. From the fire in his eyes, I expected him to throw me over the banister and fuck me hard.

But he carried me like a bride up the stairs. I clung to his neck, his flexing biceps pressing into me as we rose. At the top, he turned to stare down at the two left behind. "Are you coming?"

My incubus smirked before he blinked out of existence. Cal carried me down the sloping hallway of his house toward a sudden light flickering in his bedroom. Without pause, he kicked on the door and we both gasped. Rose petals covered the flannel quilt and trailed onto the floor. Enough candles for an eighties music video filled every open space on his furniture. Standing in the middle, slowly bringing a flame from the tip of his finger to the last wick, was Ink.

"A lady's first night in her new boudoir requires proper ambience."

"I'm…" I pulled myself up to look in Cal's eyes. "I wasn't certain if you'd want me to—."

"If you think you'll be sleeping in any bed but mine…" He tossed me onto the bed, which cradled me in. Cal pulled off his T-shirt by the back of the neck while his eyes blazed. Slamming one knee to the bed, he crawled over me. "You're wrong."

I reached up for him, when cold hands swept inside of mine. They were tugged back, taking me with, until I stared at Daniel resting on the pillows behind me. Ink sat on the bed beside me, his trousers unbuttoned and the zipper beginning to fall. The demon who never did underwear slid closer, exposing his throbbing crown. He caught my chin and kissed me while Daniel pinned my hands above my head.

Ink trailed his touch across my breast until he wedged a knee below the small of my back. Rough fingers latched onto the hips of my panties and I tried to sit up just as Cal shredded them into pieces. In just his tight-ass jeans, he drew his nose from my belly button straight down. Ink shoved me higher, and

Daniel pulled my hands until they pressed against the headboard.

With me strained to the breaking point, Cal dug his fingers under my ass and into my hips, then he sucked hard on my labia. *God!* I tried to thrust against him, my body at a boil from Ink's touch. But Daniel held me tight as he gazed down at the wolf eating me out. My demon was gentler than both, tenderly sweeping his palms across my fallen breasts, then pushing my hair from my face. I tried to reach up to kiss him, but he leaned back.

"Ink?"

He circled the tip of his finger around my ear as he said, "We want to hear you."

"Oh god!"

Cal's hungry licking around the whole of me turned into a low growl. It bounced against my vulva, causing a second slower vibration that drove me mad. He flung himself back onto his knees and kept licking me even as he struggled to unbutton his jeans. Ink drew his palm against my inner thigh, his light touch causing my skin to shiver, before Cal's two-day stubble scratched against it. My incubus strained my leg further as Daniel bent closer.

I stared into his luminous eyes as he whispered so a faint breeze caressed my forehead. "You've never looked hotter. Ride his tongue, thrust harder. Take all you want as you deserve far more."

Cal whimpered against me, his tongue tapping against my clit before he pulled back. Concern struck me first, until I realized he was crying out in need from sucking on me. Moaning, he licked deeper while toying with the tip of his cock protruding from his jeans.

"Shall we liven up the festivities with a bit of the old gladiatorial spearing?" Ink asked. Everyone stopped and stared at him. "What? That has fallen out of fashion? Shame. I refer, of course, to…"

Ink drew the flat of his palm down the curve of my back until he slipped a finger straight to my back door. A flitter of pleasure tingled from his touch and I wanted more.

"Wolf?"

Cal looked up only a moment and waved in the general direction of his nightstand. It took Ink but a moment to procure a mega bottle of lube. "Do not worry, my bond. I am as gentle as the sunrise, until you do not wish me to be."

He pushed my back up higher and I thought it'd cause my ass to sink into the bed, but Ink's finger was there before I knew it. Fuck me! The slippery glide of his touch set off a shiver clear down to my toes.

Carefully, Ink dipped the tip of his finger in just as Cal did the same with his. Pierced in both holes by two men, my body sparked with unholy fire. I struggled to breathe, Ink playfully pinching my nipple as Cal sucked hard on my clit.

I tried to shift for Cal's tongue and also Ink's finger. The swinging of my hips back and forth was just enough to strike the match. My entire body trembled from my big toe to my eyebrows as the orgasm swept over me. Cal clenched my thighs tight to his cheeks, his tongue pressing against my clit so I could ride it out.

Ink brushed his knuckle over my anus, guiding the orgasm deeper. I tossed my head back and cried out as Daniel gasped in a pleasure he could no longer feel. He dropped my hand and brushed my thumb against my lip.

I'd never felt so wrecked, and I needed more. It was Ink who read the thought first, his demonic chuckle brushing against my cheek. Cal caught on quick too, a sly smile rising as he finally tugged off his pants to reveal his mega-cock was ready for duty. I wanted all three inside me at once, I just wasn't sure how to go about doing it.

"Do not worry your perfect brow so." Ink kissed me on the lips, his body stripped in the way only an incubus could. He guided a hand under my back and, with no strain, hefted me on top of him. As I came crashing down on his chest, then his hips, his cock wedged into my butt crack and the glide of its lubed crown set off another wave.

"What if I crush you?" I asked even as I gave in to his hands plying at my breasts.

Ink's hot breath bounced against my cheek. "I would be mightily impressed. Would you be so kind, my good wolf?"

The two shared a look as if they'd coordinated this plan before. The idea of the two of them talking about how to best fuck me… I was going to come from that image alone.

Cal bent low and he let a growl rumble his lips against my skin. Then he bit, little more than a nip, but it sent me reeling. Daniel slipped his hands into mine, then the whole of my arm. With them, he pried open my legs and flicked my clit. Cal locked his hands to my cheeks, kneading them as he moaned, before he spread both and Ink's dick slipped right in.

My breath shallowed in my chest and I held it, anticipating a sharp sting of pain. Ink was no slouch in the pants department, but he felt more aerodynamic, only reaching an inch in as he drew his hands down my body. "I will never cause you pain, my bond," he whispered in my ear. "Until you desire it."

"Umf." He tentatively thrust another inch and my body from the waist down lit up like Mardi Gras. Ink nibbled on the back of my shoulder as he twisted his legs between mine and strained them apart.

Cal snatched up the abandoned mega-lube bottle and drenched his cock. "I wish I could say the same to you, babe," he said, holding his fist around the bottom of the thing that'd make pop cans feel insecure.

Carefully, he slipped between my legs when Ink thrust. I lashed out, even with Ink's leg around mine, and pinned my ankle to Cal's back.

"I don't care, I fucking need you."

Ink drew back his hips as Cal guided himself and thrust inside me. *Shit! I forgot how massive he is.* My entire body was little more than a string wrapped around his cock.

"Breathe," Ink instructed. He brushed his finger against my cheek, then Cal touched the other. The reminder caused me to pull in air until I felt like I was floating.

"Good. Now for the hard fuck you deserve." Ink thrust deep, and I nearly yelped. But Cal bent down, half his cock inside as he kissed me on the lips. He slammed his hands astride my shoulders like he was doing pushups while he thrust. All the while, Daniel kept toying with my clit with my hand, setting off a firestorm. Ink pressed on my hips, pulling me onto his cock while Cal leaned back so I could take all of him.

This was no comforting, all-body orgasm. My entire lower half cascaded into nuclear fallout. One tremor from my vagina would travel to my ass, find Ink's cock, then roll back to Cal's. The whole of my body clamped down tighter than a vise onto the two men inside me, refusing to let go. I'd never felt this burst of rolling orgasms striking harder than the one from before.

Cal growled in my ear. "You're so tight I can barely move."

I tipped my chin and caught his eye. He stopped and stared at me. Sitting up, I said, "I love you," and kissed him. His red lips softened when they fell open and he gasped against my tongue.

His orgasm face was adorable. I stared in wonder at his nose scrunching and his lip curling as if in a snarl. When it passed, he collapsed on top of me, pressing kisses to my forehead. I was pinned between Ink, Cal and Daniel, which made me the luckiest sandwich filling in the world.

"My bond," Ink said as he slipped free of me and helped to guide me up.

"My heart." Daniel smiled sweetly and he lifted my fingers to where his lips could chill them for a ghostly kiss.

Cal placed his hand to my cheek and pulled me until our foreheads met. In a voice breathy with exhaustion, he whispered, "My love."

I wrapped my arms around all three, holding them close to me. Twenty-four hours after fearing I'd lose them, my heart swelled at the care and love they'd shown me. With a serene sigh, I whispered, "My boys," and kissed them all.

# Epilogue

After twenty-four hours of chaos, the bureau was finally approaching a semblance of order. The fugitive wretches bleated and hollered from their cells where they'd be undergoing further processing. Only a handful remained missing, along with the dead they had yet to bury. But given the circumstances of total security failure, it wasn't a bad ending.

Or so Director Zimmerman kept insisting.

"Coulda been so much worse," he said. "Shame I wasn't here. We found any sign of Ms. Monvoisin?"

"Not yet," Stone answered him. The other detectives had tried to stay out of the man's path for fear he'd wipe them out after this disaster. But no one, save an oracle, could have predicted the collapse of the grid.

A fleeting touch swept across Stone's hardened lips. He stuffed a hand into his pocket and clenched his fingers around what he'd found. More accurately what the diving team had discovered clogging one of the grates after they'd drained the pool of blood razors.

Stone couldn't stop checking to make certain it remained in his pocket, as if it were capable of vanishing on its own.

"You look perturbed, Stone."

"Only concerned for Ms. Monvoisin. Do you think…?"

"That she was gored by the minotaur? We can only be so lucky. No. That witch is either hiding somewhere down here or holed up on the surface. No matter, we'll find her soon enough. The powerful ones can never keep their heads down."

*The powerful ones…* He clenched his hand so tightly the worn plastic edge cut into his palm. "If that will be all, sir. I need to file my report."

Director Zimmerman cracked the back of his neck. "We're gonna be typing for days. Go on. Dismissed and all that." With a sigh, he stared, not at the shrieking denizens, but the empty cell that had once housed their only siren.

With a curt smile to the others trapped behind their desks, Stone pulled out his chair. As he sat down for the first time in forty-eight hours, he plucked the trinket from his pocket. A sly black cat in a purple witch's hat winked up at him. Guessing by the broken loop at the top, it had once been a keyring, but whatever keys it'd been attached to were probably in the belly of a razor beast. He wasn't in a rush to lose his arm to them.

"Working hard or hardly working?" Drake asked as he walked past.

Stone gave a curt laugh in acknowledgment of the stupid comment and he booted up the database. His fingers did the moving while he stared at the keychain. It meant nothing to him—it should mean nothing to him. Why couldn't he cease touching it?

"Whatever happened to your nose?" Stone asked, turning away from his screen while he typed.

Drake touched the bandaged appendage, then winced. "Funniest thing, I can't remember. Eh, it was probably that fucking unicorn. Thank god for having a virgin on staff. Right, River?"

Stone's partner snarled at Drake's insinuation as the two fell into bickering in the way only those who had narrowly escaped death could. After one last glance at the keychain, Stone placed it into a drawer on his desk. As he did, the scent of jasmine filled his nose. He breathed deeper and turned to his report.

Instead of the boilerplate report intro he'd typed a thousand times before, his fingers had put down a single name.

*Layla.*

* * * *

Sybil's shop bell jangled just as she turned her back. "We're closed," she called out, hanging a new assortment of scarves from the hook on the ceiling.

She expected the person would apologize and exit, but the slow, methodical clomp of feet and a single strike of cane echoed from the entrance stairs. Some people never learned. Sybil wound up a spell to cast them into their deepest nightmare. "I said…" She turned to face the unwanted customer, and her heart plummeted.

He wore all white. Not ecru, not off-white, not eggshell. This was white in its purest form, from the bleached hue of his fedora, down the Southern gentleman suit to his white patent leather shoes. He clung to a cane with a small horse of pure silver rearing back on the top.

"I have no interest in your wares." He slipped off his hat, revealing a balding head and a face that would look normal in pictures. But in person, his eyes shone brighter than a nuclear bomb and his smile was sharpened to a razor's edge. Every feature screamed death was close at hand.

Sybil reached out to find his aura. Instead of a mix of colors, all she could see was a gaping void where nothing would touch. "You!" Her grandmother had whispered of such a being long ago—not a creature but a celestial walking the earth. Challenging him would be like dueling a god. Even still, she launched her nightmare at him, trying to will as much power as possible behind it.

The man didn't bat the fear hornets away, but let each hit. Then he smiled.

*What did I just do?*

"You are aware of me?" he asked.

"You're a rider!" she squeaked, hunting for an exit. Sybil took a step to run, but her feet wouldn't move. Her entire body shivered with terror as the man returned his hat to his head.

"I prefer Mr. White. It's much more congenial in polite company."

"What...what do you want?"

"You are a witch, are you not?" he asked, his tone even and calm.

Had he come to her for a spell, or had she accidentally acquired a rider's artifact? Fear and greed competed inside of her, for such a thing would be extremely powerful and worth its weight in gold. But she also didn't want to be obliterated to atoms. "Take it, take whatever you came for."

"You misunderstand me, my dear. I'm not here for any of these trinkets you bamboozle others with." He drew his fingers down one of the scarfs, then sniffed a bundle of white sage. "My long-drawn plans are at last in motion, but I cannot abide any threat to them."

He took a step closer and Sybil's sheer terror broke her from his spell. She stumbled back, but in her tiny shop there was nowhere to go. Herbs rained into her hair as Mr. White advanced. "Wh—what are you going to do?"

Mr. White tapped his cane once more and the horse glowed green. With a deepening grin that made his cheeks sink into his skull, he leaned close and whispered, "Eliminate them."

## Want to see more from this author?
## Here's a taster for you to enjoy!

# Coven of Desire: Wings
## Ellen Mint

## Coming October 2022

### *Excerpt*

"I'm late!"

My shout, ten seconds after blearily checking my phone, reverberated off low wooden beams that I was shocked had never beaned my boyfriend. Stumbling on the slick floors in my wool socks, I slid for the closet and grabbed the first shirt I found. It wasn't until I already had my arms through the sleeves that I smelled the musk of man and a hint of wet fur. Even a month later, most of my clothing was scattered between four cardboard boxes I swore I'd unpack once the semester was over.

I began to reach for the top one, hoping to hit summer tees and not sweaters, when my phone's alarm went off again. Damn it, there wasn't time. While half hopping into my sweatpants, I dashed down Cal's… No, he wanted me to think of it as my hallway too. The bathroom door was partially open. At my blur, my werewolf boyfriend called out, "Babe!"

"Yes?" I skidded in my tracks and turned to find him in nothing but a nearly see-through pair of gray boxers.

Even with his blond hair smooshed on one side and his eyes drooping after our long night cramming—of both the academical and carnal variety—he was perfect. Cal smiled with his total sunshine grin and my legs began to wobble. He slipped a hand around my waist and pulled me partially into the bathroom.

"Morning," he whispered before kissing me. "I still love doing that."

I'd had no choice but to take the leap to live-in girlfriend thanks to evil witch hunters and it'd taken some adjusting. I can't say I'd have been so quick to move in with Cal minus the pitchfork-wielding agents, but he'd been trying his best to make it all work.

Cal picked up the blue toothbrush from the cup, leaving my purple one alone. "Are you ready for the last one?"

"No," I admitted without pause.

He squirted out a huge glob of toothpaste, then stared at me. "You've got this. Or should we"—Cal cocked an eyebrow and full-on smirked—"cram again?"

A laugh escaped my lips even as goosebumps rippled up my legs and arms. It sure as hell was a cramming session with him, even using lube, but I didn't have time. "I can't." I groaned. "I'm already late. Do you know where I left my purse?"

"Maybe downstairs?" He went to town on his incisors with the toothbrush before stopping and turning to me. "How are you late? We've got at least a half hour until exam time."

"Only a half hour?" I repeated, the sarcasm thick. Talking to Cal wasn't getting me to class any faster. "I hate boys."

As I dashed down the stairs, Cal called out, "I have proof you love certain parts of us."

Upon reaching the landing, I was greeted by the sound of pans striking a stove. That could only be one thing. I gave a quick hunt about the living room. The TV was running through a mess of old sitcoms but no one was watching. No sign of my purse or book. I remembered needing it when the pizza arrived, but wasn't certain where it went after the demon and werewolf ambushed me.

If the latter didn't know, maybe the former would. Dashing down the narrow hallway, I had to cling to the walls to avoid tripping. The last lightbulb had burned out and no one had bothered to replace it. I pushed open the kitchen door with my foot and it swung in on a baking disaster.

Standing in the middle of an egg-and-flour apocalypse was my own personal incubus. Ink's go-to outfit was splattered in white powder and dough while he held a far-too-small bowl in the crook of his arm and actively stabbed it with a knife. I must have made a sound as he looked up from his concoction and smiled.

Unlike Cal's sweet sunshine, Ink's smile was panty-melting nefarious even when he was covered in flour prints. My mouth dried and I tried to think. Why was I here? I was doing something important, something that didn't involve him swiping the pans off the counter and taking me now.

"I'm late," my mouth supplied to my frozen brain.

"I assume that is not in reference to your moon cycle," Ink said strait-laced before smirking. "Unless you're far more devious than I imagined."

"That isn't. I can't even..." I slapped him on the arm with barely any force, not that it mattered. I'd seen him take knives to the chest without reacting. "I wouldn't."

"It was but a jest. Your virtue is pure."

"Ha!" It was hard to think myself virtuous when three men shared my bed, often two or more at a time. "Have you seen my purse?"

"I believe I last viewed it in the galley when I'd bent over your back and pressed your hands to the wood while the wolf—"

"Yes!" I interrupted, my cheeks hitting ten thousand degrees at the reminder of just where Ink and Cal had been. "I remember that part. Thanks."

I turned to find my purse, when Ink hefted up a tray. "My bond, before you attend your academic gauntlet…"

I stared at whatever he'd been cooking with dread rising in my stomach. "What is it?" They looked like generic toaster pastries with a smear of chocolate on top, but it couldn't be that simple.

"A sandwich of my own concoction to aid in breaking your fast."

That was what I was terrified of. Still, I picked one up. Ink had been helpful as of late. I couldn't even hazard a guess as to why he suddenly wanted to do the occasional bout of cooking and laundry, even if what he made was usually inedible. And I was never getting that dress back after it floated down the river. But turning him down felt mean. As I raised up his sandwich, I realized it was two toaster pastries stuck together. What was in the middle was anyone's guess. Could be more chocolate, or mustard or even a thickened soy sauce.

With the tips of my teeth, I nibbled on the edge, hoping to escape the answer when a brown goo clogged my throat. "Peanut butter?" I coughed out. It oozed and dripped off the sides, like he'd heated it between the two pastries.

Ink only smiled wider. "Yes. I am quite ingenious."

"Yep," I agreed.

"Do have a delightful day." He pulled me closer while I stared at the PB and T sandwich. Once the peanut butter cooled, it wasn't too bad, the strawberry in the pastry combining well. I was about to take another test bite, when Ink whispered, "Upon your return, I shall..."

He plunged his teeth to my neck just to the edge of breaking skin. The pressure rushed through me, filling me with pleasure. Ink pressed the tip of his long nose to the middle of his bite mark. "That is for your inner thigh, and this..." He darted his tongue around the wound, the slick heat causing one of my own. "You can decide where you wish it."

I groaned as my entire body lit up with anticipation and my hand clenched, shattering the breakfast sandwich. We both stared when the soggy pastry halves hit the floor. "Sorry," I muttered, struggling to get my breathing under control.

"No matter." Ink popped open the oven and, without gloves, pulled out a bright red tray. "I made three sheets' worth."

"That's...good?" I inched out of the kitchen, leaving Ink to it while silently hoping Cal wasn't counting on the mega-box of toaster pastries to fuel his wolf metabolism. An impertinent *brring* chirped from my phone and I glared at it.

"Yes, I know. I'm working on it!" I shouted at my inanimate object while walking into what should have been the dining room. A man dressed for a punk concert in the nineties hovered next to where every book in the house had been scattered across the long dining table. As quite a few were nursing textbooks, the old wood was bowing in the middle.

"Daniel? Have you seen my purse?"

"Hm?" Slowly, the book lowered, revealing my ghost from his cheekbones up. Not that I was complaining—they were fantastic. His deep umber eyes flared blue a moment and he snapped the book shut.

I reared back in shock. "You can do that now?" Last I remembered, the best he could do was push a page and maybe the cover.

Daniel dropped the book where it landed on knowledge mountain and picked up another. "Yes, I found I could move the book much in the way I sit."

"I assume you mean using muscle memory and not that you close it with your butt."

The air froze at the serious glare buffeting from Daniel's face. I swallowed haphazardly, the peanut butter still lodged at the hollow of my throat. *Did I say something wrong?* He'd been waffling between a debilitating state of sadness followed by manic bursts of certainty. I couldn't handle pushing him back to the dark side again.

Slowly, Daniel scratched his chin and he cocked his head, causing the single blue stripe of hair to fall to the side. "Is that something you'd like to see?" he asked with dead certainty.

"Ah..." I was about to laugh it off, when I remembered my werewolf boyfriend who was really into leashes and the demon that'd do literally anything. What I found hot seemed to shift by the day. "I'll get back to you on that. In the meantime, I need my purse."

"Under the table," he said, gesturing to exactly where Ink had said it was. As I bent over to pick it up, Daniel immersed himself in yet another book. I reached inside to find my spell book safe and sound. Running my finger down the spine calmed me. Ever since I had learned that a witch losing her book caused her to go mad, I'd taken to sleeping with it under my pillow. Only the dual exhausting talents of Cal and Ink could distract me from my mortal dread.

"Did you read all of those?" I asked, pointing to his stack. There had to be a good three thousand pages there.

"Oh no," he said with a laugh. "I read the whole table. Which reminds me, I have a list of new books I'll require." Daniel gestured to an old tablet Cal let him use. He couldn't pick it up, but with his ghostly powers he could use the apps and leave lots of lists.

"I'll have to look later," I said, trying to work around the book peaks to escape.

"I also discovered another three potential protection spells for the house."

"And how many of them will banish a demon?" I asked.

He frowned. Their whole ghost and incubus bromance had only lasted a few days after my rescue, then it was right back to openly hating each other. "To my knowledge none. If you'd take a look?"

"I really have to run. Last day of exams."

"That was today? Hm, I thought they'd already occurred. Or were going to…" The unsleeping ghost stared back at the dining room window as if it could act like a calendar.

"Nope. Happening in an hour. I've got to bolt."

"Why are you not going with your wolf?"

I heard him but didn't want to answer. Because was a cheap response, but also the best I could give. If it was the usual lecture day, of course I'd go with Cal, even if he'd wait until the last second to leave. But the only way I could keep the letters on the page from dancing the dyslexia steps was if I had a half hour to myself to calm down. Sitting next to Cal this close to a full moon would only make my brain more stupid.

As I approached the front door, I called out, "Bye" to the house and opened it. A very small man in a bowtie stood outside holding an envelope. I gasped in surprise and he opened his mouth.

"For Lady—"

Before he could speak, a demon's claw latched around his shoulders and hefted him off the ground. I reached over to stop Ink from damaging him, but a naked arm wrapped around my stomach and pulled me deeper into the house. "What's going on?" Cal shouted behind my ear, his words garbled from the toothbrush still in his mouth.

"They seem to have sent a spy gnome. What do they have on you? Kidnapped your gnome wife? Threatened your fox? Out with it?"

"Layla?" Daniel rushed to my side. My three guys were now standing guard against a two-foot-tall man armed with only a letter. "Gnomes are often indebted to powerful magic users."

Ink groaned and glared back over his shoulder. "Shall you read to us from the Compendium of Wikis next? We all know what gnomes are. And this one has come bearing a piece of parchment. A written threat, perhaps?"

"It's a note, you demented fucktoy," the gnome snarled, his little legs kicking in the air.

"A likely… Ah, it is a note addressed to Layla. Wolf?" Rather than pass it to me, he handed it to Cal who stepped even further back while taking me along.

He breathed in the scent of the envelope. "I don't smell the sewers, but there's obvious magic."

"No shit," the gnome responded. "It's from…"

"Allow me." Daniel was the next one to excise the letter, somehow pulling it not only from Cal's fingers, but flipping open the flap and lifting the paper free. We all watched him carefully unfold the paper.

Ink pulled the gnome closer. "If it is coated in a ghost purging powder, I will buy you a keg."

Daniel didn't respond to that, his focus on the letter.

"Well," Cal snapped. "What's it say?"

"It's a letter for Layla."

All three jerked to attention at once, as if certain it had to be a sign the witch hunters were on my trail. Daniel glanced down to the bottom and sighed, "From a Valerie. Were any of the hunters known as Valerie?"

"Val…That's the witch that saved me." I ripped the letter from his ethereal fingers to read myself, when Ink grabbed it first.

*Where is the gnome?* I stared around in a panic, only to find the small man scurrying down the stoop as fast as possible.

"'To Lady Layla, so on and so forth. I have engaged in much research…' Humans do like to prattle…oh. Oh, great." Ink's interpretation of the letter smashed to a halt and he raised his head to stare at the sky.

"What?" I tried to look closer, but Cal had the whole of my waist and he wasn't about to let me get near it just in case.

With a sigh that rattled the windows, Ink said, "It is a potion to bring back the dead."

"Really?" I gasped, tears springing to my eyes as I turned to Daniel. His mouth hung open as if he too couldn't believe it. We'd been hunting for a month, him for all hours, day and night, and had found nothing. If it was true that I could bring him back, he could touch, feel, live…

"What does it need? What do I have to do?" My excitement hit a peak, then crashed hard as Ink stared at me not in exhaustion but a distressing concern. I gulped and asked, "Don't tell me it'll cost me an arm and a leg?"

"Not quite so macabre, lest you happen to be hiding a horn I am somehow unaware of?"

A horn? I wrenched the letter away from Ink who stared in surprise that I'd dare. Damn thing was addressed to me after all. I skipped past the preamble from the witch who'd saved me from the hunters to the helpful bullet points.

*Blood of a demon*
*Piece between realms*
*Skin of a unicorn*
*Feather of an angel*
*Bone of the dead*

*Boil in a cauldron or available kettle for thirty minutes, then recite the intended's name while pouring the potion out.*

That was it. Laid out like a recipe, it felt easy, doable. I glanced to Daniel and hope shone in his eyes. Reaching over, I placed my hand above his. He took control, holding mine as we both grinned like two idiots who won a chocolate factory. Soon, he'd be able to hold me for real.

"We can do this," I whispered to him, trying to seal the promise I made.

"Ah, yes." Ink peered over my shoulder at the list he'd already read. "Only requires the blood and brains of two celestials, and a piece of the void to seal it together. A light shopping list. Perhaps your interconnected webs have an all demon and angel body part store?"

They never said it would be easy. "You're a demon…" I began to my incubus.

"Even ignoring the technicality, I am not a demon. My blood is not special enough for this spell."

"I pray I don't expire twice from the lack of surprise," Daniel cut in.

Ink's lips cut apart into a toothy grin aimed only at the ghost. "Would be much easier to simply acquire a bowl of salt and a torch."

I was about to cut in, when my phone gave its final warning. All of this demons and angels mess would have to wait. My other life needed me. "We'll figure all of this out later. I've got to get to the test." I started to fold the letter up, but Daniel held his hands out for it.

For a moment, I hesitated. Not only was it addressed to me, it was also a private letter between witches. But it was his life, literally, in my hands. I handed him the paper which he managed to keep floating a millimeter above his palms while he stared at it.

Checking my purse once more to make certain my book hadn't fallen out, I tugged open the front door. "And, if you wouldn't mind, can you dial back the 'big scary bodyguard' routine, okay? Not everyone in the world is trying to kill me."

"Are you certain of that, my bond?" the one who'd assaulted the gnome asked without pause.

I glared at Ink, then caught a quick blown kiss from Cal. Daniel broke from the letter to give me one last smile before I slipped out of the house. I couldn't blame them for being so overprotective, but it'd been a month since I had escaped the hunters. At some point, I had to return back to normal life.

"Wait!" Cal dashed to my side. It was sweet that he didn't want to say goodbye, but I really had to… He reached up and tugged my bonnet off my hair. "Didn't think you wanted to leave the house with this on."

A jab of embarrassment jolted through me. I had forgotten I even had it on. That he'd cared enough to tell me and it didn't faze him warmed my heart. I pulled him close for a quick peck and whispered, "Thank you."

"When will you return?" It was Daniel who spoke, still transfixed by the letter.

"Once this test is done, we can get to work on figuring out that potion."

"Ah, Dana's party," Cal interrupted.

I winced at forgetting my friend's 'we're free' bash. I'd been so busy lately, the only time I spent with her or Fariah was during deathly quiet studying. "After that," I promised Daniel. "Then we'll bring you back to life."

He smiled so sweetly that I ached to kiss him. It was Ink who sighed dramatically and turned. "I shall fetch the lightning rods and pitchforks then."

I really had to go. With one arm around my purse, I stepped out of the door to the walkway lined with untrimmed bushes and tried to force my brain to think about gram-negative bacteria. What would it feel like to hold him? To touch warm skin instead of cool air? To pull off his jean jacket and lift the old band shirt to touch his body below? To feel his lips on mine?

I was electrified, certain I could take on the world. *Pass my finals, bring back the dead, stop whatever evil Mr. White was, end the witch hunters once and for all.* I was unstoppable.

The bushes rustled and an arm bigger than a fencepost shot out. It wrapped around my throat and pulled me back, tightening so fast I couldn't even scream.

# About the Author

Ellen Mint adores the adorkable heroes who charm with their shy smiles and heroines that pack a punch. She has a needy black lab named after Granny Weatherwax from Discworld. Sadly, her dog is more of a Magrat.

When she's not writing imposing incubi or saucy aliens, she does silly things like make a tiny library full of her books. Her background is in genetics and she married a food scientist so the two of them nerd out over things like gut bacteria. She also loves gaming, particularly some of the bigger RPG titles. If you want to get her talking for hours, just bring up Dragon Age.

Ellen loves to hear from readers. You can find her contact information, website details and author profile page at https://www.totallybound.com

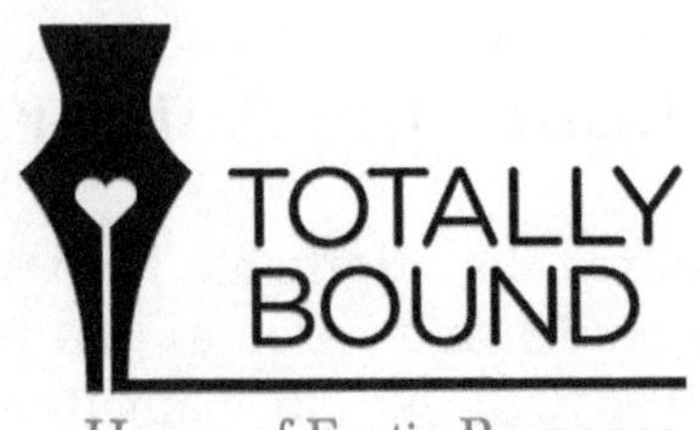
TOTALLY
BOUND
Home of Erotic Romance

oduct-compliance

2